TRIGGER

A DAMIEN HILL THRILLER

PETE BAUER

For Michael, Christopher, Paul & Josh

CHAPTER ONE

A SHOT RANG out in the distance.

Damien cocked his head, trying to track its source. He instinctively reached for his pistol, waiting for the echo to bring trouble.

Cupping his earpiece, he listened and waited, but heard nothing urgent in the crackle of police chatter. A domestic dispute. A car accident. A traffic stop. That was it.

Damien was on edge.

The summer heat was lingering into fall, and the daylight, along with his patience, was growing shorter each day. He hadn't had enough time on the job to identify the sound and not enough false alarms to brush it off. Maybe all first-year cops were like this, but knowing that didn't make him feel better.

"Hey, you with me?" Raquel asked.

She stood in the middle of the clothing store, her belly bulging with new life. It may have been her natural curves and bright eyes that first caught his attention years earlier, but it was her latest blossoming that made her the sexiest thing he'd ever seen.

"You're off the clock," she said. "I need you here, helping me."

"I'm here, I'm here," Damien said, scanning rows of miniature pink outfits hanging on tiny plastic hangers. "Fully armed in case any of these onesies make a move."

"Don't be a smart ass," she said with a laugh.

"So you want me to leave?"

"I want you to take this seriously."

"Babe, we're buying clothes our kid will eat, sleep, and crap in for three months. How serious do you want me to be? Besides, are you sure we should go all in with pink? What if the doc is wrong? What if baby Nicole ends up being Nicholas?"

"That's what receipts are for," she said. "My mami said the last trimester is going to be the hardest. Apparently, I'm going to mutate into a nesting fool."

"I wouldn't worry about that, babe," he said. "You've been mutating since day one."

Smirking, Raquel shook her head. "Can you be serious for one minute?"

"That's a long time, but I'll give it a shot."

Giggling, she turned to the row of clothes. He liked making her smile. She was the one who worried about bills, futures, and pink onesies while Damien took each day as it came. Seemed like a good approach for a cop. No sense thinking too far down the road when his next day on duty could be his last. He wasn't morbid about it. It was the simple truth. He wore a gun for a living. That wasn't for show.

Raquel said something—about her being the responsible one when he was the one who carried a weapon—but Damien didn't have a quick comeback. He was distracted by his reflection in the store window. The bright blue uniform looked as uncomfortable as it felt.

Still, he wore it well.

Examining the rows of clothes and merchandise, he made his way to the front of the store and looked out on Main Street.

Drawn forward, he pushed the glass door open and peered out into the heat. Hayeston's main road was quiet. Across the street, a homeless man rummaged through the garbage. To Damien's right, a mother pushing her baby in a stroller disappeared around the corner. The air hinted of citrus.

Everything was normal, yet nothing felt right.

"I love that smell," a joyful voice behind him said.

Benita inhaled the warm air wafting in. "Makes the store feel like home, doesn't it?" she said, her bright smile showcased by her darker skin. "My dad worked at the citrus plant for thirty years before he passed. Came home smelling like navels and hamlins, grapefruit and ambersweet. I loved it. Now, freshly squeezed citrus makes me think of that silly old man and his boisterous laugh."

"You're lucky," Damien said. "My dad drove a semi truck. The smell of exhaust reminds me of him. And he didn't laugh much."

Benita eyed his badge. "You're one of the new ones, aren't you? The next generation?"

"Yeah."

"Good," she said. "We need new blood."

"We do," he said with a sincerity that came from experience. "We love this town. And everyone in it."

"That would be a nice change," Benita said, moving back behind the check out counter.

"What do you think of this?" Raquel said, skirting around the aisle. Her eyes beamed as she held up a pink onesie with a picture of a kitten on the front.

"I think dogs will want to eat my child," he said.

"I know you hate cats," she said.

"Hate is a pretty strong word."

"That's not a denial."

"It's a clarification," he said with a chuckle. "I'm sure Nicole or Nicholas will love it as much as you do."

"Will you stop with the Nicholas thing? You're making me wonder if we're wasting our time."

He kissed her on the forehead. "Sorry honey," he said. "It's just... being in this place is making the whole thing real. We're gonna have a baby soon. I'm gonna be a dad to a little girl and it's kind of freaking me out. One day, she's going to grow up to be a beautiful young woman, like you. Then the boys will look at her the way I do you. And then I'll have to shoot them. And who wants that?"

"I think there are other ways to raise our daughter that don't involve gunplay."

"I don't know," he said. "I'm pretty sure your dad wanted to kill me when we dated."

"Maybe so," she said, "But don't worry. He'll warm up to you when he sees how you're a great dad. I know it."

Damien envied her confidence. Just then, he felt a tug on his pant leg. A cute boy, maybe four years old, stared up at him.

"Is that a real gun?" he asked, pointing at Damien's holstered weapon.

"Yes, it is," Damien said.

"Mama said guns are bad."

"They can be."

"But cops are good."

Damien smiled. "They can be."

"My uncle doesn't like cops. Says they're rook-it."

"Rook-it?" Damien asked, puzzled.

"You know, do bad things 'cause they can."

"Oh, crooked."

Bemused, Damien bent to the boy's level. "Well, I'm not one of those crooked cops. I'm one of the good guys."

"Really?" the boy asked. "Then can I play with your gun?"

"No."

The boy crossed his arms, pouting. "Rook-it."

"They're not toys," Damien said. "Your mom is right about that. Guns are dangerous. But when you get a little older, if you want to learn how to use one properly, and your mom will let you, I'll teach you myself."

"You promise?" the boy asked with a hopeful lilt.

"I promise."

"Until then, you'll protect me from the bad guys?"

Damien tapped his badge. "That's why I wear this."

He had to be on his best behavior, on and off the clock. This might have been the boy's first face-to-face experience with someone wearing the uniform. Damien couldn't allow himself to have a bad day. Not in public. It was the price that came with the shield, but a burden he was willing to carry.

"Slow day," Benita said, maneuvering around a row of baby cribs. "Are you all finding everything you need?"

Benita surveyed Raquel's shopping cart full of clothes.

"My wife has been a bit enthusiastic," Damien said, fighting a smile.

"What can I say?" Raquel said. "I love your store."

"Thank you," Benita said. "It wasn't always this nice in here. Gosh, just a few years ago, when Billy was born, this place wasn't even a dream, let alone a reality. My husband had just left me. I was broke. Unemployed. On food stamps. A lot of tears. Not much hope, until I held my boy in my arms and felt his breath against my cheek. He changed everything.

"But, when he was just a wee little one, I couldn't find any baby clothes that matched my style. They were generic and I wanted something with a little flair, a little panache. So, I saved up what I could and opened this place. Found some local designers, and here we are now. Four years of sleeping on my uncle's couch with Billy, microwave dinners, and a lot of sacrifice. Four long, hard years."

Benita surveyed her small shop, her pride barely contained.

"All days are good in this place," she said.

Raquel smiled. "I can't argue with you there."

"*10-24*," a voice screeched in Damien's earpiece. "I need assistance at Barrows and Ninth Street."

He recognized the voice. It was Ted's.

"Suspect is down, bleeding. Send paramedics. And police backup. The spectators are getting restless."

Barrows and Ninth, Damien thought. *That's just a few blocks from here.*

"I repeat," Ted said, his urgent plea nearly drowned out by screaming voices. "Things are getting out of hand."

"Ted's in trouble," Damien said. "I have to go."

He rushed out of the store and sprinted down the street, toward his friend.

CHAPTER
TWO

DAMIEN'S LEGS moved with lightning speed, the businesses and storefronts on Main Street rushing by him in a blur. The warm air flowed through his nostrils like jet fuel as he raced around the corner onto Barrows Avenue.

In the distance a crowd had formed at the next intersection and it was impossible to see over the wall of spectators.

He grabbed onto a street pole and steadied himself atop a fire hydrant. Peering over the crowd, he spotted Ted standing next to a low ride Honda Accord painted with gray primer. On the ground near the opened car door laid a man with blood pooling below his chest and what appeared to be a knife in his hand.

Damien pulled his walkie from the slot on his shoulder.

"Ted!" he said. "Are you all right?"

Ted straightened and pulled his walkie toward his mouth.

"Bad day," he said.

"I can see you. Over here, on Barrows."

Damien waved, walkie in hand.

Ted spotted him above the crowd and recognized him with a nod.

"I'm coming to you," Damien said.

"No. Stay there. The riot team is on its way."

"I'm not going to let you face down these people alone."

"Our boys with shields and batons will be here any minute. Be an extra set of eyes until they get here."

Damien spied the crowd. Familiar faces twisted with rage.

The victim on the ground looked like a gang banger he'd seen in the area. A trouble maker always looking to make a name for himself on the street, not a tombstone.

Bad day all around.

Sirens echoed against the hard buildings.

Over the crowd Damien spotted a black transport with the riot team inside. The driver blurted impatient horns as it approached, but the crowd wouldn't budge. Instead, a small portion surrounded the van, banging and pushing.

"Ted, get in your cruiser," Damien warned. "They're getting violent."

"Not a chance. It's a crime scene. My shot. I'm not going anywhere."

"This ain't an academy training exercise. They're about to turn on anyone wearing a blue uniform."

A shotgun barrel appeared out of the side van window and shot into the crowd. A smoke grenade bounced off a large man in a white t-shirt and burst into smoke at his feet.

The coughing spectators stumbled away as the van pulled up next to the gray Honda.

The back doors to the van opened and the riot team flowed out, helmets, shields, batons and non-lethal weapons at the ready.

It was ten against hundreds.

"Ted, I'm coming to get you out of there."

"No!"

Damien watched his friend back up toward his cruiser.

"You were right. Take cover."

Smoke grenades were fired in every direction.

The crowd dispersed in pockets, then reformed into

tighter bands, each attempt to push them back only bringing them closer to the riot team.

Fists raised in the air and chants to kill cops grew into a chorus of hate. The illusion of law and order was decaying into chaos.

The crowd in front of Damien pushed backwards like a wave, crashing into him, knocking him off the fire hydrant and onto the ground.

A man turned and began to offer Damien a hand, but stopped once he saw his uniform. The stranger's eyes hardened.

"We got one!" he yelled.

Damien hopped to his feet and backed away as more of the mob turned to face him.

"Take it easy," Damien said, gripping his gun in his holster.

The hardened man looked at the crowd behind him and smiled.

"I think we'll do just about anything we want. Starting with you."

Damien thought of his training. Diffusing conflict. Tactical retreat.

But his mind landed of the one thing more important than his training or his badge.

His pregnant wife, only one block away from the fury.

Damien kept his gaze on the hardened man with a stone glare as he backed away, each step faster than the last, until he turned and sprinted onto Main Street.

Behind him the mob charged in pursuit.

In front of him, at the end of the road, another chanting throng began to form.

Between the two was Benita's store.

CHAPTER
THREE

DAMIEN BURST into Benita's shop, panting, sweat and fear covering his face.

Benita jolted upright at the checkout counter.

"Do you have a back door to this place?" he asked.

"Why-"

"Raquel!" Damien interrupted.

Raquel appeared from one of the aisles, holding up a pair of miniature socks.

"How cute are these?" she said.

"We have to go. Now. All of us."

"Why? What's wrong?"

A wave of grumbling approached the store like a thunderstorm. Slow. Steady. Menacing.

"Mama, they're coming," Billy cried. "They're coming!"

His little finger pointed toward the front plate glass window as it shattered, shards raining on him like razor-sharp snowflakes.

Damien rushed toward him, his shoes sliding across the scattered glass like ice. A garbage can flew inside and crashed right next to the little boy, debris falling around him.

Damien slid in and scooped the boy up just as a tire iron spun by their heads and stuck into the chest of a mannequin.

"That was close," Damien breathed, his heart galloping as he carried the crying child away from the chaos.

Outside, yelling and chanting overwhelmed Benita's screams. A growing mob suddenly flowed into the store like a storm surge, rushing through the aisles, grabbing and stealing whatever they could.

"Get out of my store," Benita shrieked. "Get out!"

She beat on the back of one of the looters. It was a young man, maybe a teenager, his arms locked around a new baby stroller.

"Put that down," she shouted. "That's not yours. Put it down."

The teen rocked his elbow back and struck her in the head, knocking her off her feet. She spilled through a display of shoes before landing awkwardly on the floor.

Damien handed Billy to Raquel. "Get out of sight," he ordered.

"We're going to be okay, right?" Raquel asked, her hand covering her round belly.

"Go," he said, nudging her to the rear of the store. "Hurry."

This was day twenty-one on the job. There were more thieves in the store than traffic tickets ripped from his citation book.

Damien yelled into his radio, "10-24! Officer needs assistance at Benita's Baby Shop, 1754 Main Street. We have looters in the store and an angry mob outside. Get the riot team down here, now!"

Damien had two defenses at his disposal, a taser and his pistol. The taser had one shot. His pistol, eighteen.

He unholstered his Glock, trying to grip it firmly in his shaking hand.

"This is the police," he called. "Everyone put the merchandise down and leave the store. Now!"

The looters paused. One laughed. Others shrugged. The

rest continued as if he were invisible, dismantling the shop like rabid dogs fighting for scraps.

Damien seethed at his impotence.

There were more looters than bullets, and he wasn't about to kill anyone over pink onesies. He shifted from peacekeeper to protector, hurrying over to help Benita to her feet.

"They're taking everything," she cried. "They're stealing my life. I can't stand by and do nothing."

Damien moved between her and the crowd.

"The floodgates are open, Benita," he said. "We can't stop them now. We have to find cover."

He shuffled backward, shielding her as they maneuvered to the far corner of the store. Once there, they ducked into a small bathroom where Raquel and Billy already hid.

"Did you call it in?" Raquel asked.

"Yeah," Damien said. "There's a lot of shit happening out there. It'll take a while before they get to us."

Damien closed the door of the small room, his gun poised in case someone came after them.

"You're not rook-it," Billy said with wide eyes, staring at the gun. "You're a good guy."

Benita began to cry, her tears streaming down her cheeks like twin waterfalls. The lovable woman with an infectious smile had descended into a grieving heap.

"Three hours," she said, clutching Billy. "I was going to sign my insurance papers tonight after we closed. Three hours from now. Three hours…"

Damien's heart sank, helplessness welling up within him. Benita's life was being stolen by both strangers and neighbors, who picked at the bones of her store like vultures on a corpse. Years of her sacrifices and struggles gone in seconds, and Damien could do nothing to stop it.

Raquel's hand slid around his bicep and squeezed. They shared a glance, and it seemed as if she could sense his despair.

"You got this," she said.

Her words and tone flooded him with memories. She'd said the same thing to him the first time they met.

———

Nine years earlier.

Damien sat at a high top near the coffee stand of the bookstore. He felt nervous, but tried to look bored. The first time he met his tutor he couldn't appear too eager.

Being a high-school dropout had expectations. Bad boys. Troublemakers. Geniuses. They were the ones who ditched high school for the real world.

He wasn't any one of those.

Still, he didn't want it to appear he'd made a mistake. That would make him look foolish. He'd offer resistance to the idea of getting the equivalent of a high school degree. Play it as something he was doing because he had the free time, not because his job at the bookstore had become as stale as his dreams.

Besides, women liked a strong man.

Damien wasn't one of those either.

The woman on the end of the phone call sounded enthusiastic. He didn't catch her name. The signal stuttered when she spoke it. Yet, her hand written sign posted on the cork board near the bookstore time clock told Damien enough.

She was still in high school. Her writing was crisp and big, with rounded letters penned by a happy hand. Plus, she'd turned the O in TUTOR into a smiley face.

Hayeston was a one high school town and he knew most of the women who would offer a helping hand to those in need.

He didn't want her pity. He needed direction, a rudder to help guide him. He'd do the work. He did it before he dropped out in the middle of his junior year. That wasn't the issue.

He'd grown bored in school.

Now he'd become bored at the bookstore.

The electronic bell above the glass door chimed. Damien nearly hopped in his seat, then slouched back down. Dropouts rejected class bells. He'd ignore that one too.

He spotted his reflection in the opened glass door.

He looked like a punk.

He was better than that.

He straightened and put his hands on the table. Being a dropout didn't mean he couldn't be a gentleman.

Behind the closing glass door was a smiling face Damien recognized.

Raquel Domingo.

Damien's mouth grew as arid as a desert.

She bounced as she walked, her ponytail swaying behind her as she approached.

Damien felt like he was about to melt.

She held out her hand.

"I'm Raquel. It's nice to see you again."

Words fumbled in his thoughts and lost their way to his mouth.

"We were in that one class together," she said. "Remember?"

He nodded.

"I can't wait to see you get your GED."

She sat across the table from him, her heavy backpack shaking the table as it landed. She slid out a folder with a number of papers, mostly handwritten.

She gave him an update on what he had missed since he quit school, then explained his study plan.

Damien couldn't hear her. Her intoxicating eyes drew him in and the rest of his senses took the afternoon off. He wanted to fall into her beauty, but tried not to stare too intently.

"Sound good?" she asked.

"Yeah…" Damien said, his tongue desperate for moisture.

"Where do you want to be in five years?" she continued. It was a rhetorical question. That was fine with him. The speech center of his brain was losing a battle with his hormones anyway.

Slowly, her certainty about his future started to become his own and his dream of a hopeful life felt possible once again.

He sipped his hot chocolate, gazed into her eyes, offered a few nods here and there, and listened to her soothing voice.

Before he knew it, this bad boy troublemaker genius had been replaced with a smiling, excited teen.

Whatever her hourly rate, he was willing to pay it.

As their first session wrapped up, she grabbed his hand and said, "You got this."

He looked down.

She touched my hand.

He lost his breath.

"You got this," she repeated.

Damien could only nod one last time.

She gathered her backpack, then gave him a wink.

From that day forward, he'd known he'd follow her anywhere.

————

Today, that path led him into the bathroom in the back corner of Benita's shop.

Unlike their first meeting, Raquel was petrified. Damien, too, but he couldn't show it. Cops were supposed to be the calm amidst the storm.

The chaos on the other side of the bathroom door sounded like a tornado touching down. Waves and waves of grumbling and destruction shook the walls, the feet of thieves stomping through the store vibrating the wooden floor as they trampled Benita's dreams.

Damien was on his own.

One badge, one gun, one radio waiting on his calls for backup.

In the end, he had but one choice. Wait it out. Stay out of sight. If he did that, they might get out of this alive.

Billy started to squirm in Benita's arms. His eyes darted side to side, his breathing shallow and quick.

"What's wrong with him?" Damien asked.

"He doesn't do well in small spaces," Benita said.

Four people stuck in a fifty-square-foot bathroom was a tight fit.

"Mama, I wanna go now," Billy said. "I wanna go outside."

"Not now, baby. There are bad men out there. We can't leave just yet."

"But he's got a gun, and he's a good guy," Billy whined, pointing at Damien. "He's not rook-it. He can stop the bad guys. That's what good guys do."

Damien felt his chest tighten, avoiding the young boy's eyes.

"I'm scared, and I want to go home," Billy said, reaching out and grabbing Damien's hand. "You can stop the bad men from hurting us. We could walk right out there and they'd leave us alone, because they'd see you're a cop with a gun and you mean business. Right? Because I want to go home. I'm a big boy, but I'm a little afraid and you can protect me."

Damien mustered the strength to look up.

"I *am* protecting you," Damien said.

"But I have to leave now. I have to go home."

Billy squirmed from Benita's arms. Damien caught him as he reached for the doorknob.

"I have to go," Billy wailed.

"Okay, okay," Damien said. "We'll go. You and me."

"Really?"

"Yes."

"Damien," Raquel scolded.

"He's right," Damien said. "It's my job. We're all going, okay?"

"We share the loading dock with the grocery store next door," Benita said, pointing. "We could get out that way."

"Okay. Everyone, follow behind me and stay close."

"Will you hold my hand?" Billy asked.

"Sure," he said as Billy's little palm slid into his. "We have to move quick. We'll escape through the loading dock, then try to get to my cruiser if it's not in flames by now."

"We could use our minivan," Raquel said. "It's closer."

"Good idea," Damien said, glancing at everyone. "We'll do that. Ready?"

They all nodded.

"Here we go."

He turned the round knob and slid the door open a crack, waiting.

"What's wrong?" Raquel asked.

"It's quiet."

"Are they gone?" Benita asked. "Are those bastards gone?"

"I can go home," Billy said, escaping Damien's grip and running into the store.

Benita followed after him.

"Wait," Damien said, rushing out and hopping over metal skeletons of clothing racks strewn about the floor.

There was nothing left. Every shelf, every display, had been picked clean.

In the center of the destruction, flanked on either side by four armed thugs, stood a tall man with olive skin and long hair. A wide scar traveled around his right arm like a python choking its prey.

The scarred man's hands were empty.

He wasn't there to steal.

A SMIRK FORMED on the scarred man's lips, like a lion who had cornered its prey.

The armed thugs around him remained emotionless, staring straight ahead, waiting. They weren't gang bangers. Their pistols were holstered, not stuffed into their pants or bulging from their pockets. Damien counted two Glocks, a Luger, and a Taurus. Another held a Remington shotgun.

The scarred man was unarmed.

"I heard a bluebird was in here," the scarred man said. "A bluebird with a tin badge, hiding like a coward."

The first to talk. The leader. He wasn't local. His speech pattern told Damien as much. Neither were his thugs. They didn't look familiar, except one with a large tattoo on the side of his neck.

Damien attempted to lower the temperature in the room.

"It seems you just missed out on the sale," he said. "But maybe Benita will give you a rain check before you leave."

"Oh, we're not going anywhere," Scarman said. "Our day is just beginning."

"Are you and your boys running the show?" Benita asked. "You're responsible for destroying my store?"

"You can leave, sister. I have no quarrel with you."

She covered Billy's ears. "Well, I got one serious issue with you, you sonofabitch. Who do you think you are, giving me permission to leave my own store? You and I are gonna have words. More than words. I'm gonna kick your ass."

She tried to strike Scarman, but one of his thugs snatched her hand in mid-slap.

"You think you scare me?" she asked.

"Benita, stop," Damien said, pulling her and Billy back. "This isn't going to help."

"Watching 'em bleed on my floor will make me feel all kinds of wonderful."

"Listen to the bluebird, sister," Scarman said. "Before you do something you'll regret."

"Son, I haven't even started," she said.

Damien may have had the law and a gun on his side, but he knew the man standing between the thugs was in charge.

"What do you want?" Damien asked.

"I want the world to burn," Scarman said. "But Hayeston will do for now."

Damien glanced at the side exit leading toward the loading dock. Two more thugs and an avalanche of toppled shelves stood between him and freedom.

"You assholes destroyed my life," Benita said.

"Collateral damage, sister," Scarman said. "And for that, I'm sorry, but a life was taken today, less than two miles from here. Did you know that? An innocent life lost at the hands of a corrupt bluebird, like this one."

Damien thought of Ted and wondered if he'd escaped unharmed.

"The victim was unarmed," Scarman said. "Illegally stopped with a bogus traffic violation. When he got out of his car, the bluebird put him down like a rabid dog. No warning. A single shot to the chest. Just like target practice."

"That's bullshit and you know it," Damien said. "The guy had a knife in his hand. I saw it myself."

"So you say," Scarman replied. "You're bullies with badges. How long did you expect this oppression to go unchallenged? Your uniform is no better than the white sheets of the Klan."

The scarred man was the rambling voice of a revolution Damien sensed was coming.

"My wife is Puerto Rican," Damien said. "My best friend, a fellow officer, is black. And I'm trying to protect what is left of Benita and her son's future. The only bigot here is you, judging me by the color of my uniform."

"Don't lecture me," Scarman said. "You have no authority here." He pointed at the shattered front window and inhaled the gas fumes drifting into the store. "Do you smell that? Change is in the air. You can see it, hear it. They have spoken with their voices and their fists. They're screaming for justice and I'm going to deliver it to them."

"At what cost?" Damien asked.

"At any cost," Scarman said.

As if activated by Scarman's thoughts, two of his men approached, their hands clenched into fists and their muscles taught.

Damien's instincts told him to unholster his weapon and fire. A couple of muzzle flashes, the smell of gunpowder, and it would all be over. The chants outside could drown out the shots. He could end this right here, but by doing so, could lose his badge. Maybe even his freedom. In the fog of the riots, he may be able to justify his actions, but even though the threat was real, it wasn't yet imminent.

He had to live up to the uniform.

"You've already taken Benita's future," Damien said. "How many more casualties do you want?"

Scarman smirked, his eyes boring into Damien like a laser. "Just one."

Movement drew Damien's attention to his right where a thug shoved Raquel into the room. She stumbled over an overturned shopping cart and fell into Damien's arms. He caught her, one hand cupping her belly.

"Are you okay?" he asked.

"Yeah," she said, panting.

"And who have we here?" Scarman asked. "A mother-to-be with a little blue bird in the oven? How sweet."

Scarman's face was hardened by old wounds. Damien spotted a faint, thin scar near his right eye. His nose, though straight, had been broken. On his neck were a number of small, circular burn marks long since healed, perhaps from a cigarette or cigar. His strong jaw was slightly misshapen by bones that appeared to have healed outside the care of a hospital. Brutality, as a recipient or a donor, must have filled his life.

"She has nothing to do with this," Damien said. "None of them do. Your problem is with me."

"I want to agree with you," Scarman said with a sigh. "But new, beautiful pieces have been added to our game," he said, glancing at Raquel. "We can't ignore that, any more than we can ignore your crimes. You see, today is the day everything changes. The country will look back on your little town and remember this is where it all started, the epicenter of a movement that will change the world."

"With you as its leader?" Damien asked.

"Me? No. I'm a soldier, not a general. I do what needs to be done. You could say I have taken an oath to the cause. Like the one you took as a keeper of the peace."

"I knew what I signed up for," Damien said.

"Did you? You knew you'd have days like this?"

"No, but I knew there were people like you."

"Really?" Scarman asked. "Poor little man, all dressed up with nowhere to go. The pride of the bluebirds. Ready to do whatever it takes."

Damien's fingers caressed his pistol grip.

"I have a few ideas," he said.

CHAPTER
FIVE

DAMIEN EYED Scarman and his men more closely. Their calm spoke volumes.

None of the chaos surprised them. They had lived through this experience before. It was as if protests and violence were their calling cards. This was *their* story, today being retold in a different town with new actors, but only Scarman and his men knew how this tale was going to end.

Damien had run out of peaceful options. If Ted's gunfire started this mess, maybe Damien's could finish it.

It would be the bravest or dumbest thing he would ever do.

Once the bullets started flying, the few moments of shock might give Raquel and Benita the distraction they needed to escape.

It was now or never. It was time to follow his instincts.

Damien unclipped the holster strap over his Glock.

He slid his fingers around the grip.

He examined each face, the position of each target, and planned his order of fire.

As his hand tightened, he felt the cold sensation of a pistol barrel pressed against the back of his neck. He didn't have to turn around to know another hidden thug had circled behind him.

"Shit," he said.

Damien carefully lifted his hand off his gun, then held out his arms.

The hidden thug removed his sidearm and taser, stuffing the pistol behind his belt and tossing the taser to Scarman.

"Look," Damien said. "We're all just people here. We don't want trouble."

"But you have it," Scarman said. "Today's victims want justice and revenge. They will look to someone who feels their pain and isn't constricted by laws. Someone who is willing to do whatever is required to reconcile their loss. Someone like me."

"And what is required?" Damien asked.

"For someone to pay the price. A symbol. Their enemy. A punishment equal to the crime. An eye for an eye, as it were."

"Fine, it's a deal," Damien said. "I'll stay. Let the rest go."

"No, Damien," Raquel said. "They'll kill you."

"I'll be fine." He kissed her on the cheek, then whispered into her ear. "I'll see you and the baby later. Now go, before they change their mind."

Raquel's hand tightened around Damien's.

He loved her touch. Her fingers were magic. They were long and feminine, a model's hands.

"Hold on here," Benita said as she lifted Billy into her arms. "You think I'm gonna skedaddle while you all beat on this man? Or worse? What kind of a monster are you?"

"An impatient one," Scarman said. "You've suffered for the cause and I appreciate your loss, but don't try me. I'm prepared to do whatever it takes, to whoever it takes, to make my point."

Scarman aimed the taser.

Two metal probes darted from its bottom, flying across the room and lodging directly into Damien's chest. Fifty-thousand volts jolted through him. He collapsed to the ground, his body spasming in a violent seizure.

It felt like being hit with a baseball bat while being paralyzed and electrocuted at the same time.

"No!" Raquel screamed.

Scarman turned to Benita.

"Get out, sister," he said. "Before you and your boy become one more point I need to make."

Benita paused and focused on Damien, her chin quivering.

"I'm sorry," she said as she rushed out of the store clutching Billy on her hip. "I'm so sorry."

Raquel rushed over to Scarman, trying to pry the taser from his hands.

"Stop it," she said. "Leave my husband alone."

He raised his hand, palm flat, and struck her across the face.

Raquel tumbled onto the floor, protecting her stomach as she fell. She landed next to Damien, her face resting opposite his, her eyes wide and terrified.

"L-L-L-L-Leave," Damien said through gritted teeth. "P-P-P-Please."

"I can't," she said. "I can't leave you alone with them."

Pain and electricity surged through Damien as tears started to well, his body quivering uncontrollably with powerful volts. With trembling hands, he reached out and touched her stomach.

"P-P-P-Please…" he said. "F-f-for h-h-h-h-her…"

Scarman released the taser button and the pain ceased, but Damien's body continued to spasm with aftershocks.

"I-I-I said I would stay," Damien said to Scarman, the metal probes still embedded in his chest. "Let my wife go. Please."

"I'm not the one making her stay," Scarman said.

"What do you want from us?" Raquel said.

"To put it bluntly, I want your husband to die. No. For both of you to die."

"You're a pig," Raquel said as she struggled to sit up.

"I'm not a pig, Mrs. Bluebird," Scarman said, circling around them like a vulture. "I'm an opportunist. My world will welcome the downtrodden and the poor, the outcast and the angry. Division will be erased. The classes, leveled. It will be a wonderful place to live for those who understand our vision. Sadly, there is no place for you or your kind."

He motioned to his thugs.

"No guns," Scarman said. "Bullets are like fingerprints. They can be traced."

His men holstered their weapons, instead sliding on leather gloves.

"In my world, collateral damage is not only a byproduct of our work, it's encouraged."

Fifty thousand volts again surged through Damien's body. Every muscle convulsed as the thugs surrounded him and Raquel, their shadows covering them in darkness.

Raquel laid over her trembling husband, shielding him, and he could feel her love through his pain.

Fighting uncontrollable seizures, Damien lifted his hand and placed it on her bulging belly, cupping his hand over hers, begging, even praying to a God he wasn't sure was there, that baby Nicole would be spared from whatever was about to unfold.

Raquel's and Damien's eyes met, their fear replaced with a lifetime of love they'd never get to live.

"We got this," she whispered through her tears.

"I-I-I lo-love you," he said as a flurry of blows battered them on all sides.

Feet and fists pummeled. Pain and anguish. Fear and sorrow. Helplessness that he couldn't save the two people he loved most in this world. The two he'd sworn to always protect.

He tasted his own blood. Felt his ribs breaking. Heard his air violently expelled from his lungs.

Even though his body was being pulverized into bruises and blood, he kept his eyes locked on Raquel's.

They were supposed to have a life together, raising their children on his modest income, growing old, with a lifetime for him to gaze upon her beautiful eyes.

He'd never hear his baby's laugh. He'd never feel his wife's touch again. A life of possibilities stomped out by heartless extremists, one kick, one knee, one bloody fist at a time.

A hard boot swiped across Raquel's face, knocking her unconscious. Blood trickled from her nose and mouth. Her body fell limp. Defenseless.

The volts continued to surge through Damien.

He couldn't move. He couldn't stop them. He couldn't save her.

They were going to die.

All the decisions of his life, every second, every choice, led to this one moment. This was it. There were no more tomorrows.

A crushing blow rocked his head, turning light and pain to darkness.

CHAPTER
SIX

"BABY, TIME TO WAKE UP," Raquel's voice whispered in Damien's ear. "C'mon. Up and at 'em."

Damien groaned. His body felt like a discarded punching bag. Even his eyelids hurt. He kept them closed.

Where was he? Still in the store? In an ambulance? Hospital? He couldn't tell. Pain overwhelmed his senses.

"Raquel..." he said, his mouth dry. His tongue wouldn't work. His throat felt like sandpaper. Agony rippled through his body with each breath. He felt swollen and broken.

"Raquel..." he said again. Or had he? Was he speaking out loud or was it all in his head?

"Raquel," he grunted.

"He's awake," a voice said. It was deep, authoritative. Someone he'd didn't know.

Swirls of disconnected memories replayed in Damien's mind. Raquel. Protecting his baby. Scarman. Billy and Benita running. Punches. Kicks. The sadistic joy of their attackers. It was coming back in pieces. Out of sequence. Pain. Sadness. Helplessness. An incomplete story, its words and images jumbled.

"Mr. Hill," the deep voice said, interrupting his flashbacks. "Mr. Hill, can you hear me?"

Damien's hearing rose above the pain. There were other voices. Other sounds. Beeps. Whirs.

His body shifted. Agony surged through him like lightning.

The sounds disappeared.

————

"Damien?" Raquel whispered. "I know you can hear me."

He couldn't move. The world was still dark. His body felt numb. No more pain. No sore muscles or broken bones. There was a stillness. A peace. His eyes wouldn't open. His arms ignored his commands. He felt his lungs inhale and exhale. He was breathing. He was alive.

Or was he? Was he dead? Was this hell? Limbo? Purgatory?

It surely wasn't heaven. If so, infinite blackness didn't live up to its hype.

Damien felt like he was floating in a universe devoid of stars. No direction. No up or down or forward or backward. No gravity or pull. He sensed no movement. He sensed nothing but her voice.

Raquel's voice.

It was enough.

"You're getting better, babe," she said. "You're a fighter. Getting stronger every day. You'll need it. You've been through a lot. Still have a long way to go, but I know you won't give up. It's not your style."

Time was lost on Damien. How long had it been? Long enough for scars to heal? For bones to mend?

"I know I say it every time I'm with you," she said. "But I'm so proud of you. I know you think you should have done more that horrible day, but we did the best we could. Don't worry, baby. We'll make it. Together."

Her words felt like a cool breeze across his burning guilt.

"And our baby, Damien," she said. "You were right. It was baby Nicholas after all. He's so handsome. Looks just like you, in a small, lovable package with big, kissable cheeks. He has my mami's nose, which I know you won't be too happy about, but other than that, he's all you. He's such a happy baby. Not a care in the world. He's got a mischievous streak in him, too, and when he laughs, I hear you. I think he'll have your strength and gentleness. I wish you could see him. I miss you, babe. I miss your lips. I miss the way you find me beautiful no matter how I look. Most of all, I miss hearing you say that you love me."

———

The pain was back, but muted. Dull and relentless.

The world was louder somehow, yet missing Raquel's voice.

Noises. Shuffling. Machines. Murmurs.

His senses rose in him like a slow tide, soft aches and pains washing through him in consistent waves. He could feel the rough linens covering his hands. He could hear his breath flowing through his nostrils. The room was dry and cool. Air conditioned.

Scents lifted through the air. Hand soaps, industrial strength. Alcohol wipes. Latex. The smell of plastic penetrating each breath.

When he lifted his hand to his nose, he felt an oxygen cannula pressed into each nostril, its thin hose wrapping over his cheeks and behind his ears, disappearing beneath him somewhere.

He pried his eyelids open, the sting of light blinding him. Seconds later, it faded into the sterile colors of a hospital room. At Damien's feet stood a short, stout nurse with gray-streaked brown hair. She was humming a song that echoed from Damien's youth. He couldn't place it, but it was comforting. Her head bopped to the beat drumming in her mind. She appeared to be in her own world, and he was reluctant to interrupt her.

Damien's mouth was dry, his tongue enlarged, and his saliva felt like paste. He wanted a drink. Any kind would do.

He tried to speak. A gravelly gasp escaped his mouth.

The happy nurse's head stopped mid-bop and jerked up, her eyes widening at the sight of him.

"Holy shit!" she said, then rushed from the room.

CHAPTER
SEVEN

DOCTORS LIKED to use big words. They seemed comfortable with them, like they allowed them to distance themselves from the suffering they faced every day. Made sense. Had to compensate somehow.

Damien had faced plenty of pain. A lot of bones broken, from his skull to his feet. The nurse said his x-rays looked like fractured glass. The doctors were forced to place him in a chemically induced coma until his brain swelling diminished.

He was weak. Muscles atrophied. Now hypersensitive, loud noises pierced his head like hot needles.

The doctors said it was normal, all things considered.

That wasn't comforting.

Damien had been asking for his wife and son since he awoke, but was told he was hit with the MERSA virus while in his coma. He was near the end of their isolation protocol, but still had two more days under quarantine.

Forty-eight hours until he could feel Raquel's lips against his own. It would be an eternity.

The door to his room opened. A gowned man stood in the doorway. Familiar blue eyes stared at him. Through the thin hospital gown, Damien spotted the man's black clothes and white collar.

"No priests allowed," Damien said, trying to smile. "It means I'm either dying or about to be bored to death."

Jacob laughed. "Good to see your humor has returned with you. When I heard you had come back from the dead, I had to see it for myself."

"You doubted me? A Doubting Thomas? What has happened to your faith, little brother?"

"My faith remains steadfast," he said. "After all, here you are."

"My recovery is because of your faith? I doubt that."

"You would," Jacob said with a laugh. "You know, I prayed for this moment. Now, having heard your unappreciative sarcasm, I'm beginning to have second thoughts."

"Faith and second thoughts?" Damien asked. "Now you've caught up to me."

Jacob winced, obviously a familiar subject.

"For someone who was so close to death," Jacob said, "I'm surprised you haven't reconsidered the spiritual side of—"

"Let's not start again," Damien said, holding up a weary hand. "Please. I'm too tired for another theological debate."

"Fine," Jacob said. "But I'll keep praying for you, just the same."

"Go for it. Break a leg. No, wait, I did that already."

"I'd hug you, but I've been told by a very formidable nurse that no one is allowed to come into contact with you until after the quarantine. I'm lucky to have been able to come in as it is."

"That's okay," Damien said. "I'd probably break into a million pieces." He glanced out of the small window at the end of the room. Blue sky. High clouds. No trees could be seen from his floor. No indication as to the season or the time.

"How long have I been out?" Damien asked.

"Long time," Jacob said. "It was touch and go for a while. They asked if they should pull the plug, but I couldn't do it. You had too much life ahead of you. I was certain of it."

Damien tried to slide up in the bed, but his arms trembled as he struggled to lift his weight. "Shit," he said, flopping back onto his pillow.

"Don't rush it," Jacob said.

"How are Raquel and Nicholas?" Damien asked. "I heard her voice while I was under. She talked to me every day, so I'm assuming I got the worst of it."

"Damien…" Jacob started. He dropped his gaze and licked his lips, his face growing as pale as his collar.

Damien lost his breath. Licking his lips, that was what Jacob did when delivering bad news. He'd seen it when Jacob told him their father had passed away and when they discussed putting their mother in a nursing home.

Nothing good ever came from Jacob's freshly wetted lips.

"Damien…" Jacob said again.

"No," Damien interrupted, fearing the answer.

"Your wife and baby… they didn't make it."

"No. That's impossible. She talked to me when I was unconscious. I heard her. We have a baby boy. Nicholas. He looks just like me, she said, well, except for the nose. She was going to wait for me. She said we'd be together eventually…"

His voice trailed off as he replayed her words in his mind. They were cloudy now and certainty left him. Could it be true? Was he the only one to survive? He had taken a lot of blows. Perhaps his memory was unreliable or the chemicals that forced him under concocted an imaginary companion to lead him through his recovery.

He shook off his doubt. No. He had heard her voice. Had felt her touch. He probed his mind further, remembering the faint sound of his baby boy's laugh. They were more than just a memory or a fantasy. They were real. Alive. Both of them.

"No," Damien repeated. "I don't believe you." Forcing his legs over the side of the bed, he willed his weak arms to lift him to a sitting position. "If they're dead, I want to see their bodies… I mean, her body," he said. "I want to see it with my own eyes."

Medical alarms screeched as he started removing the sensors attached to his body.

"Damien," Jacob said. "Their bodies aren't here."

"Where are they?"

"They were buried. Three weeks ago. In a plot next to Dad."

Damien froze, Jacob's words hanging in the air between them.

"You buried my wife and son without me?" Damien asked, staring dumbstruck at his brother.

"It couldn't wait any longer… her body was starting to… her family demanded… it couldn't wait."

Damien trembled with sorrow as gowned nurses rushed into the room.

"Mr. Hill, you must lay down. You cannot leave this room, not until—"

"I want to see my *wife*," he screamed. "I don't care if I infect the entire hospital. I want to see my wife. I want to see her face. I want to hear…"

He struggled to breathe, his lungs gasping for air. The room began to spin and he collapsed onto the bed, tears forcing their way to the surface. The hope of his wife and son waiting for him on the other side of the darkness had faded.

"I need to see her… and my boy," he mumbled. "I need her…"

———

The saying "time heals all wounds" was a joke. Damien wasn't buying it. Days and months hadn't dulled the pain. He was certain they never would.

Today was the first time he'd been allowed outside on his own without a hospital leash. No more physical therapist. No more generalist. Or surgeons. Or psychologists. No more crutches or canes. No more pain medication.

No more.

He'd had enough.

Whatever aches lingered, he welcomed. It fueled him, giving him the strength to wake up each morning in an empty bed.

Life was going to be harder. Everything once stable was now fluid, including his career. He'd wanted to be a police officer since he was a teen, but now he wasn't sure if he could ever wear the uniform again. His reflection would force him to revisit Benita's store.

He was left with a conundrum.

He was still breathing, still living, but he couldn't exist in the vacuum of loss forever. Eventually, he'd have to find a new reason to get out of bed.

The large hill on which his wife and child were buried was a challenge for him. His once-toned legs started to quiver halfway up the modest incline. His breathing was quick and shallow, panting like a dog on a hot summer afternoon. Damien had never been this frail in his life. A stiff wind could crush him.

He hadn't been to the cemetery since his father was laid to rest. Damien didn't see the point. If his brother was right, his dad's soul was either with angels or demons. Most likely, the latter.

Under the dirt was just a rotting corpse. No need to stop by and chat, especially with him.

But, this was different. Everything was now.

He needed to see where his wife and son were laid to rest for himself. He had so much he wanted to say, so many conversations that were left unsaid. Most of all, he needed to say goodbye, or at least try.

With a few more heavy steps, he reached the top of the hill, the veins in his neck throbbing with each heartbeat. As he caught his breath, he gazed across the well-manicured grounds and wondered how many tears had fed the grass below the myriad of granite tombstones.

To Damien's surprise, Raquel and Nicholas were not alone. A tall figure stood in front of their new headstone. He was holding a large bouquet of flowers.

CHAPTER EIGHT

DAMIEN RECOGNIZED the man standing at his wife's grave. Ted was nearly six-four, with long arms. His natural height and strength had suited him well on the high school basketball team, and it made him an imposing figure in his crisp uniform and police cap.

Ted's head was drooped forward, his nose dipped into the flowers as if he were taking a long inhale. He then placed the flowers on the grave, took off his hat, and bowed his head in a short silent prayer.

Damien wasn't prepared for a conversation, not with the living, but to do nothing would communicate even more.

"Been avoiding me?" Damien asked.

His voice startled Ted. His friend straightened as if he were back in the academy, standing at attention.

"At ease, soldier," Damien said.

"Sorry," Ted said.

"Four months I was stuck in that hospital. Not one visit from my best friend."

"I'm sorry about that. I was here most days."

"Praying to grass and granite?"

"Paying my respects. Asking for her forgiveness. I'm the

reason she's here. It was my shot that started it all. My decision to fire."

"It was a justified shooting," Damien said. "The man was a gangbanger with a knife, had long record with an outstanding arrest warrant."

"The police commission is officially determining my culpability. I expect an announcement any day now."

"They'll rule in your favor."

"Doesn't matter. I know what I did. I saw the cost to you, Raquel, and your baby."

"Is that why you've been hiding from me? You think I blame you? I saw the man who put my wife and son here, and he was a lot uglier than you. That's the sonofabitch you should be angry with."

Ted finally showed enough courage to look Damien in the eye.

"I'm so sorry," Ted said.

"No need."

"Please, don't dismiss me like that."

"I forgive you. Is that what you need to hear? Fine. Consider it done."

Damien knew it wasn't enough, but he had nothing else to offer.

"Look," he continued, "I don't need you beating yourself up. I need your help finding the man who ordered my wife's death."

"You're coming back to the force?" Ted asked.

"I haven't decided. I've been waiting for a tipping point one way or the other."

"I understand. I don't know if I can do it anymore. Not after—"

"Stop it," Damien said. "You can't quit. Not you. You're the one who was going to fix the police force, remember? Lead by example. If you leave, you'll be telling Hayeston you were a dirty cop who shot an innocent man. Is that what you want? Is that what you think Raquel would want?"

Ted remained stoic.

"You quit now and you'll never get past this," Damien continued. "One of us has to be strong, Ted, and it can't be me. Not right now. The only way we get out from under this, both of us, is to hunt that scarred bastard down, put him on death row, and watch them put a needle in his arm."

"That could take a while," Ted said.

"I've got nothing else to do."

Damien watched his friend's gaze as it returned to Raquel and Nicholas' tombstone.

"Ted, I'll make a deal with you. If you stay on the force, I'll come back and we'll finish this. Together."

"It won't be easy. Your guy… he's a ghost. Vanished. That day of the shooting, things were crazy. More crime than we had cops and more criminals than we had jail space. By the time we found you and Raquel in the store… and then tracked down the store's owner—"

"Benita," Damien said. "Are she and Billy okay?"

"Yeah. They got caught in a wave of people outside her store. Bumps and bruises, but otherwise okay. She asked about you and Raquel a hundred times. She gave us a description of the assailants and the ring leader…"

"I call him Scarman."

"By the time we went looking for him, he was in the wind."

"He didn't stay around and gloat? He seemed the type."

"No."

Damien grimaced. "Of course he's hiding. He's a cockroach. They always run from the light."

"I'm sorry."

"How long had Scarman been waiting in Hayeston?" he asked.

"Our CIs said he'd been in town recruiting for a few days

before the riots," Ted said. "He was seen talking to Hector and some of his friends a couple of hours before things went south."

"And his thugs?"

"Gone, like him."

"That doesn't make any sense," Damien said. "Why would he pull the plug on the riot? They had momentum. He wanted the world to burn, and he was going to start with Hayeston."

"Well, he got the first part right. You've seen the damage."

"Some of it," Damien said. "From the hospital windows. What was the point if he wasn't going to stand atop the rubble and proclaim his manifesto?"

"It was like a jab, not a knockout punch," Ted said. "I have a feeling the fight isn't over."

"No, you're right about that," Damien said. "Whose on the hunt? State agencies? The Feds?"

"Yeah, they're doing their thing, and we're doing ours. It's the best we can do shorthanded."

"What do you mean?" Damien asked.

"The department isn't what it used to be. Commander Decker was fired, our sergeant resigned, and the governor has ordered a reevaluation of the entire force. We're starting over. New psychological exams. Better accuracy on the range. Higher test scores. Faster runners. I don't know if anyone will be left when they're done. We're not Seal Team Six. We're a bunch of cops trying to do our job."

"No amount of training could have helped us that day," Damien said. "It was simple math. There were a lot more of them than there were of us."

"A lot more," Ted repeated.

"How are Denise and the kids? Are they okay?"

"Yeah. They've been great. You know Denise, she thinks hugs can cure anything. She didn't let go of me for weeks.

Even now, she puts her arms around me the second I get home."

"Good," Damien said, looking at Raquel's tombstone in earnest for the first time. "How was the funeral?"

"Your brother gave a wonderful eulogy. Raquel's family was devastated, of course. It was all so unbelievable at the time. Even now when I come here, I can still hear her family wailing over her casket."

"Was it an open service?"

"No."

"Good."

Raquel was the most beautiful woman Damien had ever met. Better everyone's last image of her was a pleasant memory than the work of a funeral director.

"Have you talked to them?" Ted asked. "Her family?"

"Briefly," Damien said. "Nothing to say, really. They probably blame me for her death. Raquel and I weren't married long enough for me to be accepted into her family, not completely."

"Do you want me to talk to them?"

"Not your fight."

"Understood." Ted checked his watch. "My shift is about to start. Still riding a desk."

Damien offered his hand, but Ted stepped passed it and gave him a powerful hug.

"Denise is rubbing off on you," Damien said.

There was desperation in Ted's grip.

"I forgive you, my friend," Damien whispered.

It was the first time Damien had said it and meant it. It didn't change the fact they were standing at Raquel's grave, but he hoped it would end Ted's compulsion to return there.

His best friend nodded, then backed away without another word. As Ted disappeared down the hill, Damien realized he was finally alone.

Really alone.

No matter how many times he was told Raquel and Nicholas were dead, there was a part of him that refused to accept it. Even standing at their grave, he still doubted, fighting the urge to dig the soil with his hands and pry the casket open.

Raquel couldn't be dead. That wasn't the way it was supposed to work. Their love was greater than a room full of bullies. They had plans. Talked it through.

Raquel liked that. Her life centered around an evolving five-year plan. She'd write it on paper, then tape it to their bathroom mirror. What she wanted to accomplish this week, this month, this year, three years from now, five years from now. It was all sketched out.

She wrote in pencil because life needed erasers, but it was important to her. Their plans were their future. A future that existed after Benita's store.

This month: *get the baby room ready*. This year: *have a healthy baby*. Three years from now: *regain her pre-baby body or maybe get pregnant again*. Year five: *get a part-time job after their baby entered kindergarten*. There were other things too. Their vacations. Date nights. Baptisms because she was into that. House projects. Family reunions.

Damien saw it every morning, stared at it every time he brushed his teeth. Each week, she'd check an item off. Each month, she'd update it and tape a new version to the mirror.

It was all there. Their life. Written out. It felt like stone, not dust.

All that was gone now.

Damien stared at Raquel and Nicholas' tombstone with a date too recent. He waited for the tears to come. The anguish. He'd been both dreading and wanting this moment, to say something to them and bring some sort of closure, whatever that meant. But his mind was blank, his emotions dry. No torrent of tears or waves of sorrow.

Nothing.

Just silence. Hollow silence.

Damien felt his finger twitch. His hand started to quiver. The flowers Ted had laid on her grave suddenly lost their color. The world spun off its axis and Damien's body started to convulse.

He gritted his teeth, his neck stiffened, and he stared at the sky. The cloudless day grew pale as Damien passed out.

CHAPTER
NINE

"THAT WAS PRETTY DRAMATIC," Raquel said. "Passing out at my grave."

Damien awoke with a jolt.

His eyes tried to focus, staring up at familiar lights. And that smell. That awful smell.

He couldn't believe he was back in the hospital.

Standing over him was Doctor McShay, Damien's neurologist. She preferred to be called Shannon. Her red hair spilled over her shoulders, her green eyes probing deep into his.

"Mr. Hill, are you with me?" she asked.

"You have freckles on your cheeks," Damien said. "Never noticed them before."

Smiling, she straightened. "I can see your vision is returning."

"And so is my sense of smell. How do you work in this place?"

"You get used to it." She pulled over a chair, then sat next to Damien's gurney. "We have some things to talk about."

"I figured," he said, sitting up.

As Shannon flipped through a series of brain scans, Damien's nose caught another scent. Familiar. Comforting. Impossible.

"Do you wear perfume, Doc?" he asked.

"Not here, in case my patients are sensitive. Why, are you smelling something? Can you describe it?"

"It'll just make me sound nuts."

"Try me."

"My wife's perfume. It's unique. She gets it from Puerto Rico, where she was born. It smells like roses and jasmine. It's just… I swore I smelled it."

"Could be a sense memory flooding back."

"Sense memory?" he said. "You mean my brain is lying to me?"

"Not lying. It's just working things out."

She placed his file on her lap and clasped her hands on top of it.

"Your brain took quite a beating, Mr. Hill. Neural pathways were damaged and, as they heal, they'll form new connections, if they can. This may make things a bit unpredictable for a while."

"Are you saying I'm going to hallucinate?"

"No. However, some areas of your brain may be heightened temporarily. Other parts were more severely damaged and have not yet recovered. Your brain may have to figure out how to work around those areas."

"Is that why I passed out?" Damien asked.

"Possibly. You had what is similar to an epileptic seizure, which is why I recommended you continue your therapy with me."

"No deal, doc. I've got to move beyond this place."

"And, yet, here you are," she said with a smile. "At this point, I'm not sure if unpredictable responses will become a chronic issue for you, but it is something we'll have to deal with as it comes."

She paused and bit the inside of her lip. "And there is something else."

She opened up his file and flipped through his brain scans

once more.

"You've had extensive damage to the supramarginal gyrus in your cerebral cortex where your temporal and frontal lobe meet."

"Sounds interesting. Now, imagine I don't have a medical degree."

"Sorry. Those areas of the brain normally control certain emotions, such as empathy and sympathy. You may struggle to feel them for a while."

"How long?"

"That's uncertain at this time. But, there is a slight possibility they won't fully heal."

"You're saying it may be permanent?"

"We don't know. Only time will tell."

"Wait, wait, wait," Damien said. "I'm a cop. I've read psych reports. I know people without empathy or sympathy —the prison is full of them. They're murderers and molesters. They're like the guy who killed my wife and wanted me dead. Are you saying I'm going to be like him?"

"No," she said.

"Then what are you saying?"

"I'm saying you've had brain damage, and you're healing."

"And that I may never be the same again," he said. "What's the term for someone with my condition? Someone who can't feel empathy or sympathy?"

"Mr. Hill—"

"No, I want to hear you say it. What would a psychologist call someone like me?"

"I'm not a psychologist," she said.

"Humor me," he said.

"Clinically? Someone incapable of feeling either of those emotions is often classified as…"

"A what?"

"A sociopath."

CHAPTER
TEN

DAMIEN'S HAND wrapped around his pistol for the first time since the day it happened. The Glock was heavier than he remembered. Bulky.

He methodically pressed the bullets into the clip, one after the other, in no rush to fire. Officially, he was still a cop with a few weeks left on medical disability and he was taking his time. He was allowed to use the shooting range as much as he wanted, but he'd been avoiding it.

After his conversation with the doctor, he didn't trust himself anymore, questioning every thought, every impulse.

He'd never considered the right way to think. He saw things, interpreted them, and acted accordingly. That used to be enough. With two of his six cylinders no longer firing, everything he took for granted was gone.

Every action was preceded by one question. *Would I have made this decision before?*

Living in a world without empathy or sympathy would be cold and calculating. Sociopaths used guns as easily as they would a harsh word, whatever it took to get what they wanted.

People were pawns to be used in their own personal chess

match, their value tied directly to what they could get from them. Use or abuse, it didn't matter.

A sociopath's wants superseded everything else.

He'd seen hints of it in his father, actions that didn't make sense to anyone but him. On the rare occasions he'd been home, he liked to stir the pot, setting everyone against the other, with him changing sides just to keep it interesting. It was one big game to him, and he'd been indifferent to their tears and frustration.

The deeper the divide, the better.

He watched his father strike his mother when she tested him, a test for which only he had the answers. And had no qualms about putting his belt against Damien or Jacob's backside for the slightest offense.

His moral compass spun in circles, with him at its center.

If his father was indeed a sociopath and Damien's brain left him no alternative but to follow in his footsteps, then his time on this earth would be short.

The day he looked in the mirror and saw his father's reflection would be his last.

There had only been one certifiable psychopath in Damien's life, someone he least expected to be a killer. From the mouth of that childhood friend, he heard the inner thoughts of a cold-blooded murderer.

Ted and Damien grew up with Mark, a chubby kid with sandy-blond hair. They all liked sports and movies. That was enough at that age. Shared interests, shared experiences. That was all boys needed to gain friends.

Like most childhood relationships, they started to separate in middle school. Their worlds no longer shared the same orbit.

During this time Mark began to show signs of change. Puberty was a tricky thing. Hormones running through their bodies, altering their brain chemistry and making them horny as hell. This was when Mark grew interested in videos.

Disturbing videos of executions or news footage of horrific acts. Somehow, people's suffering became entertainment to him.

Damien dismissed it at first. Every kid stumbled across something they had never seen before, fascinated, or maybe disgusted, by it at first.

Turned out Mark never made it to the second part.

He started doodling on his school notebooks, covering them with pictures of violent acts and over-sexualized women.

Damien had no idea what demons were swimming around in Mark's mind. Five years later, he found out.

A high school cheerleader went missing after a football game. Her name was Cathy Richie. She was blonde, bubbly and a straight-A student. She was going to hang out with her friends at a burger joint across the street from the school. She said she needed to get her cell phone out of her car—that she would be back in a minute.

She was never seen again.

A year later, another blonde girl, Daisy Hicks, a cashier at the local grocery store, went out by the loading dock to have a smoke.

She vanished.

Two weeks later, they found her body buried under the porch of an abandoned house. She had started to decompose. Some small animals had fed off her remains, but there was enough left for the coroner to determine she was raped, tortured, then strangled and stabbed.

One hair changed Mark's life. A single strand stuck around Daisy's earring led the cops to his front door. He was a pizza delivery man by then. Could travel anywhere, knock on any door, unnoticed.

At over three hundred pounds when they arrested him, he could have put up a fight, but he entered the county jail without a word. He confessed to Daisy's murder, but that was it. Detectives were certain he was responsible for Cathy, and probably a number of other unexplained disappearances of cute blonde girls, but they couldn't prove it and he wasn't talking.

During his cadet training, Damien went to see Mark in prison. He was still big, but it had become more muscle than fat. He was imposing and hardened. Gone was the kid with odd fascinations and strange doodles. Through the prison bars was a killer who shared a face with someone Damien once considered a friend.

Over the next few months, Damien visited Mark seven times and they talked for over five hours. At first, it was about the old days, sneaking into the movie theater to catch the latest blockbuster, playing kickball in the empty field next to the orchard of grapefruits. Nostalgia.

Eventually, the real Mark started to drive the conversation. He hinted at the pain he'd caused his victims and the pleasure it brought him. He was arrogant, proud of what he had accomplished, and thought he was smarter than everyone else.

It was then Damien asked the simple question.

Why?

That was when his visits became trips into the mind of a sociopath. A sadomasochist. A rapist. A murderer.

The more Damien probed, the more he saw behind Mark's facade. Even when they were kids, Mark was hiding his true nature. He didn't know why he felt the way he did about people, but he could tell from his family and friends that it wasn't normal. So he played along, learned the rules of society so he could fit in and get what he wanted.

Mark washed the dishes, not out of love, but so his mom wouldn't take away his game console. He did his homework, not because he liked school, but to avoid getting another lecture from his dad. He joined the theater department in middle school, not because he loved the arts, but because he wanted to get into Susie Marriot's pants.

Everything he did, everything he cared about, was to fulfill his own desires. He eventually grew tired of rejections from people like Susie, lectures from his dad, and stacks of dirty dishes.

In middle school, he started to embrace the way he was made. In the next few years, he delved into any perversion he could get away with.

He'd drug the "school sluts," as he called them, and have his way with them.

He'd vandalize the cars of the bullies in school.

He even tried to poison Mrs. Kerry, his guidance counselor, after she suggested he get psychological counseling.

It was a slow and inevitable progression from thinking things to doing them. Now, thanks to Scarman, Damien and Mark shared the same moral flaws.

Standing at his wife and son's grave, he felt nothing. He would have died for his family. He wished he had. He would have taken that beating gladly to save his wife. He'd take a bullet for Ted, and he'd risk everything to protect Jacob and their mother.

Was all that gone now, lost amidst misfiring neurons and scar tissue?

He studied his pistol. It was now in the hands of a mentally altered law enforcement officer. Same palm, same fingers, different man.

Mark wasn't deterred by society's rules. He didn't see the lines between right and wrong. They didn't clarify things, as they did for Damien. They just got in the way.

Damien was drawn to the police force because it provided him with the structure he needed. Rules. Accountability. Consequences. Those didn't exist in his father's house.

Mark didn't care. Lawlessness opened his mind to a world of possibilities that most people, including Damien, found repulsive.

Now Damien was left with a choice he never dreamt he'd have to make—be the cop or become someone like Mark.

"You're not going to be like him," he heard Raquel say.

"I could be," Damien said out loud.

"You're kind. You're loving."

"That's all past tense."

"You don't know that," she said.

"And neither do you."

He looked up to an empty room.

He'd grown accustomed to hearing her voice. He didn't question it anymore. He was probably going insane or, as Doctor McShay—sorry, Shannon—would have said, he was dealing with the residual effect of a brain still healing. Maybe. There was still a chance, albeit small, he'd end up like he was before, but with each passing day, that felt more like a fantasy than a diagnosis.

No matter the reason, mental or miracle, Damien didn't want Raquel to leave him. Her voice was comforting. Kept him steady. If her presence, imagined or otherwise, was the one gift he received from Scarman's beating, he'd take it.

He returned to the gun in his hand. Whether he would end up being Dr. Jekyll or Mr. Hyde, stayed a cop or killed Scarman without remorse, he needed to hone his shooting skills.

He clipped a virgin target onto the mechanical track and pressed the button, moving it twenty yards away. First time out, sixty feet could be a challenge, but anything closer and he wouldn't know how much his skills had degraded. If the new police commission wanted better-stronger-faster cops, he didn't have much time to get there.

He secured his gun range earmuffs atop his head, then slapped the clip into the pistol grip.

His palm was sweaty. His grip, loose. Not good enough.

He thought of Raquel's words. "You're not going to be like him."

He loved her optimism.

Holding the gun with both hands, he placed his feet shoulder-width apart. He bent his knees to a semi-seated position, leaning forward slightly to balance his weight.

He closed his left eye and lined up the targets on the gun, his hands struggling to remain still.

You're not going to be like Mark.

His finger squeezed the trigger, and the range echoed with his shot. The pistol chamber recoiled, ejecting the shell at his feet, and the smell of gunpowder drifted in the air.

Gazing down the range at his latest shot, he smiled.

First time, right between the eyes.

He'd always been a natural, and it was nice to know Scarman hadn't taken that away from him. Turned out it was like riding a bike, one that traveled twenty-five hundred feet per second.

In the field, agility was as important as accuracy. Not every target would be immobile twenty yards away, waiting for him to plug its forehead with a kill shot. He called the agility routine Muzzle Juggling. Thirty shots with both hands. Fifteen with the weak hand. Fifteen with the strong. Thirty shots in sixty seconds. Hand strength played a part. Fatigue, too, as well as the pressure of time. All real-world concerns if a situation required a drawn gun.

With his full clips ready for reloading, he aimed his pistol and prepared to fire. The excitement of the challenge was invigorating, but one uncomfortable realization overtook him.

The sociopath was still a marksman.

DOCTOR MOIRA JONES was a tough nut to crack. All business, no fun. Dressed in her pants suit and with glasses too large for her face, she scanned through the results of Damien's psychological exam. Her expression offered no hint as to her findings.

Impassive, like an unflattering statue.

The police commissioner's new admission standards were daunting, but Damien had been given a bit of leeway. His injury afforded him a little more time to prepare. He'd been training hard, but his muscles were still weak. Didn't matter. He couldn't wait any longer. He was going stir crazy sitting in his apartment, surrounded by Raquel's pictures and baby items she'd purchased.

He probably should have packed them away by now, but they kept him grounded. Sometimes he'd lay on the floor, surrounded by Nicholas' toys, and wondered what his son would have been like. His personality? Would he have been cranky or fun? Demanding or relaxed? Would he have been into cooking like his mom or a bookworm like his father? Smart or clever?

There were many things Damien wished to do with him. Play hide and seek. Take him to his first baseball game. Play catch. Teach him to ride a bike. Tell him about girls. Show him how to treat a lady. All the things Damien's dad had never done. Instead, Damien was left being a father who would never hold his son.

At night, when he was at his weakest, the pain of Raquel's death hurt the most. Sleep was difficult to find, the space next to him impossible to fill. Nothing had eased his pain until last Saturday, when he rummaged through their dresser, hunting for an old pair of cuff links. As he sifted through the drawers, the smell of Raquel's clothes began to fill the room. Along with it, her scent. It felt as if her presence moved around him, through him, like a dance. Now, when his heart ached in the dark of night, he laid one of her shirts next to him and imagined her beautiful body filling it.

It wasn't a healthy way to live, but it kept him sane for now.

At his last checkup with his neurologist, Damien expressed his worry about the changes occurring in his brain. He told her about Mark, but not Raquel. Shannon reminded Damien that he and Mark would never be the same. Mark was always a sociopath and, as such, never experienced the world like the rest of us. Damien had over two decades of life experiences Mark couldn't understand. Mark never felt love or mercy. Damien had lived with both.

She may have been right, but whatever progress he felt he was making in the light of day, his nightmares were still filled with Scarman's eyes and the persistent impulse to put a bullet between them.

Shannon urged him to see a psychologist. He did. He was sitting in front of her now. Not for healing. For reinstatement.

Damien watched Dr. Jones' eyes dart back and forth as she read the results of his psychological exam. Somehow, a series of vague questions and obtuse scenarios was the key to unlocking his psyche. He tried to answer them honestly. Well, the way he would have answered before the riots. It was a long exercise of second guessing and trying to say what he thought the police force wanted to hear. Maybe it was enough to keep his new flaws a secret from his superiors and the frumpy psychologist.

"The last time you cheated on a test, you got suspended, remember?" Raquel's voice said.

Damien fought the urge to respond.

"Tenth grade biology midterm," she continued. "I remember. It was before you dropped out. You sat in the middle of class, I was sitting three seats behind you. I thought you were cute, even back then. You'd always been smart. Too smart for that class. I couldn't believe someone like you would do something so stupid. Why did you cheat?"

"To see if I could," Damien said out loud.

"I'm sorry?" Dr. Jones asked. "Did you say something?"

"I just wanted to see if I could look at the results of my exam?"

"In just a minute."

Damien nodded and leaned back, peering over Dr. Jones' shoulder, where his eyes beheld a vision he believed was relegated to his memories.

Raquel stood on the other side of the room. Full bodied. Present. As real as Damien himself.

She was wearing his favorite outfit. The simple yellow sundress and sandals she wore on their first date at the beach. Damien loved the fact Raquel didn't need makeup to look beautiful. She had that naturally, in abundance. The dress was short enough to show off her tan skin and tone legs. The top was tight enough to suggest the rest. She was radiant. Alive. More stunning than ever.

Damien wanted to jump out of his seat and wrap himself around her, but he didn't move, afraid she'd disappear in his arms.

"Hi," she said with a smirk. "You're wondering if you're

going nuts, aren't you? Good question. Truth is, I don't know. All I know is that I'm here."

She pulled a chair up next to Dr. Jones and sat down.

"You look like shit, though, babe," Raquel said. "You need to take better care of yourself. Time you started getting on with things, don't you think? That means stop eating mac-n-cheese and pizza and throw in a couple of vegetables every once in a while. You've got up to thirty-seven years ahead of you. Don't waste them on regret and fatty foods. Do something with your life. You're a good man. I know you are."

Damien bit his lip, desperately trying to keep from talking. There was so much he wanted to say. She was so close he could smell her perfume and the minty scent of her lip balm. Closing his eyes, he relished them both

"Mr. Hill?" Dr. Jones asked.

His eyes shot open as he straightened in his seat.

"Sorry," he said, relieved Raquel hadn't vanished. "I was thinking of my wife. It's calming."

"Of course," Dr. Jones said, adjusting her glasses. "I appreciate your patience. My workload didn't allow me time to go over your results before our meeting."

"That's understandable. Especially with all the cadet changes coming down from on high. So, Doc, what's the verdict?"

"Before I start, I just want to say I'm sorry for your loss and what you've been through. Your scores in the academy were some of the best we've ever had. I was excited to see you start your career with us."

"So was I," Damien said.

"When the riots broke out, I never expected things to end as poorly as they did."

"That's one way to put it."

"It's commendable how far you've come in a relatively short period of time. You're an inspiration to many of us."

"Thanks, Doc, but I hear a but coming."

"Yes. No matter my personal feelings, there are some things outside of my control." She took off her glasses, then rubbed the bridge of her nose. "This is the least favorite part of my job. I'm sorry to have to tell you, but you did not pass the new psychological exam required to retain your position as a police officer."

"See," Raquel said. "You suck at cheating on tests."

"It's not all bad news, however," Dr. Jones said. "Because of your unique situation and the fact your injuries occurred in the line of duty, the department is willing to offer you a disability pension. It would be about half your current salary, which wouldn't be a lot, but it would continue for the rest of your life." She placed his file in a stack of many. "It's the best I could do for you, all things considered."

"Thank you for your honesty, Doc. Can I ask one more question?"

"Certainly," she said.

"What does your test say about me?" Damien asked.

Shifting in her seat, she returned her oversized glasses to her small face. "It tells me you're driven. Smart. Skilled." She paused. "And potentially dangerous."

He nodded, wishing her response was a surprise.

"Well, at least it doesn't say I'm completely dangerous," he said with a forced smile. "There's still some wiggle room, right?"

Dr. Jones didn't return his playful mood. "Please don't do anything stupid, Mr. Hill. I wouldn't want to have to testify against you in a courtroom."

"Wouldn't be my first choice either, Doc. I'll do my best to stay out of your crosshairs."

Damien stood, staring at his file. One test in one folder and that was it, his career was over. Some overpaid politician changed the rules and now he was no longer qualified to wear the badge.

It pissed him off.

He could still be a good cop. A great one, given a little patience and some guidance. Sure, he was damaged goods. Synapses misfiring here and there. So what? Cops didn't give out lollipops; they did the dirty work no one else wanted to do. Arrested drug dealers and pimps. Saved girls from the sex trade. Stopped drunks from mistaking headlights for brake lights. Kept husbands and wives from killing each other.

He didn't need sympathy to do that.

"Is there anything else?" Dr. Jones asked.

"No," Damien said. "What else is there?"

It wasn't Dr. Jones' fault. She was trying to help. Damien should have been grateful. He wasn't, but remembered what gratitude felt like.

"Thank you, Dr. Jones," he said, extending his hand. "I appreciate your honesty. I'm sure your job isn't easy, especially now. Thank you for sharing your expertise with me. It means a lot."

That was what he was supposed to say. Not because he cared, but because it was expected. Living with his new brain wasn't going to be easy.

Raquel joined Damien at his side as he started for the door.

"It's okay, babe," Raquel said. "You'll find a new path to take. The world is full of them."

"You sound like a Hallmark card," he whispered.

"Thinking of you during this troubling time," she said with a smirk. "Buck up, little fella. The sun rises on all of us, even the newly unemployed."

Damien chuckled.

"One more thing, Mr. Hill," Dr. Jones called. "If you don't mind, you can leave your badge with me."

"I don't mind, Doc," he said, turning and placing it in her small hand. "I hope it goes to a good home."

As Damien opened the office door, a number of new

cadets hurried down the hall, excitedly talking amongst themselves.

"What's the emergency?" Damien asked.

One of the cadets stopped. "The police commission is about to release their findings on the shooting that started the riots. We've been called into crowd-control duty in case things go bad again."

The police commission rarely found an officer culpable in a shooting, even as one as public as Ted's. The citizens or the media never got access to all the details, nor did they understand the department's rules of engagement.

Cops on duty didn't get second chances in life-or-death situations. They had less than a second to decide if their lives were in danger. If so, they were trained to end that danger as quickly as possible.

All their practice on the gun range wasn't a game. It was for a moment when a gangbanger running from an arrest warrant exited his car with a knife. When Ted couldn't talk that knife out of his hand, he let his bullet finish the conversation.

Cops couldn't risk being wrong, not if they wanted to keep breathing.

Damien wasn't worried about Ted being exonerated.

When the news hit the streets, he feared his small town would end up descending into madness once again.

THE POLICE STATION buzzed like a hive of angry bees, and Damien couldn't help but feel invigorated by the energy. With the heavy flow of cadets rushing past him, he instinctively held his hand out to Raquel before realizing the absurdity of it.

"Stay close," he said.

He no longer had his badge, but Damien didn't expect the paperwork for his dismissal to be finished until later that day. For the next few hours, he was still a cop and his city needed him.

No doubt the police leadership must have been anticipating what could happen after the announcement. In bigger cities, they'd call in their SWAT or SERT teams, or accompanying sheriff departments, to handle any potential blowback, but Hayeston was still a nothing town in the middle of nowhere. The best the attorney general and governor offered were a few more openings on the force to be filled with high-quality candidates who met their new criteria.

Damien assumed the majority of the experienced officers would be fanned out to expected hot spots in the city while the new cadets were likely to serve as a reserve force in case the current police presence couldn't keep things under control.

If all that failed, the National Guard would have to come to the rescue. Two hours by truck. Thirty minutes by helicopter.

Damien pulled out his cell phone and called Ted.

"Are you in the station?" Damien asked.

"No. I couldn't sit there, surrounded by my coworkers, and watch the guillotine fall. The sergeant assigned me an unmarked car. Told me to go home or somewhere out of sight. I couldn't go home. That would be worse than the station."

"Where are you?"

"Where no one will find me. Not until after the dust settles."

"Keep your head down, just the same," Damien said.

"How'd your psych eval go?"

"You weren't the only one facing the chopping block. Turned out, my head was expendable."

"Sorry," Ted said. "We'll still get the guy who killed Raquel."

"Oh, I know. That's gonna happen whether I have a badge or not."

"I figured. Just don't do anything crazy, all right? Let's meet up for beers at Chancers Bar later and we'll come up with a plan of attack."

"As long as the scarred fucker doesn't cross my path before then," Damien said. "Stay safe."

"You too," Ted said.

Damien followed the group of cadets through one of two doors into the Read-Off room. The briefing room held five long tables and chairs, a wooden podium, and a large cork-board with announcements and departmental initiatives. On the wall above the corkboard, a television showed a live news feed from the police commissioner's office three blocks away. A local female reporter, Casey Lane, stood outside.

None of the cadets were seated, but stood in front of the television like fans at a sports bar.

"It's been four months since the small town of Hayeston turned into a war zone," Lane said. "That's when police officer Ted Sherman shot Hector Martinez, a local resident, who allegedly refused to drop a knife."

"Allegedly?" Damien said.

He hated how the press had spun the event. They downplayed Martinez's criminal past and turned Ted's act of self-defense into something criminal. It was ass backward. But, burning buildings and dead bodies made for great television.

"Hayeston had not only become a site of civil unrest," Lane continued, "but also a battlefield of ideas regarding police brutality and the abuse of power. The commission's findings could either start to mend the rift or tear open the social wounds once again."

Damien fumed. "So, the only sane thing for the police department to do is sacrifice Ted's career on the altar of political correctness? Is that it?"

No one in the room replied, but they no doubt felt the same way. The ends justified the means. It had become America's new battle cry.

A tall male cadet pushed by Damien, weaving past him into the crowd carrying a stack of white papers. He moved toward the front of the room, placing a sheet of paper at the end of each table. With all eyes glued to the television, no one even bothered to glance at them.

Something was odd about the cadet's cap. It didn't sit right. It reminded Damien of when Raquel tried to fit all her hair beneath a baseball hat. Male cadets weren't allowed to have long hair. It had to be high and tight, that was the rule.

Curious, Damien tried to follow him, moving through the crowded space in his thin wake. The more he eyed the tall cadet, the more he stood out. His posture and gate were undisciplined. His uniform incomplete. His shirt was too small for his long arms, and his black belt held no cuffs, holster, or taser.

"This just in," the reporter said. "We have word from the police commission that the shooting involving Officer Ted Sherman has been ruled justified. No punitive action will be taken against him or any member of the Hayeston police department. Officer Sherman could return to active duty as early as today."

The officers in the room cheered, but the celebration didn't last long. How could it? Everyone was gearing up for a riot.

"Need to be prepped for secondary coverage in ten minutes," an officer yelled. "Let's help the town make it through today without incident."

The room flurried with activity as the cadets readied themselves.

All but one.

The tall cadet slithered to the front of the room and paused at the door, his hand grabbing onto the doorframe.

Damien saw it then—the serpentine scar twisting around his right arm. He snatched one of the sheets of paper left on the table.

It had a picture of Ted and his family.

Wanted: Dead or Alive. $50,000 Reward.

And added at the bottom:

Collateral damage is encouraged.

The tall man in the uniform turned to Damien and smiled.

"Stop him!" Damien yelled, pushing through the crowd.

Scarman tossed the stack of remaining wanted posters into the air. Behind the paper snowfall, he disappeared into the hall.

"Stop him!"

Damien's cry barely made it above the chatter. He forced

his way forward, pressing through the wave of anxious men and women, and into the hallway.

The long hall with cement walls and a hard tile floor was littered with Ted's wanted posters, but Scarman was gone.

The air in the hall suddenly shuddered as an unholy groan shook the building. The Read-Off room next door, full of nervous young cops, exploded into a ball of flames.

CHAPTER
THIRTEEN

DAMIEN FOUND himself on the ground, leaning against the far wall, its cinderblock construction offering him no comfort from the powerful blast that tossed him there.

"Raquel..." he mumbled, staring into the room billowing with smoke and screams. "Raquel? Are you all right?"

"Are you serious?" she asked, sitting next to him. "I already died once. It'd be cruel to make me go through that again."

"Right..." Damien said, pushing himself to his feet. "Sorry."

Alarms sounded, water raining down from the emergency sprinkler system. Large cracks scarred the wall supporting the Read-Off room where the bulk of Hayeston's remaining police force lay dead or dying.

Smoke and dust filled the air. Cries of anguish followed them into the hall.

Damien squinted, trying to wave the cloud of debris from his eyes, and spotted a bloody hand escaping the smoke, reaching out for help. He grabbed hold and escorted the officer from the room, the young man's hair singed to the scalp, his clothes and skin shredded like grated cheese.

The officer collapsed in Damien's arms, and he struggled to keep his grip on his bloody body.

"Hold on," Damien said as he laid the wounded officer on the tile. "Help's on the way."

He held the man's blood warm hand. The young cop, probably less than a week out of the academy, stared up to him and tried to speak, but only blood and saliva pushed out of his mouth.

"Stay with me," Damien said. "Just hold on."

The cadet gurgled, his grip growing limp.

Damien pressed his fingers against the man's neck.

No pulse.

Unsure of what was to come next, Damien took the pistol, cuffs, and keys from the dead cadet. Clip, full. Cuffs, undamaged.

Officers from the far side of the building entered the hall. They raced past Damien into the smoldering briefing room.

One of them stopped. "How many are in there?"

"Twenty," Damien said. "Maybe more."

"Wait here," the man said before running into the room after the others.

A moment later, the floor trembled and a second blast on the other side of the wall exploded, throwing Damien down the hall.

The fractured cement wall splintered into pieces. Sections of the roof collapsed above him. Damien rolled into a doorway, escaping chunks of metal and wood, and braced himself.

Creaks, snaps, and thuds surrounded Damien as the building crumbled around him. Time seemed to slow. Sounds deadened. Flashbacks of fifty thousand volts coursing through his body jolted him. The rush of fear paralyzed him. Fending off kicks. Trying to save his wife. Trying to protect his child. Failing them both. It all flooded back. Helplessness. Worthlessness.

The guilt of survival.

Between him and the Read-Off room laid a pile of broken cement, wooden beams, and smoke. No way to get back in to see if anyone had survived.

Damien needed more help.

Through the fallen roof, shafts of light pierced the smoke, lighting a path down the hall and away from the epicenter of the blast.

"Let's go," he heard Raquel say. "Get moving. You're not done."

"Where are you?" he asked.

"Stop asking questions and go. Now."

Her voice was the only other sound penetrating the ringing in his ears. His head throbbed with pain, and he struggled to find his footing. Water and debris covered the uneven slick tile. Sparks from failing electrical systems pulsed around him like a dying heartbeat as Damien stumbled toward a side exit.

With the police either dead or vastly outnumbered, Scarman and his team could move about the city with impunity, inflicting whatever damage they wanted.

What was he up to?

Damien raced through possible targets. The main employer was the citrus facility. There was a power plant on the edge of town, feeding electricity to Hayeston and surrounding areas, including all the medical facilities, both big and small. If he wanted hostages, Hayeston had one school, kindergarten through twelfth grade, about five hundred students in all.

Political targets included the mayor's residence, City Hall, the police commission offices, and the headquarters for whichever political party Scarman opposed.

None of that accounted for the stores, strip malls, public parks, and churches.

Churches, Damien thought. *Jacob.*

Jacob wasn't a fighter; he was a counselor. Sometimes, Damien wondered if they'd grown up in the same house.

He shoved his shoulder against the metal door leading outside and forced it open, spilling into the alleyway. The light was overcast with smoke, the air filled with the stench of burning flesh, and Damien tumbled onto the uneven brick between the buildings.

His breath pushed wisps of sand out from within the crevasses, and Damien stared down the alley.

As the ringing in his ears began to subside, Damien heard the sounds of cheers and chanting nearby. The voices drew him to the front of the building where a massive crowd had gathered. Hundreds of people stood outside the collapsed structure, holding up signs that called for the destruction of the police force and death to all cops.

"Who the hell are these people?" he murmured.

Damien scanned the crowd. Most of the faces he didn't recognize. Only a few citizens from Hayeston peppered the group. The rest were unknown. Probably agitators. Scarman's soldiers. It was hard to tell.

What was happening in town was more than just another groundswell of discontent. This was organized. Bigger. Planned and executed. Hayeston had once again become ground zero in Scarman's war. The battle lines between anarchy and the rule of law were drawn on its streets. It was early in the fight, but the mob was winning.

Sirens of approaching fire trucks and ambulances drowned out the protesters. As if with one mind, the riotous crowd turned and rushed toward them, forming two lines, blocking their path to the station. Rocks and Molotov cocktails followed, forcing the first responders to stop blocks from the burning station.

Within Damien grew a voice. It was urgent and angry. Not

Raquel's. This one was new, yet familiar. From his own darkness emerged a side of Damien that had been silent. One fueled by rage and inspired by violence. It was a beast borne from his own flesh and bone, coexisting inside him, now formed and seeking approval to act.

The more he listened he came to realize it was the other side of himself. It was the Mr. Hyde in every person. The persona that abandoned morals for personal justice, sought vengeance for the sake of closure.

Its influence had never been this strong before, and Damien wondered if this was the sociopath in him making his presence known. He couldn't control his thoughts. They were racing, both sides of him, the cop and the beast, fighting for supremacy.

Anger boiled inside him from a depth he'd never experienced. An uncontrollable fury. His rewired brain didn't include a governor, and he wanted to kill every person stopping the paramedics.

Put them all down and count the bodies later. Casualties of a war Scarman started.

"You're better than this," he heard Raquel say.

"Am I?" Damien said aloud, his fingers caressing the pistol.

"Don't become one of them. Tearing something down is always easier than building it up. Don't be a wrecking ball. The world has enough of them. Be better than that. Be the man I married."

"He's gone."

"No, Damien, he's not. You'll always be my husband."

"You expect too much," he said.

"No, you expect too little."

He tried to push aside Raquel's words, but her voice stayed with him.

He reluctantly shoved the gun in his pocket.

He stood in the alley as screams and pleas from the station were replaced by the crackling of fire and snaps of a collapsing structure.

Damien swallowed his anger and walked away.

Finding Scarman in the crowd would be impossible. He needed to tap into the police radio. Find out who was left to help hunt the terrorist down before he became another ghost.

The police cruisers parked in front of the building had been set ablaze. Other cars were tipped over or vandalized. None were drivable.

A police parking lot was a block away, home to marked and unmarked cars. No doubt it was already in flames, leaving Damien only one option. The departmental auto shop. It was also nearby, tucked away in a nondescript building adjacent to a defunct bakery. No one would know it was owned by the city unless they went inside and found the cruisers under repair.

That was his best shot.

He turned and jogged away from the mob, running down the uneven brick alley. As he approached the next intersection, he found another protest group behind the station, smaller, mostly strangers, blocking all the roads leading in.

These anarchists were determined to make sure the cops inside died slow and agonizing deaths.

What drove them to hate so openly and take joy in the public slaughter of innocent people? How did they exist, hidden from society for so long?

Damien fought the urge to empty his clip into the crowd. Instead, he clenched his teeth and scanned the police garage a few storefronts away. It was free of flames and protestors. Just the road and sidewalk littered with thousands of pieces of paper. Not just on the ground, but affixed to every pole and building.

They were Ted's wanted posters. The city was covered

with them. Anyone in the town could cash in by killing Damien's best friend.

The beast inside Damien started to engulf him again. This time, he had no interest in extinguishing it.

Raquel would have to forgive him for what he was planning to do.

CAUGHT ON A WAVE OF AIR, one of the wanted posters brushed by Damien's foot. He pulled out his cell phone to warn Ted and his family.

"We're sorry, all circuits are busy."

He tried Jacob.

Same thing.

He tried nine-one-one.

Same response.

Hayeston was an island in a sea of citrus. It wouldn't take much to isolate it from the rest of the world by disabling or blocking the cell phone towers.

Damien had no way to warn the others what was coming.

He'd use the car radios in the police auto shop, if they still worked. The garage appeared untouched, and Damien didn't want to draw attention by breaking in through the front.

He'd only been inside once. It was wide and hot. Harsh light from lines of old fluorescents were offset with the addition of two expansive skylights overhead, adding a warm glow and unwanted heat.

They also offered Damien an entry point hidden from the protestors below.

Sliding under a weak board on the side of the closed

bakery, Damien slipped to the rear of the store and up a maintenance ladder to access the roof. From atop the building, he could see spires of smoke dotted across the town. City Hall. The bus station. Buildings in the industrial park. A number of storefronts on Main Street. A few other houses scattered in neighborhoods near the police station. The chaos was spreading.

Jacob.

He glanced in the direction of his brother's church. No fires or flashing emergency lights, but destruction was heading that way. Damien tried to call his brother one more time.

No luck.

The two skylights were about ten feet apart, made of clear plastic that had long since faded to a cloudy white. Around their base, years of the bright Florida sun had taken its toll on the tar and caulk. Damien used his keys to separate the base from the dried and cracked frame. With a jerk, he tilted the skylight up and peered into the garage below.

It was quiet and still. Just the dull sunlight from the smoke-filled sky illuminating the cars and trucks in the shop.

The drop from the roof to the floor was at least twenty feet.

Time to get creative.

Dipping his head into the opening, he spotted a wooden cross beam spanning the width of the building. Located midway between the two skylights, it was a good five feet away. No easy jump. Nothing there to catch his fall.

Damien sat on the edge of the opening, his legs dangling through the hole. Gripping the skylight frame, he eased himself down, hanging in the air, facing the crossbeam. The rusted edges rising above the dried tar started to cut into his fingers and his forearms started to burn. He'd never felt so fragile in his life, his own weight almost too much to bear.

Like an unskilled gymnast, he started to swing his legs

back to front, each movement forcing the frame deeper into his flesh. With shaking biceps and knuckles that felt like they had turned to glass, he let go, lunged forward, and snagged the wood with his left hand.

When his body jerked to a stop, pain shot from his arm to his side.

"Oh, shit," he grunted, certain he'd torn a muscle. He dangled momentarily, the pain increasing, his arm too weak to stop his momentum, his shoulder straining to hold his weight.

He reached up and grabbed the beam with his free hand, but wasn't strong enough to lift himself up. Scanning the length of the beam, he spotted a chain-linked storage enclosure on the other side of the room.

Hand over hand, one painful inch at a time, Damien moved down the beam and across the garage, his feet hanging above the cement floor. The cars and trucks below him would not welcome his fall.

Ignoring his ripped muscle, failing strength, weakened fingers, and bleeding palms, he swayed back and forth one more time, gaining enough momentum to fling himself at the chained enclosure. With a loud *clang*, he crashed into the fencing halfway to the floor, scrabbling as he fell. The loose chain links slowed his momentum and he landed on the ground with a survivable, but painful, *thud*.

Damien rolled onto his back, trying to breathe through the pain, and stared up at the crossbeam above him.

"Shit, that hurt," he said.

He rolled over, then pushed to his feet with a grunt.

He tore paper towels from a roll on a tool chest and held them against his bleeding hands. The cuts weren't deep enough to need stitches, but the blood wasn't going to stop without a little help.

Surveying the garage, he spotted two police cars—one a cruiser, the other unmarked—along with a tow truck, a pickup, a motorcycle, and a meter maid cart most in varying stages of disrepair. The walls held tool chests, rags, cleaning supplies, oil, fuel, buckets, garbage cans, and a first aid kit.

Damien sprayed antiseptic onto his hands, the liquid dousing his skin with searing pain. His fingers trembled as he then wrapped gauze around each hand, but they felt more stable after he taped them tight.

Inside two of the cars, Damien found police radios, but only one still worked. Once he slid into the front seat of the unmarked car, he clicked it on.

"Another Crown Victoria," Raquel said, suddenly sitting next to him.

"Shh, I'm trying to listen," Damien said.

She ran her hand across the cloth lining drooping from the ceiling. "How the hell did I fall for you when you owned one of these?"

"That car lasted us a long time," he said. "It was well maintained, cared for—"

"And ugly," she said. "A gas guzzler. Smelly, too."

"Okay, okay, I get it. Not the most elegant of cars, but dependable."

"Like you," she said with a smile.

"Wait. Are you saying I'm dependable, ugly, or smelly?"

She responded with a grin before crawling over the seat into the back.

"Wow, I forgot how roomy it was back here," she said.

"Big enough for two criminals," Damien said. "Or a canine and one criminal. Or two canines."

"Or a hot wife and a horny husband."

Pausing, he grinned. "Right..."

"In the parking lot of the town fair. Surrounded by families and kids with balloons… what were we thinking?"

"I was thinking of getting you naked," he said. "I have no idea what you were thinking."

"I was thinking you were handsome and that we should wait."

"Wait? Why? You got the ring. You got the wedding. And you got the Crown Vic. What more could you want?"

"We hadn't been married very long," she said.

"That's what made it fun."

"I was worried about what could happen."

"The same thing happened that always happened. I satisfied your every need."

She sighed. "Oh, baby. I love that you think that."

Damien climbed over and joined her in the back.

"Well, don't tell me any different, because I can't do anything about it now."

"Baby, you were amazing," she said with a lustful sigh. "You made my toes curl."

"That's better," he said with a laugh. "I remember it was a lot of fun. Hot, sweaty, naked fun. What were you worried about?"

"I was…" she said. "That was the night we got pregnant."

"What?"

"That was the night Nicholas was conceived."

"Holy shit, really? In the back of our Crown Vic? Why didn't you tell me?"

"We got rid of the car soon after," she said. "It never came up."

Damien smiled, the realization elevating his Crown Victoria to an even higher standing.

"One hell of a car," he said.

The police radio beeped alive, the speaker buzzing with excited chatter. Officers frantic, calling for help. There was a lot of background noise of protests and yelling, but he was able to recognize a few of the voices.

All the officers were struggling to keep their area under control. Too many people, some armed with bats, rocks, and homemade flammable cocktails.

The area near the police station was a total loss. No way to gain control of that section. A few cops were holed up inside City Hall trying to keep the mayor and his staff safe. The National Guard had been called, but it'd take them time to get here, maybe longer if Scarman treated the feeder roads like he did the cell towers.

At least help was on the way. It also meant one other thing. If Damien wanted to hunt and kill the scarred asshole, the clock was ticking.

Other cops had taken refuge in the undisturbed areas of town. They were trying to round up any willing citizens to help them defend what was left of the city.

Blockades had been structured in those outer areas. Some townsfolk had even taken up their own arms, joining forces to stem the tide of destruction.

Another voice crackled over the speaker.

"This is Sherman," Ted said. "Can anyone hear me?"

Damien hopped into the front seat, snatching the radio handset up. "Ted, this is Damien. Can you hear me?"

"Damien?" Ted asked, the signal muddled with static. "Is that you? I can barely hear you."

"Ted? Ted?"

"My car was set on fire, barely made it out alive. I got beat pretty bad. I think my leg is broken. I'm holed up in the old Hayeston Herald printing warehouse. I think I'll be safe here for a while, but send a paramedic as soon as you can. Can't get through to nine-one-one."

"The first responders are swamped with—"

The radio was interrupted with loud static.

"Ted?" Damien asked.

"Has anyone heard from my family?" Ted asked. "The last time I talked to my wife, they were heading to St. Simeon's."

Jacob's church.

"Ted, I'll come get you," Damien said. "Wait there. I'll get there as soon as I can. Can you hear me? Wait there. I'm on my way."

"If anyone can hear me, please provide Denise and my kids with safe passage to the church. I'll meet them as soon as I can get out of here."

"Ted." No response. "Ted."

Damien tossed the broken handset against the dashboard.

He was left with two choices. Save Ted or save his family. No way to protect them both.

Damien would have to pick one.

DAMIEN TURNED off the police radio, then double checked his pistol clip. Fifteen bullets. Not enough to start a war, but maybe enough to finish one.

He was one of the few people who could identify Scarman. Pain meds or alcohol hadn't been able to remove his face from his nightmares.

Scarman's wanted posters made Ted his prize. Saving Ted became Damien's only concern. His best friend was hiding out in the warehouse district on the other side of town. The ten-mile drive through a war zone wasn't going to be easy with crowded streets full of angry people.

Denise and her kids were already heading toward Jacob's church, away from the violence. Chances were, they'd make it okay, but Ted had a bull's-eye on his chest and thousands of people searching for the target.

Damien exited the Crown Vic, checking out his options. The pickup's engine had been removed, and the tow truck had a bad axel. The police cruiser would be a prime target on the streets, and the unmarked Crown Vic was no better.

The motorcycle was his best bet. It was plain and old, probably from the eighties. Damien had no idea what the roads were like between here and the warehouses, but the cycle only needed a path wider than its handlebars to make it there.

The bike seemed to be in good shape. Tires were relatively new. Cables fresh. Oil clear. It was just missing a spark plug. Damien entered the enclosure, scanning the storage room for a replacement.

From behind the wall of supplies, he heard the sound of a key entering a door lock and the bolt clicking open.

Ducking, he pulled the gun from his pocket.

Two men entered the garage. One was about six foot, a little on the heavy side. The other, a thin younger man, about twenty, looked familiar. A local.

The heavy man placed the key in his pocket.

"See if you can find a light switch," he said.

The young man reached behind one of the toolboxes. Clicked on the lights.

Damien shifted behind a stack of boxed oil filters, keeping his eyes on the intruders through the chain-link fence.

"He was right," the heavy man said. "Looks like we'll able to salvage a few of these for the cause. Take inventory and see what needs to be done."

The young man popped the hood of the police cruiser.

"So, you're getting paid?" the young man said.

"Yup," the heavy man said. "A lot. Too much, if you ask me. But with the plant closing in Percy, you take what you can get. Someone offers you a thousand bucks to get on a bus to Hayeston to chant and throw stuff, I don't complain. I ask where do I sign up?"

Percy, Damien thought. *That's over two hours away.*

"That's all you gotta do?" the young man asked. "Protest and throw rocks?"

The heavy man pointed to the vehicles. "And borrow some transportation."

"Why?"

"I don't know. I don't ask questions. I pocket the cash and

nod like a happy puppy. Not like some of the other folk. Some on the bus were a bit more enthusiastic about taking on the cops. I didn't talk to them much. They weren't right in the head. Me? I'm just looking for enough dough to keep the lights on until my unemployment checks start coming. They got no openings at the citrus facility here in Hayeston, but I got an interview over in Breston. I'm not too hopeful, though. Everyone from the Percy plant is trying to snag one of them jobs. Four hundred people applying for twenty positions. Gonna be tough."

"I hope you get it," the young man said.

"Me too. But I tell ya, I'm not putting 'borrowing cop cars' on my resume," the heavy man said with a laugh.

Damien stepped out from the cage, gun drawn.

"You think this is funny?" Damien asked. "Men and women are dying across the street... and you think this is a joke?"

"Whoa," the young man yelped.

"A cadet died in my arms," Damien said, pointing to the young man. "No older than you. Is that funny? Want me to put a bullet in your brain for another punchline?"

"No," the young man said.

The heavy man pulled out his cell phone.

Damien charged him. He tackled him into the tow truck, knocked the phone from his hand, and struck him in the face with the pistol butt for good measure.

"Wait, wait, wait," the large man said. "I don't want any trouble."

"Then you should have stayed in Percy. Who do you work for?"

"I'm unemployed."

"Don't give me that shit. Who hired you to come to Hayeston?"

"Some big fella, tattoo on his neck. Don't remember his name. Something like Dog or Tick or something like that."

"Still making jokes?" Damien shoved the gun in the babbling man's mouth. "Go ahead. Make me laugh."

"Leash," the young man next to him said. "They call him Leash."

Damien aimed the gun at the teen. "I know you. I've seen you around. What's your name?"

"Freddy."

"You live in Hayeston?"

"Yeah. Over near the laundry mat."

"Then what the hell are you doing here?" Damien asked.

"Got nothing else to do."

"Nothing else to do? People are dying, Freddy. Good people who would do just about anything to save your life. What in the hell is wrong with you? You think killing people is a way to fill your time? I got a few minutes to spare. You want me to kill you? What would you like, a slow death or a fast one? I mean, I'm just filling time."

"No! I didn't know people were going to die. I heard on the street that shit was getting real today. That I could up my cred by joining in."

"Your cred?"

"You know, harassing the cops. Shit like that."

"How many lives does it take to max out your cred, Freddy?"

"Look, man, I ain't gonna kill no one. Ever. That's not my thing."

"Not your thing?" Damien asked.

"No."

"Who was your contact? On the street?"

"I told you. Leash."

"Leash. Is that his given name?"

"I don't know who gave it to him, but that's what he's called."

"Fine," Damien said. "Get out of here. If I see you on the street—holding a sign, throwing stuff, or just looking grumpy—I'm gonna shoot you where you stand. You hear me?"

"What kind of cop are you?" Freddy asked.

"I'm not a cop. Not anymore."

Freddy scurried out of the building.

It was the first time Damien had said it out loud. It felt right, and the beast in him agreed. No longer restricted by the law, he could enforce justice in its purest form.

Damien turned his focus to the heavy man. Scum. No principles. No soul. Just in it for the money.

"Where'd you get the key to this place?" Damien asked.

"The key? I, ah, I got it from a guy on the bus. Told me to come over and see if there was any transportation they could use for the cause."

"What cause?"

"I don't know," the man said. "Whatever cause that pays. Look, I'm sorry about what happened to you and the others. I didn't have anything to do with that."

"But you did," Damien said. "You're here to destroy my town. Hunt down my friends. You… you killed my wife and child."

Grabbing the man by the shirt, he spun him around. He opened the back door of the police cruiser, then cuffed the man to the interior cage. "I think it's time you and I had a little quality time."

"Look, mister, I didn't kill anyone. I'm sorry about your wife and—"

Damien slapped him across the face.

"Don't you *dare*!" Damien screamed. "You don't have the right to talk about her. As a matter of fact, you have no rights at all, not in here, not with me."

Damien pocketed his gun and tossed the drawers of the toolbox, searching through each one.

The man tried to free himself, the cuffs clanging against the metal screen separating the front and backseats.

"You don't look good," the man said. "You got that look in your eyes, like those boys on the bus."

Damien pulled a pair of jumper cables from a cabinet. He used a hacksaw to cut off one of the ends. After he pulled the protective covering off the exposed wires, he shoved each one into an electrical socket. Sparks flew off the metal jumpers as he tapped the remaining battery connectors together.

"What's your name?" Damien asked. "No, don't tell me. It'll make it easier if I don't know."

"Wh-wh-what are you going to do with those?"

"I don't know yet. The possibilities are endless."

Raquel appeared from behind the cruiser.

"Damien, what are you doing?" she asked.

"I'm having a chat with my new friend," Damien said.

"Who are you talking to?" the man asked.

"Shut up," Damien said.

"I saw this once before," Raquel said. "I saw a man send thousands of volts through your body for fun. You were scared. Helpless. Do you remember that?"

"Of course I remember, but I already lost you. I'm not losing Ted or Jacob. No more people are dying today. Not on my watch."

He approached the man, stroking the jumper cable ends together, shooting sparks into the air.

Damien smiled. "So... what should we talk about?"

CHAPTER
SIXTEEN

ANGER COURSED through Damien's body, a font of hate and distrust. The man cowering in front of him was both an obstacle and an opportunity.

He was also a coward. Damien half expected the man to urinate on himself the first time the electrified jumper cables grazed his neck.

"Who is your contact?" Damien demanded. "Who gave you the key?"

The man quivered, cowering away from Damien and falling into the backseat of the cruiser. "I told you, the man on the bus."

"What was his name?"

"I don't know. He didn't tell me."

Damien tapped the jumper cables across the metal grate near his cuffs, the current shocking the man's wrist.

"Think harder," Damien said.

"He didn't give me a name!"

"I don't believe you."

"Look, man, I don't know what else I can say except what happened," the man said. "This wasn't a dinner party. And the guy who gave me the key wasn't the talkative type. He wasn't asking me what I wanted to do. He was telling me. He was kind of scary, you know? The kind of fella you tried not to irritate. Kind of like you."

"Wrong answer," Damien said, moving the jumper cables near his neck. "Let's try again."

The man started to beg, but the beast didn't care. He didn't ask the man to be here. The man made his own decisions. He'd taken the key. He'd unlocked the door. He'd even walked passed a burning police station to move into Damien's path.

Actions had consequences, and justice required sacrifice.

"Damien!" Raquel said.

"Not now," he replied.

"Damien Michael Hill!"

He turned to find Raquel standing next to him, her hands on her hips.

"What do you think you're doing?" she asked.

"Having a conversation with my new friend."

"You're going to torture this man?"

"I'm going to get answers," Damien said.

"It's only been a few months since I died, yet you're already becoming just like them. A sociopath. Is that what you're turning into? You're not even going to put up a fight? Who will you be in a year? Or two years? Will I even recognize you?"

"What the hell do you want me to do? Nothing? Stand by and watch the world burn?"

"No," Raquel said. "I want you to do what a law enforcement officer would do."

"He'd be wasting time. Scarman is out there laughing as our town destroys itself. He killed our cops in front of our eyes, blew them to pieces without any mercy. He killed you and our baby for fun. He's put a bounty on Ted, Denise, and the kids. He deserves to die. So does anyone on his side."

"Listen to yourself, Damien."

She stepped closer to him, her eyes glistening with tears.

"Baby," she said. "I don't want to lose you."

"You won't."

"But I will. I can't be with this version of you. I won't. I'll start to loathe you. Detest you. Eventually hate you. My heart cannot stand the idea of hating you. I would rather remember the man I loved than watch you become… this."

Damien paused, peering into the eyes that had lifted him up from his own failing before, wondering if they held enough strength to do it one more time.

"You'd leave me?" he whispered.

"No. You'd be leaving me."

Dropping his head, he noticed shadows of himself cast by the numerous overhead lights, his shape split into multiple weaker versions of itself, each facing a different direction.

That was how he felt. A man shattered from the inside, fighting the collective wills diverging away from each other.

The beast and the cop. The old Damien, or the new.

Damien tossed the jumper cables aside and sat on the floor, leaning against the cruiser. He couldn't be two men. He had to pick one. Right now, at this moment, he chose the one who had married his wife.

"What's your name?" Damien asked.

The man remained silent.

"What's your name?" Damien repeated.

"Oh, now you're talking to me?" the man asked.

"Yes."

"Oh. Charlie. Charlie Beckman."

"Charlie Beckman. What did you do in Percy?"

"Worked on a manufacturing line. Made computer boards for cars. I was in the quality department, running diagnostics on parts before they left the plant."

"How long did you work there?" Damien asked.

"Nearly fifteen years. But technology, you know. It changes quick. Got replaced by a robot."

"That's tough. It's hard when life throws you a curve."

"It can be."

"Where did you get approached about protesting in Hayeston?" Damien asked.

"At the unemployment line. Me and a hundred other folk were waiting to sign up for our checks when the guy, Leash, he shows up flashing a lot of cash and asking people if they wanted to make a couple of hundred for taking a ride on a bus."

"You told Freddy you made a thousand bucks."

"I know what I told him. I exaggerated. You know, trying to impress the kid. Then maybe he'd listen to me. Think I was more than I am."

"How many people decided to take Leash up on his offer?" Damien asked.

"Most. Wasn't a hard decision. You'll do just about anything when you got nothing to lose."

Damien glanced at the jumper cables on the floor. "Yeah, you do," he said. "You ever meet a guy with a long scar down his right arm?"

"No. Don't think so."

"Long dark hair. Olive complexion. Italian, maybe? The scar twisted around his arm like a snake."

"No, sir. Never met him."

"So, what were you supposed to do with these cars?"

"If any of 'em work, me and the kid were to drop them off for Leash and his boys."

"Where?"

"I got the address in my pocket." Charlie tried to reach the note, but needed his cuffed hand. "Excuse me, I can't get it unless you uncuff me."

"Sure," Damien said, tossing Charlie the key. The man quickly uncuffed his hand, rubbing his raw wrist.

"Didn't think I'd make it out of these alive."

"I didn't either."

Charlie retrieved the paper from his back pocket and handed it, along with the keys to the handcuffs, to Damien.

Damien read the address aloud. "Fourteen hundred Pearson Drive." His eyes widened, and he hopped up. "Fourteen hundred Pearson Drive."

"That's what it says. What is it?"

"Leash is waiting there for you?" Damien said.

"Yeah, he and his boys. Is that bad?"

"It's the police armory. If they take that, they'll control all the department's weapons."

CHAPTER
SEVENTEEN

THE SCARRED MAN sat atop the water tower, gazing over the town of Hayeston. His finger traced along the twisting scar on his arm, stopping at his wrist. He did this often to remind himself of his greatest failure and the lessons he learned from it. His youth and hubris nearly cost him his life that day. He was never going to make that mistake again.

More pillars of smoke began to rise into the muggy overcast sky. The spread of the riots had continued as planned. Nothing about today was a surprise to him. Human nature was a puzzle, not a mystery.

Income. Family structure. Unemployment. Church attendance. Tribal violence. Education. Corruption. Greed. Want. Need. Homelessness. Social tensions. Secular compassion. Religious hypocrisy. Drug of choice. Frequency of use. Prostitution. Domestic violence. Fatherless homes. Gang infiltration. Racial disparity. Historic bias. Engrained distrust. Simmering anger. And that was just the beginning.

For the people of Hayeston, these were real issues affecting lives in tangible ways. For him, these were nothing more than ingredients to a recipe.

High unemployment. A history of prejudice that fueled

resentment. Disenfranchisement of a segment of the population. Weak infrastructure. Isolation.

After that, the rest was just flavoring to tailor the outcome to his needs. How quick did he want the rage to burn? How violent did he want the citizens to act? How many would he be serving with this recipe? A city block, like months earlier? Or an entire town? A state? Country? Or the world?

Each in progression. All in time.

The recipe needed to be refined with each attempt. Lower church attendance? Add more racial tension. Diminish secular compassion and infuse more greed. Months of planning, seeding, nudging, and inflaming.

Despite human nature's redundant behavior, individualism was always a problem, for it was nearly impossible to predict. Collective minds, however, demanded less variations of thought. The more people added to the mix, the less things he had to get them to agree upon.

Mobs were stupid. Single minded. Reactionary. Emboldened by the perceived noble actions of others, they would follow the lead like lambs to the slaughter. A plumber, by himself, would never burn down a local store in which he shopped, but if mixed in a mob, that same plumber would happily set fire to the whole town in order to vent his frustration.

Scarman liked the violence. The rage, pain, and confusion. It reminded him of home. His childhood was stained by the blood of others, and he welcomed it wherever he went. It was a sign of his eventual victory.

However, the pawns below Scarman didn't realize they were the distraction in a sleight of hand for a greater purpose. Hayeston not only had the elements for the recipe in Scarman's revolution, but it also held a weapon that no one knew existed. It was benign in its creators' hands, but full of global, destructive potential in his brethren's.

The world would eventually burn, as Scarman had predicted, but not for the reasons the lemmings roaming the streets in Hayeston believed.

Nothing below was as it seemed.

Just the way Scarman had planned.

CHAPTER
EIGHTEEN

DAMIEN KICK-STARTED THE MOTORCYCLE.

He tossed Charlie onto the streets with the same warning he'd given Freddy. Even though he hadn't tortured the unemployed factory worker, the thought of what happened lingered with Damien.

Torture. It was an option now.

The boundaries that once separated right and wrong in him were gone. His rewired brain didn't recognize those limitations anymore. Damien wanted to hurt Charlie. He wanted to make him feel his pain and know, firsthand, the suffering of which he had taken part.

He wanted vengeance. Cruelty over compassion.

The beast felt fully justified. Pressing electrified jumper cables to the cuffed man's neck was the right thing to do. The clock was ticking. Lives were at stake. Secrets could be discovered. All good things.

Would Benita complain if Damien had killed Scarman the first time they met? No. She'd have her store, her future. Ted and his family wouldn't be in hiding. A room full of cadets would still be alive. Parts of Hayeston would be more than fire and rubble. Raquel and Nicholas would be home, waiting for Damien's shift to end.

The beast understood the power of action and that collateral damage was part of the math. Charlie became an acceptable loss.

Hearing and agreeing with those thoughts were what ultimately saved Charlie's life. Damien had effortlessly moved from cop to killer. Knowing he could turn into all that he hated terrified him.

Damien was speeding through life without guardrails now, and his thoughts were betraying the beliefs that had guided him so far. He didn't want to lose the man he was—become one of the faded shadows on the auto shop floor—but he didn't know how to stop it.

The mind was the filter through which the world made sense, but all that was now gone. His thoughts used to inform his will, but now his emotions were in the driver's seat. His will was at the mercy of his impulses. His morals at the whims of his emptiness and anger that accompanied it.

Damien was broken. Unlike his bones, the damage felt as if it were permanent. There was no light at the end of his tunnel, just more darkness and a destination he feared awaited him.

Damien wasn't a religious man, not like Jacob. However, a childhood growing up with an abusive father made some sort of afterlife a requirement, because that awful man got everything he wanted, no matter the cost. Someone as despicable as him had to pay the price for his actions. It surely didn't happen in this life. It had to in the next.

Otherwise, his father's tombstone represented the rewards of a selfish life, never having to pay the tab for years of taking from others.

If his father's eternity was of his own making, then so was Damien's. He wasn't sure how, with faulty synapses and evil urges, he could possibly make it to the place Jacob called heaven?

Shaking his head, Damien tried to dismiss the idea.

He was missing guardrails again, unable to control his thoughts. He didn't believe in God or heaven, yet he couldn't stop thinking about it. He never worried more than a day in advance, yet all of eternity consumed him now.

Damien had to get his introspection under control. He wasn't on his way to see a priest to confess his sins; he was heading to an armory where the tattooed man who killed Raquel was probably waiting. If they crossed paths, the farthest thing from Damien's mind was forgiveness.

The armory was located about halfway between the auto garage and the warehouse district where Ted was hiding. It was out of the way, but a necessary stop. Damien had to know what sort of firepower he was facing. If Leash was there, Scarman may be as well. If not, one of Scarman's minions must know where he was hiding.

Damien was going to find out.

He weaved through the backstreets and alleys, avoiding the hordes of protestors and agitators. The drive was taking longer to navigate through the city than Damien wanted, but the route kept him away from suspicious glares.

As he approached the back of Benita's burned-out store, he could see more wanted posters littering the neighborhood. In the distance, he heard the cry for the public execution of Damien's best friend.

He pulled over and turned off the engine, unsure of what drove him to stop. His wife and child were buried four miles away, but this was where they both died. It was the one place he promised himself he'd never see again, yet here he was, staring at a collapsed brick wall and smoldering embers streaming upward like incense.

"What happened in there was a tragedy," a voice behind him said.

Damien turned to find an old man approaching him. His wrinkles were deep, his face a dark tan, like he'd spent his life working outside in a state where the sun rarely hid.

"They say where there's smoke, there's fire," the old man continued. "Well, I think that smoke is where all this fire started. Bad things happened in that building. Bled into the rest of the city. Corrupted good people. Turned the wicked loose."

"What are you talking about?" Damien asked, knowing the answer, but drawn by morbid curiosity. "What happened?"

"Good folk died in there. A young man. A cop, I think. And a woman. I heard she was pregnant at the time, poor soul. When all the ruckus started, they got caught up in it, became the avenue for some sick people's anger. Beat them to a pulp, for no real reason I could understand."

Damien tried to bury the flashbacks pressing against his conscious.

"Sounds awful," he said.

"Got worse, too. What they done with them afterward, I mean. Propped their bodies up in the store windows like bloody mannequins, as a warning to others about what was to come. A dead pregnant woman in the window of a ransacked baby store. People took it as an omen. A portent."

Damien gritted his teeth, balled his hands into fists as the beast fed off his anger.

"How long were they there?" Damien asked. "In the store window?"

"A couple of hours at least. This here store was the center of all the ruckus. Being so, it was the last place to get calm again. I heard some parents were showing their kids, pointing at the bodies, telling them they deserved it. Awful thing to say to a young mind. No one deserves something like that. Not here. Not in Hayeston."

"Not anywhere," Damien said.

"That's right. Not anywhere. Not in a world I want to live in. Why would people do something like that? How does inflicting such pain cross someone's mind?"

"Because they're evil," Damien said. "It's no more complicated than that."

"Well, if that's the case, then evil is winning and Hayeston is smack dab in the middle of hell."

Damien kicked the motorcycle to life, pointed it in the direction of the armory.

"You're heading the wrong way, son," the old man said, "Things only get worse the farther you go that way."

"I know," Damien said.

"What's so important you gotta ride into that?"

"The devil and I have something to settle."

CHAPTER
NINETEEN

THE ARMORY, though small, was well stocked.

The last time Damien visited the hardened building, it included three M-16 A1 assault rifles, two Remington 700 sniper rifles, five tactical 12-gauge shotguns, a gas gun, ten standard police shotguns, and thirty handguns.

If Leash had access to those weapons, then Scarman's little war had entered dangerous territory. Two sniper rifles in skilled hands was enough to lay siege to this little town. From the tallest buildings, it would be easy to see to its borders and very little of the population would be free from the scope of an accomplished shooter.

Damien was glad Scarman and Leash didn't know he was coming.

The armory was surrounded by houses that had been rezoned into small businesses. A dentist. An injury law firm. An accountant. A veterinarian.

In most districts, the armory would be housed within the police station itself. It would have worked that way in Hayeston had the police station not once been the town post office. At the time, the city couldn't afford a bigger building. The station didn't even have jail cells. Those were in another location that used to be a book depository, which was near the water treatment plant. The hodgepodge of buildings wasn't ideal, but seemed to work well enough. There wasn't enough crime to justify changing things.

Damien needed to understand what he was facing. For that, he required a clear line of sight of the armory without being visible to Leash or any of Scarman's soldiers. His best chance was the Barrett Supplies office building three blocks away. Sold construction supplies to the area. Businesses only. No retail or foot traffic. It was catty-corner and three stories high, giving him a good view of the front and side of the armory.

Damien knew the building well. Raquel worked there for a short time after they got married, but had to quit when pregnancy complications put her on partial bedrest.

The first story of Barrett Supplies was a storeroom. The second held Barrett's offices and cubes, including Raquel's old desk. The third floor was being remodeled, the last Damien heard.

He'd been called to the building a couple of times while on duty. Juvies were stealing copper from the jobsite when the building was getting the air conditioners replaced, and Damien became familiar with the location's security. If Barrett Supplies hadn't yet been set on fire during the riot, it was a good bet he could get to the roof without much trouble.

The deeper Damien rode into Scarman's territory, the more lawless the little town became. Small gangs ran through the streets. They vandalized homes and businesses, harassing people who were trying to stay out of harm's way.

Random gunfire would occasionally echo through the neighborhood. It occurred so frequently, Damien no longer flinched. He would never confuse that sound with another again.

It appeared many families had either left town or hunkered in their houses, blinds drawn. While others sat on their front porches, nervously holding pistols and rifles for everyone to see. People were doing anything to convince the roving bands of outlaws to skip their homes and move on.

So far, it appeared to be working.

The Barrett building was in sight, but Damien needed to take a detour. There was one other location he needed to check.

He took a left through two empty lots onto Trammel Street, where he was greeted by a blockade of cars and men with guns. He recognized them.

"What do you want?"

The question was asked by Robert, Raquel's oldest brother. He was a stocky man, all muscle. Six years older than Damien, he had a tattoo of a dragon on his chest, its tail peeking out of the neckline of his t-shirt.

When Damien and Raquel started dating after she graduated high school, Robert was their most vocal critic.

"I wanted to make sure you guys were okay," Damien said.

"Like you'd protect us," Robert jabbed. "As you can see, we can take care of ourselves. We're fighters. We'd die protecting those we love."

"As would I."

"I guess we'll have to take your word for it."

Damien nodded, knowing this wasn't the time to offer olive branches or build bridges. When it came to Robert and Raquel's family, that time may never come.

"What streets do you control?" Damien asked.

"We got a three-block radius," Robert said. "Trammel to Vine. Vine to Akins. Akins to Horton. Horton back to Trammel."

"Nice work."

"We're not cowards."

"No, you're not," Damien said. "Have you seen a man with long hair and a scar down his right arm, twists around and stops above his wrist?"

"No. We haven't seen much of anybody. Word is getting out this ain't a neighborhood to play with."

"What about a guy with a large neck tattoo?" Damien asked. "He's called Leash."

"No."

"Good. The less you see of them, the better. Listen, be careful. The people behind this, they're the same ones who killed your sister and our baby. I think they're controlling the armory."

"You're shitting me," Robert said.

"No. A lot of cops are dead. Won't be help for a while. Stay low. And don't kill anyone. The *defending your castle* law doesn't apply when you're not on your own property. Out here, murder is murder."

"Don't worry, anybody we shoot will end up on our property one way or the other."

"I'll pretend I didn't hear that," Damien said.

He wanted to leave, but knew he may never get this chance again. He didn't blame Robert or anyone in Raquel's family for their feelings about him. Raquel married a cop. She signed up for all that entailed.

Her family hadn't. They attended a wedding, received a birth announcement, had a big party, then lost their daughter and future grandson in an attack they'd never be able to forget.

The only survivor was the man whose mere existence put their daughter in peril. Damien didn't expect forgiveness, no matter how much he craved it.

He walked over to Robert and embraced him, catching him by surprise. Damien finally understood how Ted felt at the gravesite.

"I am so sorry for what happened to Raquel," Damien whispered. "I tried to save her. I would have died a thousand times to stop them. Please tell your parents I'm sorry."

Robert stepped back as Damien let him go, staring in a stunned silence.

Damien hopped back on the bike. Started it up.

"Where are you going?" Robert asked.

"The armory."

"But isn't that where all the bad guys are?"

"Hope so."

LEASH CHOSE HIS NICKNAME. Some people thought it made him sound weak, but he knew otherwise. He'd watched the pitbulls fight in his uncle's ring. They were killers, trained to destroy their opponents. They were powerful and cruel. They weren't afraid of the fight. Blood didn't scare them. They dreamt of the battle. And when they were set free, only the strong survived.

That was the way he saw himself. A pitbull on a leash. Not a pet, but a weapon waiting for the chance to act.

The boss had given him a book about the art of war. He said Leash needed to learn how to think ahead instead of after things were already going crazy. He tried to make it through the first chapter, but he didn't learn much reading before he dropped out of school. His mom said that was why he got angry so much, because he couldn't read.

Maybe.

Didn't matter much. He liked being angry. He was good at it. Being big and strong made people listen. Didn't matter what books he finished or what grade he got through. He had muscle. On the street, that meant more than brains. Other people could do the thinking. He didn't mind. He liked the fight.

Like the pitbull.

He'd been fighting since he was a boy. Picking on the kids in the neighborhood. He'd learned how hard to push, when to threaten and when to pounce. Only one kid ever had the guts to fight back. Always protecting his friends. He wasn't stronger than Leash, but he was fearless. Brave, even.

That same kid became the cop who killed that gang-banger. That cop was a pitbull, too. Maybe not. A German shepherd.

That made Leash laugh.

German shepherds were cop dogs. So, if the cop was going to be a dog, he'd be that.

When he got a bit older, Leash started his own gang. Not as good as the one that listened to him now. But they were good. Got money doing the easy things. Drugs. Stealing. Whoring out a few girls. He was doing good. Never got arrested. Stayed under the radar. Knew how the street worked and used it to his advantage. He thought he'd reached the top of the heap when his boss saw him beating a john who refused to pay. He said he could help him reach his potential.

Leash never thought about his potential. Wasn't much point. Not in Hayeston.

His boss asked him if he wanted to be a recruit. Leash didn't want to join no military. The boss said it wasn't that type of army. His army followed different rules of engagement. Leash hadn't known what that meant, but figured it out the more the boss talked. He'd liked what he heard.

The boss said Leash had skills. Said he could work his way up, be his second in command.

Skills. Potential.

Stuff no one ever said about him. They were too scared to say much when he was around, which he hadn't mind, because he didn't have much to say anyway.

His boss wasn't scared of Leash. He was impressed. Boss

wanted to hear what he thought. He told Leash he was smart. Street smart. Stuff more important than book learning. Real world smarts.

Skills. Potential. Smarts.

Boss said he could earn his stripes by helping make things happen in Hayeston, which he did. Now he had ten men guarding the armory.

Boss said be ready for anything, which didn't make much sense, since anything could be anything. No one could be prepared for anything. Leash could be ready for some things. A few things. But not anything.

He could be ready to fight. He could be ready to kill. He could be ready to eat. He could be ready for sex.

That wasn't anything, but they were the most important things. Plus, he had his smarts, skills, and potential. The boss was counting on those, too.

And the armory full of weapons.

CHAPTER
TWENTY-ONE

THE AFTERNOON SUN glowed darker than normal. Smoke from a number of fires had filled the stagnate skies with a haze. The darkness worked in Damien's favor.

After he stashed the motorcycle in the shed of an abandoned house, he hoofed it two blocks over to the back of Barrett Supplies. He remembered the storage room door off the alley had dry rot in the doorframe near the hinges. He'd noticed it while arresting the juvies, and hoped they hadn't fixed it since then.

Blended into the surrounding sounds of distant gunfire, chanting, and yelling, Damien's kicks and bangs went unnoticed. It took a few hard strikes with his shoulder to loosen the frame, but with one final kick, he knocked it into the building.

The silent alarm would alert the security company, but no police would be responding to their call. Not today. Damien moved into the dark storeroom. With a huff, he lifted the door and lodged it back into place.

He weaved through pallets of boxes wrapped in plastic to the back of the room, then rushed up a little-used stairwell to the second floor and snuck into Barrett's offices.

This floor was also dark, with dim sunlight pressing

around closed shades, giving the long room an eerie hue, like dusk moments after the sun dipped below the horizon. Manager offices lined one wall while a conference room and a supply closet lined the other. In the middle were a series of desks, including the one Raquel used to occupy.

Damien sat in her old chair, now apparently used by a woman with an unhealthy love of cats. A cat calendar, cat pictures, cat paw stickers, and a cat mousepad dotted the cubicle.

Damien shivered, and it wasn't because he loathed felines. The air behind him changed.

He could feel Raquel's presence.

"Do you think things would have been different if you'd worked here through the end of the pregnancy?" he asked out loud.

"Yes," she said, moving next to him. "I wouldn't have been with you when the first riot happened, which means you'd probably be dead and I'd be a widow."

"I would have preferred that," Damien said.

"Well, I wouldn't. It wasn't just you and me, you know. Our baby had something to do with how things turned out. Complications, doctor visits, bedrest. I couldn't hold down a job and deal with that at the same time, even if I wanted to. That day at Benita's baby shop was the first time I'd been out of the house in, what, two weeks?"

"Still," he said. "Things could have been different."

"Is that the game you wanna play? Yes, things could have been different. We'd be alive if we never got married. Or if you never dropped out of high school. Or if my parents hadn't moved here when I was seven. I could keep going on and on."

"You don't have to mock me."

"And you don't have to wallow either, babe."

"I just miss you," he said. "It hurts. Every morning I get up, I'm still surprised you're not lying next to me."

"I miss you, too," she said. "We both do."

"Why don't you ever bring Nicholas with you?"

"I'm not allowed."

"Says who?" he asked.

"I don't know, but your son *can* see you. Watches you. He thinks you're pretty cool, except when you get all crazy and violent. I cover his eyes when that's happening—tell him you're having a spell."

"A spell?"

"What can I say, it works. I can't wait for you to see him. He's four now."

"What? Already?"

"Time, babe. It doesn't exist where we are."

"Then why is he four?" he asked. "And not seventeen? Or thirty?"

"I don't know. He just is."

"You're not making any sense."

"Well, I've never been dead before," she said. "This is new to me too. I can only tell you what I know and what I don't. And I know he's four. The same age as Billy, Benita's little boy."

"Can Nicholas talk?"

"Of course. He's four."

"What does he say?"

"What every four-year-old says. I love you. Mommy. Daddy. Can we play? I want more toys. The usual."

Damien shook his head, trying to make sense of it all. "If you can see me, can you see Ted? Is he safe?"

"I don't know."

"What about Scarman?"

"I don't know. I'm not all-seeing. I can't travel around and be your spy. You see me, and I see you. That's it."

"That's it?" he asked.

"Yup."

"Then where are you when you're not with me?" he asked.

"With Nicholas. And family."

"Where?"

"I never thought about it before."

"Heaven?"

"Maybe," she said.

"Is that even real?"

"Depends."

"Depends?" he asked. "On what?"

"Am *I* real? Because if I am, I have to exist somewhere, right?"

Damien sighed. "Never mind."

"Hey, you brought it up, not me."

Damien stood and turned, but Raquel was gone as quickly as she appeared. He hadn't spoken to anyone about seeing her for fear any investigation would prove her to be an illusion. He'd rather be insane with her, than sane and alone.

He continued to the far end of the floor, then up the main stairs to the unfinished third floor. Two-by-four studs had divided the long space into smaller rooms. Stacks of drywall boards were piled inside each one. The floor was covered with a thick layer of concrete dust, except for a fresh set of footprints headed toward the far wall.

Damien had company, and he definitely wasn't hallucinating.

If someone was there, he didn't want to have to use his gun. Too many eyes would follow its sound from atop the building. In the hopes of remaining under Scarman's radar, he picked a broken two-by-four off the floor and followed the prints to a ladder used to access the roof.

CHAPTER
TWENTY-TWO

WINDOWS on the third floor were high enough for Damien to get the view he needed of the armory, but if someone else was on the roof, one of Scarman's thugs, then he wouldn't be able to approach the building in stealth.

Damien climbed the metal ladder attached to the back wall, getting off on a small landing the width of a man. To the right was a metal door to the roof, which emanated heat from the afternoon sun. He opened the door a sliver, finding the sunlight brighter than he expected. The granular surface of the roof had faded to white, bouncing the light directly into his eyes.

Shading his face with his hand, he squinted through the brightness, trying to see past the small gap and out onto the rooftop. His view was limited. Over half the building behind him was out of his sight. In front of him, air conditioners and exhaust vents offered plenty of places for someone to hide.

Damien grew aware of his breathing. Short, excited panting. He hadn't been face to face with one of Scarman's thugs since the original attack. Exacting his revenge was on his mind, but the reality of it caught him by surprise. He still wasn't one-hundred-percent healthy. He might never be. Adrenaline would only compensate for weak limbs and a fragile body for so long. If he couldn't out-muscle them, he'd have to outthink them.

He tried to calm himself and focus.

Take it slow. Don't rush.

Damien ducked and crept onto the roof, gently closing the door behind him. The open sky made the top of the building feel more expansive, like a sandlot football field three stories in the air.

His eyes were drawn to the numerous columns of smoke rising into the sky, as if the city was crying for help.

Damien took a few steps toward the armory when he noticed two shadows on the ground. One his own. The other directly behind him.

Before he could turn, a muscular arm swept under his chin and pulled back, choking him. Startled, Damien dropped the two-by-four and instinctively clawed at the arm. His attacker was strong and tall. Damien was six one. This guy had to be six five.

The assailant lifted Damien off the ground, the tips of his toes dragging across the roof. Damien grew lightheaded, the sky started to go dark, and the world around him began to slip away.

Damien had seconds.

Screw stealth. He dug into his pocket. After yanking his pistol free, he shoved the Glock against the attacker's hip and fired.

The man let out a scream. Together, they fell onto the rooftop. Damien rolled over him, tumbling over the side of the building.

For a moment, he felt as if he were hovering, nothing but air surrounding him. He reached out and snagged the edge, tearing his torn muscles further.

Damien cried out in agony as he crashed into the side of the building. Frantically, he searched the side for gutters or fire escapes. No help.

He couldn't hold on for long.

The muscular man on the roof cursed in anger. Damien could hear him dragging himself to the edge, his huge body scraping against the sandpaper roof, his blood no doubt dotting the white with smears of red.

Promising to finish the job, the attacker peered down at Damien, the bright sky hiding his face. He was bald with oversized ears that bowed out like a dog's.

"You fucking shot me, you piece of shit," the man said with a deep voice. "I'm going to enjoy watching you die."

"It's nice to see people who take pride in their work," Damien said. For the first time, he realized he was no longer holding his gun.

Sarcasm without weapons was a bad idea.

The man's hand clasped onto Damien's and squeezed.

Damien's knuckles started to crack, pain shooting up his arms.

Falling was inevitable now. Fortunately, the fall would only last a few seconds. The sensation of air whisking by and then it'd be over.

Not a bad way to go.

"Tell your boss I'll see him in hell," Damien said.

Another shadow appeared over the attacker, holding the two-by-four in his hands. The board struck the attacker's head with a sickening *crack*, and the man's grip relaxed.

Just as Damien's fingers had lost all strength, the unknown shadow reached down and grabbed his arms, pulling Damien onto the roof next to his bleeding, unconscious attacker.

"Are you all right?" the stranger said.

Damien recognized the voice.

"Robert?" he asked.

"You are one crazy motherfucker," Robert said. "Stupid. And crazy."

"What are you doing here?"

"Besides saving your ass? I figured if you were dumb enough to take on an armory full of bad guys, you'd need a little help."

"You shouldn't be here," Damien said, rubbing his torn muscles that pulsed with stabbing pains. "This isn't your fight."

"To hell it isn't. The men who killed my baby sister are down there, like this motherfucker right here." He struck the unconscious man in the head, then kicked him again for good measure. "It's my fight as much as it is yours."

"I can't let you do this," Damien said. "I've hurt your family enough. If anything happens to you, I can't be the reason for causing your parents more pain."

"I'm a grown man with a grown man's will," Robert said. "This ain't on your tab."

"Robert…"

"If I hadn't shown up, you'd be dead. So consider this a bonus round, and let's get on with it."

Robert was bullheaded, as immovable as his stocky frame.

"Fine," Damien said, standing. "Then let's figure out what that guy was doing up here."

Damien was grateful, but he didn't want a partner. It complicated things. He was running with blinders on. He needed to stay alert and concentrate. Didn't have time to keep an eye on anything but the prize.

After Damien found his Glock a few yards away, he and Robert walked the roof, finding what Damien had expected.

A sniper rifle sitting on a six-inch bipod pointing away from the armory, toward the heart of the town.

"Shit, is that what I think it is?" Robert asked.

"If you're thinking it's a Remington 700 sniper rifle, you'd be right."

"So we could start plugging those motherfuckers from up here? I love it."

Damien sighed.

Overconfidence was a personality trait rampant in Raquel's family. Damien didn't know if that was strength or foolishness, but now wasn't the time to find out.

"Robert, have you ever killed anyone?" Damien asked.

Robert paused, revealing a crack in his machismo.

"I've been in plenty of fights," he said.

"Not the same. Killing someone isn't a game. It's unnatural. It stays with you for the rest of your life."

"How do you know?" Robert asked. "You kill someone?"

"No, but I've talked to cops who have. Even when they were completely justified in their actions and would have died had they not taken the shot, they never stop thinking about what they could have done differently. We may have to kill today, Robert. You may have to end someone's life."

He could see Robert's enthusiasm erode.

"You may have to watch the light leave their eyes," Damien said. "The way I saw it leave Raquel's. Do you want? Because it will remain, every second, for however many days you have left. If you have to kill today, know the cost."

Robert grew introspective, his furrowed brow alien to him. This was a first for Damien. He'd never witnessed anyone in Raquel's family stopping to think things through.

Damien picked up the sniper rifle before crawling across the roof toward the armory. Robert followed behind him.

"I'm not afraid," Robert said. "I know this ain't no day at the park. Real shit is happening down there."

"I'm not talking about being afraid. I'm talking about consequences. Once the trigger is pulled, there's no stopping the bullet."

At the building's edge, Damien steadied the bipod, the tip of the rifle peeking over the side, and peered through the tactical scope, the crosshairs waiting for a target.

Two thugs walked the perimeter of the armory. No cops in sight.

"Shit," Damien whispered. "They've got the armory."

He followed each thug, the crosshair tracking the center of their heads, wondering if they were Scarman's men from Benita's store. The faces from that day were a blur, mixed together with terror and panic.

Damien may have given a nice speech to Robert, but he had already paid the price for making the wrong decisions. Killing those responsible for his wife and son's deaths was the only right decision he had left.

The thug under Damien's crosshair turned, glancing toward the armory entrance. He shifted the rifle to follow his gaze.

Leash exited the armory, barking orders.

The two thugs scurried inside as Leash remained near the door, staring out with a broad grin. He was smug and proud, like Scarman, and had a sniper rifle pointed at his forehead.

Damien held his breath, slowly tightening his finger on the trigger.

CHAPTER
TWENTY-THREE

LEASH'S broad face sported a wide smile, confident, drinking in his new power, or so it seemed from Damien's viewpoint. He didn't really know what was going through the killer's mind. It could have been anything. For sociopaths, wanting tacos and wanting to kill someone held the same weight, its priority only changed by its immediate value.

Damien wasn't hungry for Mexican food, but didn't mind having a taste of the second option.

"Don't do it," Raquel whispered.

Damien's finger remained poised on the trigger.

The crosshair split Leash's head into four sections. One flinch of his finger and the monster's head would explode, wiping that conceited smirk off his face.

"Is that the neck tattoo guy?" Robert asked. "Leash?"

"Yeah," Damien said.

"What are you waiting for?"

"Don't do it," Raquel said again.

Letting out a frustrated exhale, Damien released the trigger.

"He's not the target," Damien said. "His boss is."

"Did he have anything to do with killing Raquel?"

"Yes," Damien said.

"Then pull the fucking trigger. If you don't have the balls to do it, I will. I'll take a lifetime of regret to feel the pleasure of putting that man down."

"No," Damien said. "I need him alive, for now."

"You're such a pussy. What did my sister see in you?"

Damien looked him in the eye. "Potential. The first day we met, she said I had potential."

"Potential is just another word for pussy."

"I never knew you were such a wordsmith," Damien said, sarcasm coloring his tone.

"You can call me whatever you want as long as you give me the rifle."

The rumblings of an approaching car drew their attention back to the armory.

Damien peered through the scope.

The car was an old white station wagon. It was tricked out, riding low on thick tires with raised white lettering around its edges. The car roared with more than a stock engine, and Damien could make out the shapes of two people in the car.

The station wagon slowed to a stop, and Leash walked down the armory steps to greet it. From the passenger side, an arm appeared, holding out a small piece of paper. Damien pointed the scope at the transaction. He noticed a scar on the hidden man's wrist that traveled up his arm.

Scarman.

Damien felt flushed. He fumbled with the sniper rifle, his quick breathing causing the images in the scope to rise and fall like lapping waves.

"What is it?" Robert asked.

"Shh!" Damien said, pressing the butt of the rifle against his shoulder and resting his head behind the scope.

The magnified image vibrated in tremors, the gun shaking in Damien's hands. This was the moment he'd been dreaming of, praying for, *needing*, and it was slipping away.

Focus.

Damien took a deep breath and tried to steady the rifle, moving the crosshairs to the car roof where Scarman's head should be.

His finger wrapped around the trigger.

With no hesitation, he pulled.

Click.

"Damn it," he hissed through clenched teeth, recycling the weapon, forcing a bullet from the magazine into the chamber.

He gazed through the scope again.

The minute Leash took the paper from Scarman's hands, the white station wagon sped away, screeching its tires as it left.

"What the fuck just happened?" Robert asked. "You pulled the trigger. Was that the guy? In the car? Was that the motherfucker who killed Raquel? That was him... and you *blew* it?"

Damien remained silent, rolling over to his back and dismantling the rifle into pieces. He handed the scope to Robert.

"Stay here and keep a lookout," Damien said.

"Where are you going?"

"To have a little reunion with Leash."

"What are you going to do? Threaten him with your finger?"

Grabbing Robert's shirt by the neck, Damien yanked him forward.

"Listen, you cocky sonofabitch," Damien said. "I don't need your running commentary. You puff your feathers and think you're someone important when you and your brothers are just a bunch of assholes. You all talk a tough game, pick on the little guy, and, at the end of the day, go back to your nice houses, crack a beer with your families, and brag about how the world feared you." Damien pulled out his pistol. Thrust it under Robert's chin. "You may think I'm a pussy, that I was never good enough for your family, but from now on, keep that sanctimonious bullshit to yourself. The day your sister died, things changed. I'm not the man you used to know. Doubt me and I will put a bullet through your skull to prove it."

Robert leaned back. "No man, I hear ya."

"Then take the scope and do what I say. Otherwise, crawl home to your mami and embellish the story about how you saved my life. Paint me with whatever brush you want. Make yourself the hero, if that's what your fragile ego needs. Right now, you are either helping me or getting out of my way. Do you understand?"

"Yeah, yeah," Robert said. "It's crystal, man."

Damien crawled away from the building's edge.

It felt good to get that off his chest. For years, he'd been putting up with their shit. Disapproving looks. Snide comments. Wagging heads.

They didn't see the way Raquel looked at him. They weren't there, in those intimate moments, when they talked about the future they were going to make together.

They didn't have to like their relationship, but they should have respected the fact that Raquel saw enough in Damien to choose to spend her life with him. That should have counted for something on their marriage day and after. Even here, on Barrett's roof.

Out of the armory's line of sight, Damien returned to his feet and headed for the door.

He had every intention of killing Robert. One wrong word, one sideways glance, and he would have shot him, yet Raquel said nothing. She hadn't come to her brother's rescue or tried to talk Damien out of it.

She'd been silent. Was *still* silent.

Something was wrong.

He crawled down the ladder to the third floor, then the

stairwell to the second, before he spotted Raquel sitting at her old desk.

"What's up with this lady and cats?" she said.

"Where the fuck were you?" Damien asked.

"Hey! Language."

"I put a gun to your brother's chin and threatened to kill him."

"You weren't going to hurt him."

"Yes, I was."

"No, babe. You were just trying to scare him."

"No!" Damien slammed the pistol onto the desk. "I was going to kill him."

"Thinking about something and acting on it are two different things, babe. Like having cat stickers and owning cats. How many cats do you think she owns?"

"You can't do that. You can't disappear on me. I can't trust my own judgement. I don't have control anymore. My brain doesn't think twice about killing. I want to hurt those who hurt you... and there is *nothing* in my head telling me to stop. All I have is you. Don't leave my side. Ever. If you do, you and I will never end up in the same place after this one."

"I have faith in you," she said.

"Well, stop it," he yelled. "Stop looking back. I'm not there anymore."

Smiling, Raquel tilted her head. "I see what I see, babe. I see all of you, not just the bad parts."

Damien swiped the pistol from the desk. "Well, I don't," he said, charging down the stairs. He was officially losing it. Rubber room and straitjacket kind of losing it. Even his dead wife didn't understand him anymore.

Real or not, she just might leave him one day. After this thing with Scarman was over, assuming Damien survived, she could bolt and never return.

Then he'd have a lifetime alone to face his demons, unfit for such a battle.

Coursing with simmering rage, Damien crossed the street and approached Leash, who cocked his head at him, gaze curious. Damien had forgotten how big Leash was in person. Wide. Strong. Scary.

"Do I know you?" Leash's voice was cold. He wasn't asking—his question was a demand.

"We've met."

"Well, you can turn your ass around and go home. This ain't visiting hours."

"Great," Damien said. "Because this isn't a social call."

"Then what's your problem?"

"I just had a fight with my wife," Damien said.

Then he punched Leash in the face.

CHAPTER
TWENTY-FOUR

DAMIEN WAS FORCED into a hard wooden chair in the middle of the armory storeroom. The floor around the chair was splattered with blood. Apparently, he wasn't the first cop to sit there today.

His gun had been taken from him. His hands and feet were zip-tied to the wooden arms and legs. Three armed thugs, along with an angry Leash, surrounded him.

The punch to the face hadn't been necessary to get Damien inside the building, but he figured it was the most direct. While being dragged through the entrance doors, he was able to reacquaint himself with the lay of the land.

At least ten of Scarman's thugs were inside. Most were armed and impatiently waiting. They had already done so much damage to the town of Hayeston. What was left on their to-do list that had them so excited?

Most were carrying police-issued arms, but not all. The leftovers were in the storeroom. A few shotguns. Some tear gas canisters. Around ten pistols. That was it.

It was a nightmare scenario. Every weapon in their hands was another one not being controlled by a cop.

Whatever Scarman had up his sleeve wasn't going to take long. He had to know the National Guard was on its way.

That law enforcement from distant counties could show up at any minute. By bombing the police station, Scarman's gang had assured Homeland Security and any number of three-lettered agencies would bring more lethal guns and better soldiers than he could cobble together.

Scarman was under the gun, so to speak.

"I'm usually a patient man," Leash said. "But I don't tolerate getting coldcocked by a local."

"Don't lie," Damien said. "It's not your style. You're *not* a patient man. Own it."

"If you think so, then all the more reason punching me in the face wasn't a smart thing to do."

"Yeah, but it felt really good," Damien said, his flash of bared teeth more a snarl than a grin.

Leash laughed. He had a hearty chuckle, one of those contagious kinds that rumbled from deep within his belly. He'd make a great Santa Claus one day, hopefully from prison.

"I hope it was worth it," Leash said. "Because it's the last good thing you'll feel in your life."

"See, ruthless. I knew it the first time I saw you."

Leash scrunched his brow. "We've met before?"

"Let's just say I know you like Orsini leather gloves and wear a size thirteen steel-toed boot."

With his interest clearly piqued, Leash paced around Damien, studying him.

"You and I don't run in similar circles," Leash finally said.

"Doubtful, unless you bowl?" Damien said, his conversational tone at odds with the rage he felt for the cold-blooded murderer in front of him.

"Do I look like I bowl?"

"You look like a human redwood. Doesn't mean you're not a killer on the lanes. There's this one guy, Davy Gerts, he's wide as a truck, but nimble like a ballerina. Odd combination, really, but when that ball leaves his hand, its magic."

Leash's thick hand connected with Damien's cheek with a resounding *thwack*. Damien reeled from the force of the blow, ears ringing and his vision dimming at the edges.

"Shut up," Leash growled.

"Still don't remember who I am?" Damien asked, trying to shake away the cobwebs forming in his skull. Grinning at Leash through bloody teeth, Damien said, "I'll give you a hint."

Damien whistled an odd bird song, but then stopped, considering if he even had the song correct.

"I'm not sure what a bluebird sounds like," Damien admitted. "But that was the best I got."

"A bluebird?" Leash asked, seeming confused before his eyes widened, recognition dawning. "The bluebird from the baby store."

"Ding, ding, ding, ding. We have a winner."

"You survived?"

"Unless you believe in ghosts, which I personally would not recommend. They can put a damper on doing things your own way. Nag, nag, nag."

"If you survived, why did you come back?"

"That's simple. To kill you."

The room echoed with another one of Leash's belly laughs, inspiring his men to crack up along with him.

"You're going to kill me?" he asked.

"That's the plan," Damien said, no qualms about admitting it.

"And how do you expect to do that, in your current situation?"

"Well, if I tell you, it will ruin all the fun, don't you think?"

Truth was, Damien had no plan, but he had two goals. Lock down the armory with as many of their thugs inside and find out where Scarman was located. He needed to get inside the building to do that and he wasn't going to get an invitation, so he'd have to crash the party the old-fashioned way, with a right hook.

Zip-ties weren't difficult to break, if you didn't mind getting a little bloody. It wasn't a matter of *if* Damien could escape, but *when*.

Damien had to gather as many people into the storeroom as possible, break free, hit the alarm button next to the exit, and scoot outside before the cage dropped, locking them all inside. Between now and then, he also had to get Leash to spill Scarman's location. Unfortunately, it would probably take more of Leash's punches to get there.

"Not a lot of people excel in their work," Damien said to Leash. "Not like you. Do your boys know what you did with us after you thought we were dead? That couldn't have been your boss' idea."

Damien scanned the thugs around him.

"It was inspired."

The thugs looked to Leash, but their tattooed leader wasn't sold yet.

"Maybe I'm wrong," Damien said. "Maybe your boss is the brain, and you're the brawn. Some people are leaders. Others, followers. There's no shame in that."

Damien turned to the thugs.

"Ask the guy with the scar on his arm when he gets back. Obviously, I overestimated Leash's influence."

Damien's head rocked with another punch. Leash's fist felt like stone, and the room spun like a top.

"You talk too much," Leash said.

Damien spit blood from his mouth, where they joined the other splatter at his feet. "That's probably true," he said. "And not just to the living."

Across the room, Raquel stood in the doorway, tears forming. Lowering her head, she covered her eyes and walked out of sight.

"Do you want me to tell the story?" Damien asked. "Or do you want to do the honors?"

"Okay," Leash said. "You want to hear how I put them in—"

"Shh!" Damien interrupted. "Don't ruin the ending. Walk them through it."

One of the thugs leaned out of the door and whistled, calling a few more inside the storeroom. It wasn't all of them, but it would have to do.

Leash scanned the eyes locked on him, every thug hanging on Leash's every word.

"This is a bluebird," Leash started. "Months ago, during the catalyst, we cornered him in a clothing store down on Main Street."

"A clothing store for babies," Damien interjected. "My wife was pregnant."

Leash glared at him.

"Details are important," Damien said, shrugging. "Gives the story context and weight." He focused on the thugs. "My wife was nearly six months pregnant by then, and we were shopping for outfits for our first child. Onesies. Pink ones with cats on them. Not a fan. Doc said our baby was going to be a girl. We were going to name her Nicole." He motioned to Leash. "Okay, go on. I think I've captured the moment before your brilliant conclusion."

"The boss wanted them dead, but not in a way that could be traced back to us," Leash said.

"Bullets are like fingerprints," Damien said. "They can be traced. That's what the boss said."

Leash sighed, irritated by Damien's continuous interruptions.

"We all knew what that meant," Leash continued. "So, we took care of it."

There was a palpable, drawn-out pause in the room.

"That's it?" Damien asked. "You took care of it? No, no,

no. It was more than that. Leash here, he led the way. He put on his nice Orsini leather gloves to avoid leaving any DNA. That's when the beating started. My pregnant wife tried to protect me, but that wouldn't stop him. No, sir. Inspired by his leadership, the others joined in. They punched and kicked me and my wife, deliberately and repeatedly aiming for my child in her womb. They laughed at our pain, relished the sounds of our breaking bones, and got off on beating us to death. Well, almost. Obviously, I survived. But my wife and son didn't. Yeah, turned out we were having a boy after all. Nicholas. I know, not that different from Nicole. I'm not as clever as Leash. But your boss, the one with the scar, he was smart. He didn't get his hands or shoes bloody at all. Nope. Scarman shot a taser into my chest and had me convulsing on the floor. He laughed as I tried to stop them from killing my wife and unborn child. Your boss was a real leader that day. Not a coward, like many people would think. He led by example. No mercy. No prisoners. The cause above all else."

Damien caught his breath, trying to hide the pain reverberating from that awful day.

"But Leash's expertise came in after," Damien continued. "After he thought we were two, well, two and a half, corpses. Okay, tell them, Leash. What'd you do with us? And don't undersell it. This is your moment."

"We were going to leave," Leash said. "But I thought it'd be a shame to keep our handiwork wasted in a trashed baby store. So I suggested we prop them up in the windows, like the plastic things that pose with clothes on."

"Mannequins," Damien added.

"Right," Leash said. "So, I lifted them up and put them in the window like the…"

"Mannequins," Damien prompted.

"A warning to people not to mess with us. That we meant business. If we ever crossed their paths, they know better than to challenge us."

"Like walking up to the armory steps and punching you in the face," Damien said.

Leash's nostrils flared.

"Yeah," Leash said. "Like that."

"Mission accomplished," Damien said.

This was it. Leash was distracted with rage, his men were focused on the story, and Damien had quietly broken his bonds. Lock them in, get them to talk, or start shooting until they do. This could work. It was time to make his move.

"Sir," a voice yelled from the hall.

"In here," Leash bellowed.

"I found this loitering near the back of the building," a new thug said. "What do you want me to do with him?"

The thug threw the man into the room.

It was Robert.

His presence screwed up everything.

ROBERT LANDED at Damien's feet, his bravado replaced with the cowering of a five-year-old waiting for a belt lashing. He was in way over his head, and he knew it.

Damien's life was now at risk, too. Well, more so than it was before. If Leash found out Damien had broken his zip-ties, he'd be bound in a way he'd never escape. This small room would end up being his last sight before being beaten or shot to death.

Worse than that, it would mean Scarman would have won.

"Damn, Leash," Damien said. "Now you're going to have to tell that story all over again. Your man in the hallway didn't hear it."

"Story time is over," Leash said.

"Then may I add one small addition to your tale? A plot twist?"

"I said story time-"

Damien continued. "What would really make your accomplishment resound for the ages would be a hidden motivation, subtle at first, but present in all aspects of the story. A theme. An overriding impulse. Take this new guy you just tossed in here. You'll probably torture him, kill him, and then dump his body somewhere that will never be found. Me too, for that matter.

"But wouldn't your story carry greater gravitas if there was more to it than just beating people up and killing us? Like, for instance, what if this poor soul at my feet was, I don't know, I'm spit-balling here, but what if he was, let's say he was related to me or my wife. Right? See where I'm going? Adding depth? A twist? And what if he wasn't just some passerby who mistook the armory for the post office, but instead, was here to enact some sort of revenge? Or better yet, what if he and I were working together?

"What would be the odds of that, right? But it wouldn't just be about revenge, because you killing us or us killing you, that's all the same act, no matter the motivation. What would make this story resonate with your men, expanding your legend, as it were, was if you and your men, somehow, no matter how fanciful, actually were responsible for your own deaths? Right? Like who would see that coming? Unlikely. Impossible, even, considering you have all the guns and tear gas," he said, subtly motioning to Robert. "I mean, tear gas. Like overkill, right?"

"What's your point?" Leash asked, both irritated and intrigued.

"My point it, Leash…. You read the bible? Okay, bad question. I'm not a big fan either, but my brother loved to spin tales from that book. One of his favorites was David and Goliath. Little man takes down gargantuan warrior with a sling and a rock, of all things. No wonder they wrote that story down, right? So, what I'm saying is, you have to decide whether you're David or Goliath. Because that is the key, the crux to whether your story is remembered over a cold beer or one that Hayeston will be talking about for decades."

"You mean I get to choose?" Leash asked.

"Of course. This is your story, your saga, your tale, your mythos. Are you Paul Bunyan or the ox? Are you Ozzie or

Harriet? The Beaver or Wally? Kirk or Spock? You see where I'm going with this?"

"No." He sighed.

"Really?" Damien asked.

"Really."

"I'll count it down for you. Three. Deep inside of you is the pivot point in your life where you decided to become the man you are today. Two. That man ended up in here, with me and this stranger in this room, full of guns and an emergency locking mechanism by the door, for what will inevitably be the heroic apex of your criminal life. And one…"

"One?" Leash asked.

"Yeah. Three, two, one. Now!"

Damien and Robert burst into action. Damien bull-rushed Leash, hitting him at the waist, and then drove him into the hall. Behind him, he could hear Robert fighting thugs and activating the tear gas canisters.

"Get out of there," Damien yelled to Robert.

A stunned Leash grabbed Damien and spun him around, tossing him like a doll. The gas wafted into the hall, burning Damien's eyes, its harsh fumes moving into his lungs. He looked back through blurry eyes to see Robert struggling to free himself from the group of angry thugs. He fought two men, then three, four.

Damien reached out for him.

"Robert," Damien yelled, but Leash grabbed his arms and yanked him away.

Unable to free himself, Robert pushed his stocky frame forward, forcing the group of men toward the exit. "Finish it, you pussy," Robert said.

With a free hand, he reached out and pressed the emergency lock. A metal cage slammed down, locking him inside with Scarman's men.

Seconds later, he and the thugs disappeared behind the wall of smoke.

"Robert," Damien yelled.

Leash slugged Damien in the head while dragging him down the hall. Gunshots rang out from inside the storeroom.

"Robert!"

No reply. Just coughs and banging against the cage door.

Damien grabbed onto Leash's arm and twisted, spinning to his feet, but couldn't break free from the man's strong grip. He was dragged behind him like a skier behind a boat.

The two remaining thugs Damien had spotted from Barrett's roof rushed up to Leash.

"What's going on?" one asked.

"Follow the smoke and get our men out of there," Leash said. "I'll take care of this one."

The thugs raced into the cloud of tear gas as more shots were fired from the storeroom.

"Robert," Damien said through a spasm of coughs.

Leash kicked opened the front doors, then tossed Damien into the daylight and down the steps.

He rolled down the hard concrete stairs, dizzy and bruised, each breath forcing out another cough. Damien rubbed his eyes as they began to clear. His returning sight found Leash standing at the top of the stairs, glaring down at him.

He met Damien's eyes with a cold stare, the same expression he had in Benita's store.

"I'm gonna beat you to a pulp," Leash said. "I'll make sure you're dead this time."

Damien could try to run. It didn't appear Leash had a gun, but the tattooed redwood was his only ticket to Scarman.

"You like telling stories," Leash said. "Let's make us a sequel. Death of a bluebird."

"Sounds catchy," Damien said, pushing off the ground, searching for anything he could use for defense.

Suddenly, a familiar sensation returned to Damien, one he hadn't felt in months.

"No," he mumbled, gritting his teeth.

His fingers began to twitch. His hand started to quiver. Leash began to lose his color. Damien's knees grew wobbly as his muscles started to convulse.

He was going to have another seizure.

He'd have no defense for whatever Leash had planned for him.

Damien's neck stiffened.

The world went black.

THE FIRST TIME Leash took a life wasn't all that special. He felt it should have been. Firsts in things should be something worth talking about. Not killing, though. Not for Leash.

It was embarrassing now. Looking back, he wished he would have done better. Either chosen not to kill that day or made more of a show of it. He'd just had the urge. That was the problem. He'd been wondering what it would be like to let his anger do more than scare people.

Sometimes, fear made people fight back.

Killing was the ultimate knockout punch. No one got up from that.

First time he beat someone to death, he did it alone. No one watching or cheering him on. No one to show off to. Just him and the punching bag.

A waste, really.

That was why he didn't like the boss' orders. He wanted to kill Damien for good. Use him as an example, like he tried before, except, instead of propping him up in the store window like a mann... mann... plastic person, he'd hang Damien from City Hall with a sign around him saying "Don't fuck with us." Or something like that.

The bluebird embarrassed Leash in front of his squad.

Allowed him to lock 'em up with no way to get out. No way to get his cred back. He'd never work his way up to the boss' second in command with this cop still breathing. He'd have to make amends somehow. The easiest way would be to string him up for show, telling everyone—both in the cause and those on the outside—that Leash wasn't no fool. He was not to be messed with. He was a stone-cold killer.

But the boss said it'd make the bluebird a martyr, a symbol that worked against the cause, and he didn't want that. He said nothing was more humiliating for the bluebird than burying a body where it would never be found. Information was power, the boss said, and since Leash would be the only person in the whole world who knew where he buried bluebird, he'd have power over him for eternity.

That sounded good. Power was good.

Plus, Leash was allowed to kill him anyway he wanted. Slow or fast. A knife, his fists, his feet, a gun, a rope, poison, acid, a bat… anything. Or all of 'em. That was up to Leash, the boss said. He told him to be creative. Make sure that when he was done with the bluebird, he didn't have any regrets. He said a life with regrets was a wasted life.

Leash didn't want his life to be wasted. Besides, killing the bluebird any way he wanted would bring a peace to him.

No regrets. No mercy.

Kill him. Bury him. Be the only one who knew where they could find his bones and never tell a soul.

Leash liked that.

Killing the bluebird away from everyone's eyes, like Leash's first murder, would be different. He wouldn't feel cheated this time.

This time, killing would be a victory.

His and his alone.

CHAPTER
TWENTY-SEVEN

DAMIEN WOKE up in the darkness once again. He wasn't in a hospital, not this time. No smells created by manufacturing sterility.

Probably not in a coma. Raquel's voice was silent.

He wasn't outside the armory anymore either, unless the moon, stars, and streetlights had all lost their light.

His head vibrated against the floor. He was bent in an awkward position, twisted and curled. The hum of an engine. The oscillation from tires. The smell of exhaust.

He was in the trunk of a car.

His ribs hurt. His side hurt. His right eye was nearly swollen shut. A large welt now resided on the back of his head. The rest of his body throbbed with a constant pain.

Some of his injuries were the cost of falling on cement steps. Damien guessed the others were at the expense of Leash's size thirteen shoes. His attacker wasn't above beating an unconscious man.

Damien tried to collect his thoughts.

Robert.

That stubborn sonofabitch. Stupid, curious, heroic bastard. He injected himself into Scarman's war, but the armory wasn't his fight. He should have stayed on the roof, out of harm's way. Instead, he was probably dead, stuck in a room full of his killers, his body the object of mockery and vengeance.

How would Damien be able to explain that to Raquel's family?

When he got out of the hospital months earlier, still reeling from the realization his wife and child hadn't survive, he tried to reach out to her parents. In many ways, they were the only parents he had left. The mistrust, the dysfunction between them, felt like home in a screwed-up sort of way.

Damien's father was dead. His mother was in a nursing home, slowly losing her mind. He hoped he and Raquel's parents could share in the grieving together. Loss was such a lonely experience, especially in the dark of night, surrounded by memories.

He hoped they'd all mourn and heal together. He wished, as an adopted member of her family, they'd find a way to honor the life of the woman who saved him from himself. That her tragedy would make them closer for having survived the void she left behind.

Hadn't turned out that way.

If he wanted solace, he'd have to go elsewhere.

Left alone to cope with Raquel's death, without any family from either side of the marriage aisle, Damien struggled with dueling desires. He could treat every memory of his wife as if they were as necessary as oxygen or he could try to erase them from his heart, sparing it from beating in a world without her.

Her inconsistent visits from the other side were a clear indication his rewired brain hadn't come to a decision either way.

Pain clarified things. Put them in priority. Stuff. Accomplishments. Praise. None of that mattered anymore. The only thing he ever valued was six feet under the ground with his unborn child. A nice house wouldn't replace them. Nor a car, money, or jetting off to exotic locations.

Nothing would. Ever.

He knew people would tell him to move on. That there were more years ahead full of possibilities when, to him, all that mattered were the years that had already passed.

As long as her memories remained, so would his pursuit of those who caused her death. And one of them was about eight feet in front of him, driving the car.

Damien could feel the pavement shift from smooth to rough. They were heading out of town.

Plenty of remote locations to bury a body.

DAMIEN HAD skirted death a number of times already. He wasn't confident there were any more chances left. Still, as long as he was breathing, he was winning.

Damien pulled out his cell phone. No signal. He turned on the flashlight app, feeling around the trunk. To steal a few more breaths of life, he'd need more of a defense than harsh words. A tire iron would've come in handy right now.

The car took a sudden turn, jostling over uneven ground. Damien could hear tall grass scrape across the bottom of the car. They were no longer driving on a road.

The car bounced from side to side, tossing Damien inside the trunk, his sore body caroming around like a pinball. The car wasn't designed for this sort of terrain, and it wouldn't be able to take much more.

Seconds later, the car jerked to a stop and was thrown into park, but the hum of the engine remained.

Leash wasn't planning on taking long.

This is it.

The driver's side door creaked opened. Damien could feel the car lift as the heavy driver stepped out.

Damien frantically searched the trunk again. There had to be something he could use to defend himself.

Nothing.

His pockets.

Empty.

His belt?

That could work.

He unclipped his leather belt and slid it from his pants, twisting one end around his hand, leaving enough to wrap around Leash's thick neck.

The trunk *clicked*, opening a crack, the afternoon light peeking in.

Damien noticed his hands were bloody. Was it his?

The trunk lifted up and Damien swung his belt, the metal clip striking Leash in the face. Dazed, Leash stepped back. Damien leapt out, knocking them both to the ground. They landed in the tall grass, its long stalks hiding their struggle.

Leash fell onto his side. Damien rolled onto the larger man's wide back, his weight forcing Leash face down.

Before Leash could gather his wits, Damien shoved his belt under his neck and pulled.

The big man flailed, grabbing at Damien's hands.

David was choking Goliath.

Damien slid the belt through the clip, then yanked it tight. The leather pressed against Leash's neck, and he began to wheeze.

Leash lifted himself onto his hands and knees. Damien held on, riding him like a bull. With unsure legs, Leash staggered to his feet and rushed backward, crushing Damien against the car.

Damien's body jolted with unhealthy cracks as pain shot through his chest. Fractured ribs were added to a body with too many scars.

Damien gasped, trying to regain his breath, each wisp of air pressing against fractured bones. This wasn't a wrestling ring, and Damien couldn't tap out. He was fighting for his life.

Shaking off his aches, Damien pressed his feet against the side of the car and pushed, forcing Leash to stumble forward. Damien hopped to the ground, holding him like a dog on a leash. With a swing and a pull on the belt, Damien yanked Leash to the side, throwing him against the opened trunk. Grabbing the lid, he slammed it against the back of Leash's head.

Blood splattered across Damien's face.

He gripped the trunk lid and, again, rammed it into the man's skull. Then again. And again.

"Stop!" Damien heard Raquel yell. "You've done enough."

"No, I haven't." Damien panted. "He's still breathing."

Uncontrollable hatred moved through his body like blood. Months of suffering, anger, and loss fed the beast. Each crushing blow, an act of justice. An eye for an eye. Tooth for a tooth.

Damien yanked the bloody and dazed Leash from the back of the car and spun him in a circle, tossing him head-first into the back door.

Leash collapsed onto the ground.

"Please," Raquel begged. "Don't do it. Stop. Before it's too late."

"Leave me alone," he said.

"You're killing him."

He was and he knew it. Wanted it. Was enjoying it.

Damien stared into Leash's eyes, now wide with fear, and wondered if that was what he looked like before the man kicked his steel-tipped boot into Damien's side over and over again.

"You've been found guilty," Damien said to him, kicking him.

"Guilty of hate."

Kick.

"Murder."

Kick.

"Killing my wife."

Kick.

"Stealing my child's life."

Kick.

"And turning me into one of you."

Kick. Kick. Kick.

"Damien," Raquel yelled, tears streaming down her face. "Stop it! Please. You're killing us. You're better than—"

"I am not!" he yelled. "Not anymore! For the last time, leave me alone!"

He ended his sentence with one last kick before glancing up from Leash's pulverized body.

Raquel was gone.

Damien stood in the middle of the tall grass, the car idling next to him, Leash's bloody body convulsing at his feet. No more whispers or desperate pleas from his wife. No hint of her perfume or visions of her worried stare.

She'd done as he commanded. She had left him. For the first time since Leash and his men had beat him to the precipice of death, Damien was truly alone.

He dropped his eyes to see his attacker, the man's faint breathing accompanied with a sickening gurgle. Each inhale, softer. Each exhale, weaker.

A few moments later, they stopped altogether.

Damien spotted his reflection in the car's side window. His face was covered in blood splatter. His clothes stained with the fruits of his wrath.

He stepped forward and bent down, examining his face.

These are the eyes of a murderer.

He appeared older. Harder. Lines in his skin pronounced with the tint of blood trickling down their creases.

Damien wanted revenge. He wanted to kill him.

And now he had.

Closing his eyes, he waited for the regret to rise to the surface. Second guesses.

They didn't.

Either his broken mind couldn't tap such emotions, or he didn't care. He couldn't tell anymore.

Regret wasn't the only feeling that was missing. So was satisfaction. Closure. Accomplishment. Peace. Damien had taken a life, committed a mortal sin, as Jacob would tell him, and it meant nothing. His wife was still dead. His son, unknown to him. Scarman was still out there. Ted, still in hiding.

Nothing had changed, except Damien had lowered himself to the level of those he hated. All life, even one as repulsive as Leash's, should have meant something. Damien used to believe that. Surely, belief was more than just a feeling? It had to be more than synapses firing in his brain. Right and wrong must be more than chemical reactions.

Then what had happened to him? Knowing the terror Leash had inflicted on him and Raquel, how could he so easily have done the same?

Yet, he had. Unrelentingly. Brutally. The guardrails were gone. His mind, free to wander to the darker recesses. Nothing to stop him now. Not even Raquel.

Studying the blood drying on his hands, he wondered if this would be the last time they would kill.

Damien slipped his belt from around Leash's neck, then tossed it into the passenger seat. A search found no weapons on the man, but he did retrieve the piece of paper handed to him by Scarman.

Steven West. Digital Slate.

Digital Slate. The name rang a bell. Maybe a new tech company located in one of the old warehouses. Sounded right.

Was West Scarman's ally or a target? Didn't matter. Either way, he was on Scarman's mind. Damien had to find out why.

Damien pulled out of the tall grass and sped back into town, leaving Leash's body in the same space intended for

Damien's grave. There was a little poetic justice in that. He almost smiled, but stopped.

His first emotion after killing someone couldn't be happiness.

CHAPTER
TWENTY-NINE

DAMIEN GAZED out at the road ahead of him. It was quiet, peaceful. Open fields abutting citrus orchards, grazing cows chewing soft grass, soaring birds watching overhead. For a moment, he allowed himself to believe all the tragedy that occurred today was an illusion and his former life awaited him. His small town was back to moving at a comfortable snail's pace, while Raquel was at home painting the nursery a bright pink.

It was fantasy, but a pleasant one.

His reflection in the rearview mirror reminded him of who he was and what he had become.

The numbing hum of the road allowed his mind to wander back to Leash's body in the tall grass. The scene, the event, felt oddly familiar.

Dusty thoughts revisited. Buried images flashed in his mind.

He remembered a grassy field, but at night. The grass was shorter, illuminated by the yellow lights from a large truck. Damien was younger. Maybe ten. Maybe older. There was a shovel and something the size of a body wrapped in a painter's canvas drop cloth.

Young Damien was afraid and confused. Woken from his

sleep, he was brought there in the middle of the night to do something he couldn't remember. His thoughts were disjointed, scattered, buried deep enough that their sudden presence confused him.

What is going on?

His mind raced with these new, yet old thoughts. Present, past memories. He was there, as a child, standing on the wet soil wearing dirty socks, staring at the drop cloth, afraid to ask what was wrapped inside. He wasn't to question. That was made clear. He was to do as he was told and nothing more. He was to never talk about this to anyone, ever, or he would end up similarly wrapped in an empty field, never to be heard from again.

He believed him. The voice warning him had never lied before, not about punishment. His was swift and savage. His threats were never hollow. His retributions as predictable as the sunrise.

Damien didn't want to be wrapped in a cloth. He didn't want to be forgotten. He wanted to go home and climb into bed. Wanted to bury his head under his pillow and imagine none of this had ever happened. He'd eat breakfast in the morning and act like the night in the field was just a dream.

It couldn't be reality. Children didn't bury bodies.

Not with their father.

A honking horn shifted Damien back to the present.

He veered back into his lane, barely missing a pickup truck heading in the opposite direction. The driver waved a middle finger, screaming a colorful metaphor as he passed. Damien returned an apologetic wave.

Focus.

Damien buried the images ricocheting in his mind back into the hole from which they came. He didn't trust them. He couldn't believe anything his damaged brain manufactured. Not at face value.

If Damien had helped his father bury a body, it would

have taken a lot less than a similar near-death experience to retrieve the memory. During his cadet training, he'd been to crime scenes. He'd seen dead bodies. He'd witnessed the way the ruthless treated corpses like trash. There were a thousand opportunities for it to pierce his consciousness.

There was only one thing that was new.

He had never killed before.

A psychologist would chalk up his new childhood memories to projecting his guilt onto the person he liked the least, and Damien wouldn't be able to refute it. It was the most logical reason.

His father was many things, most of which were awful, but he wasn't a murderer.

Damien paused.

Wouldn't Jacob say the same thing about him before today?

Truth was, Damien wasn't sure what to do with these new memories, but he was certain of one thing. They wouldn't help save Ted or catch Scarman.

They'd have to wait. The dead weren't going anywhere.

The smell of distant smoke started to flow through the air conditioning vents. Damien was getting close to town. The warehouses weren't far now. A few miles at the most.

He pulled over to the side and headed up a rough dirt road, stopping at an abandoned scenic overlook of the Braden River. Actually, river was an exaggeration. It was more like an aggressive creek. It once flowed with brackish water, originating from Lake Patchett and downstream into nearby Jackson Bay.

Before citrus became a Hayeston staple in need of thousands of gallons of water, and a sub-division redirected the river flow to create a recreational inlet a few miles north, the Braden River had cut deep into the soil. A nearby scenic overlook once hung above wide and dangerous waters, but now stood above sand-covered rocks littered with an assortment of trash.

Damien stopped the car atop the scenic overlook, then searched the vehicle for weapons.

None.

Just a lighter in the glove compartment and a bag of Fritos.

He took both.

Damien exited the car and scurried down the embankment, hunting for a healthy-sized rock. Once found, he trekked back to the top and started the car, placing the oblong, heavy stone against the gas pedal.

The engine screamed, grey exhaust expelling from behind the car in a constant flow.

Tying his belt around the shifter, he slid out of the car, making sure not to jar the gearshift out of park. He closed the door and reached through the opened window, carefully wrapping his fingers around his belt. Once firmly gripped, he jerked the belt and the car lurched into drive.

Damien let the belt go, watching Leash's car soar down the embankment in a metallic swan dive. With a loud crash, the grill and front end stuck into the muddy shoreline below, the back wheels still spinning, searching for ground to propel the car further.

The car tilted like the leaning tower of Pisa. With the vibration of the racing engine, the vehicle continued falling forward like a domino. It splatted upside down into the middle of the river, the impact apparently jolting the car out of drive.

The engine slowed to an idle, and the wheels came to a stop.

Damien nodded with satisfaction. The water should do a good job washing away evidence. By the time anyone found Leash's car, Damien's presence in it would have disappeared into the depths of Jackson Bay.

He turned his attention back to Hayeston. The warehouses were thirty minutes by foot, fifteen if he jogged. With cracked ribs, it would be twenty at the least.

After he tightened his shoelaces, he started toward town, ribs screaming with every step he took. It appeared the small startup Digital Slate had something to do with why Scarman was here. Time to find out what his nemesis was up to.

As his walk broke into an even more painful jog, Damien realized he had no idea what he was going to do next. No longer bound by God's or man's laws, he was now capable of anything.

For the first time, it felt like an advantage.

CHAPTER
THIRTY

THE WAREHOUSE DISTRICT wasn't planned. It sprang up out of necessity, built over seventy years as the town grew out of citrus and blue-collar industries. The buildings and roads followed no logical path. Some warehouses backed up to long-forgotten railroad tracks. Others faced the direction of the Braden River.

The district was a maze with short roads and quick turns, weaving through a hodgepodge of structures, big and small, rectangular and square. The area appeared as if it were planned by dropping a handful of Legos on the ground and using their arbitrary location as a guide.

It was random and confusing to outsiders. All of which gave Damien an edge.

For Ted, too. It was the perfect place to stay out of sight. Ted said he'd be hiding in the old Hayeston Herald building, the defunct town newspaper.

Damien approached the warehouses from the railroad tracks. It was the farthest from Digital Slate's location, and it would give him three different ways to approach it. Direct, indirect, and out of the way.

The ache in his ribs slowed his jog to a determined walk. Through the pain, Damien was surprisingly calm. A switch inside of him had been flipped. He felt like a long-distance runner having pushed passed the physical plateau, where endorphins flooded their bodies and each stride becomes effortless.

The task before him was clear enough, and he held no reservations about completing it.

Save Ted, kill Scarman.

Didn't have to be in that order, either.

He couldn't let another man like his father go to the grave without paying for the consequences of his actions. Justice had to be served, inside the courtroom or out. Damien was content being the one to deliver it.

With no cell signal or access to a police radio, Damien had no idea what was happening out of his sight. The plumes of smoke had faded, the distant crack of gunshots diminishing, but that didn't necessarily mean order was being restored. The fires could have run out of fuel to burn. The thugs may no longer need to pull the trigger to maintain control.

He tried to remain optimistic. There was still hope in Damien. Not for himself, but for his town and those whom he loved. Help was on the way. The National Guard should arrive soon. Law and order would eventually rule.

All that being said, he had a more immediate need.

He had no weapons.

The homeless were not an uncommon sight in this area of town, and every one of them hiding in the shadows gave Damien pause. It wasn't beyond Scarman to seed the vagrants in the area with some of his men. It was the perfect disguise, their layers of clothes able to hide pistols, knives, rifles, and shotguns with little effort.

Damien needed to blend in. In his current dirty and bloody state, it wouldn't take much work. He leaned against the back of a warehouse, overlooking the unkempt railroad tracks overgrown with grass, and wondered what John

Hayes, the town's founder, would think of his once-proud train station.

"I know you," a voice said.

Damien whipped around, his fists clenched.

A young man with a shaggy beard and greasy hair stood behind him. He was short and thin, but not frail. Some of his teeth were missing, but still sported a happy smile.

The man eyed Damien's bloody clothes.

"Have a bad day?" the man asked.

"Hit and miss."

"Looks like you've hit more than missed."

"So far," Damien said.

"You're a cop," the man said.

"I used to be," Damien said.

"No, you're a cop. I've seen you. You fed me. At St. Mary's shelter. You were in your uniform. You and a pretty lady. It was a Thursday. They serve breakfast burritos on Thursdays. Then grilled cheese and tomato soup for lunch. Burgers and hot dogs for dinner, with a side of potato salad. I love Thursdays. You were there for the breakfast shift."

"Right. Yes."

That was months ago. Volunteering at the shelter was Raquel's idea. She said they needed to give back. Damien argued his job fulfilled that requirement, but she didn't accept his take.

"Doing things because you have to isn't the same as doing it because you want to," she said. She loved comparing intention with action.

"What if I don't want to do either?" Damien joked.

"Impossible. I know the man I married. He's not that selfish."

She also had a way of stating what she wanted as the truth. Sometimes, Damien believed her. He didn't want to get up at four in the morning before his shift to scramble eggs for people who'd made a bunch of bad decisions, but she saw them differently, the same way she saw him the first day they met.

She saw their potential and humanity.

Through her eyes, she looked into people's future with the rosiest of glasses.

It was why everyone loved her. It was why he loved her. Her heart was big enough to welcome family and strangers alike. She was more than his better half. She was their whole.

Without her, even the hallucination of her, Damien was a hollow man. He kept hoping he'd hear her voice whispered in his ear one more time. "You're better than this," she'd say, and he'd argue with her while she tried to convince him otherwise, but this time, she remained mute. Damien had told her to leave him, and she'd abided his request.

"Let me ask you something," Damien said to the man.

"You look different," the man interrupted. "You've got that look, like you lost something. I see it a lot around here. People always losing stuff they can't get back. I'm not talking about stuff you can touch, I'm talking about other things. You lose something like that, something you want back?"

"Yes. Who doesn't? Life doesn't have a rewind button."

"Now that would be something," the man said. "Think of it, being able to rewind, fix what needed fixing, and keep what needed not to be lost. The world would be a happier place, that's for sure. No more regrets or bad memories. Lessons wouldn't cost us nothing, you know? We could learn from it, go back, and keep from doing it in the first place. If I had that button, I never would have joined the military, that's for sure."

"You served?"

"Two tours," the man said. "First one was fine. Didn't do much really. Patrolled, prayed we wouldn't step on something that'd blow us to pieces. Made it home without a scratch."

"And the second?" Damien asked.

The man scratched his frayed beard.

"The second time… that was different. A forward position. A lot of firefights. A lot of them. One lasted twelve straight hours. A mind can only keep it together for so long. Twelve hours of bullets and bombs. A half a day staring evil in the eye and I was the one who blinked. I finished my tour the way I started. Committed. I'm no coward. But coming home, I found I lost something on that bloody sand. Part of me stayed there, like evil took a part of my soul. This," he said pointing to himself, "is all that was left. Not a lot of people want to spend time with half a person."

Damien spotted his own shadow on the railroad track.

"I don't miss the fighting, that's for sure, but I do miss working toward something with my team. We all need a purpose. I thought I would have found mine by now."

"What's your name?" Damien asked.

"Dexter Holt. You can call me Dex."

"Damien," he said, shaking his hand. "Thank you for your service."

"And thank you for yours."

Damien nodded, looking Dex in the eye. They were about the same age, stood the same height, and Dex's light brown eyes carried with it a weight of sadness. They'd both seen things they'd rather forget, but Dex's burden had taken a greater toll.

The homeless vet was a good fifty pounds underweight and hadn't bathed long enough that it couldn't be hidden, yet he still stood with military pride. Straight back, chin up, eyes forward. He was both fragile and strong, and Damien felt a kinship with him.

"I'm on a mission of sorts," Damien said. "Buddy of mine, my best friend, fellow officer, is hiding out down here. Last I heard, he was in the old Herald building. People are trying to hunt him down, but I aim to save him. You interested?"

Dex cocked his head to the side, sucking air through his teeth.

"How many people are after him?" Dex asked.

"Just about everybody."

"What sort of weapons you carrying?"

"None."

Chuckling, Dex shook his head. "Man, you're up shit creek without the creek," he said.

"Look, man, you've given enough to our country," Damien said. "There's no dishonor in sitting this one out. I just wanted to offer. I've made it this far on my own."

"I live in a box under the powerlines. My social calendar is not exactly filled. And I don't have much left to lose."

"Your life," Damien said.

"Like I said." Dex wrapped his fingers around his beard, stroking it. "I wouldn't mind getting me another chance to look the devil in the eye. Maybe I could get back what he stole from me."

"Then you and I have the same mission," Damien said.

"I knew it. I saw it in your eyes."

"So, you're in?" Damien asked.

"Yeah, I'm in. But I don't think your buddy is in the Herald building anymore. A bunch of angry men showed up, found a cop, and took him with them."

"Where?"

"The Digital Slate building."

CHAPTER
THIRTY-ONE

THE MEN around Scarman moved with speed and purpose, preparing for what came next. The endgame was near, and he allowed himself a moment to enjoy the excitement. Months of planning had culminated in this day, and the last few domino pieces were about to fall.

Scarman knew the subtlety of his plan would be lost on most. The layers of symbolism confused by distraction was a work of art. He was a master of chaos, and few were able to appreciate his work. Still, he wasn't above hearing praise by those smart enough to see the web he had woven.

Thus far, none had spoken up.

He would have to relish in his brilliance alone, as he had done his entire life. Those on the streets who had fallen prey to his charms were fighting a battle of no consequence.

He didn't care about the victim whose death started the riots or the bluebird who pulled the trigger. They were gasoline and matches. Moves and countermoves. The world was his chess board, and Hayeston was a pawn to be sacrificed for the greater good.

The first move in a global game.

His family had trained him well. When building a new world, suffering and bloodshed were tools, like a hammer and saw. Death was inevitable for everyone, inconsequential, unless used as another weapon in the tool belt.

These were the lessons the world would have to understand. Mankind was built on strength and conquest. The spoils went to victors, and the weak were purged from society like chaff from wheat. Only those worthy of life would keep it, and the survivors would grow stronger with each generation.

That was the way it had to be. That was the way he was raised.

He wished he would be alive to see the next phase of the plan, but that was not his mission. His orders were specific and limited to Hayeston.

He didn't question his orders. They made perfect sense.

Yet, there was a part of him that thought his death would be a waste. He had so much more to offer them, so many talents he'd yet to hone. So much he could still do, but those decisions were made by people smarter and wiser than him. Their job was to scheme, his was to act.

For the last phase of his mission, he'd laid out the pollen, set the trap, and waited for the bees to flutter in. Despite the rush of seeing it to fruition, it felt anticlimactic. The cost of being so good at his job.

He'd enjoy the last minutes of his life and hope, by some miracle, something would catch him by surprise.

DEX TOLD Damien that Ted was taken into Digital Slate by eight armed men wearing black who walked and talked like soldiers. Dex thought they were mercenaries. Damien feared they were some of Scarman's true believers.

Dex's breath still reeked of alcohol, but Damien trusted his intel. He spoke with clarity and speed, and the details didn't change no matter how many times Damien asked.

Months earlier, before being run off by a site foreman, Dex squatted in a building adjacent to Digital Slate during its construction. Digital Slate's skeleton was a steel frame while the floorplan split the building into two halves. The front appeared to have been designed for offices, bathrooms, and conference rooms. The back was one large space bigger than two basketball courts with a loading dock on the right side between the two buildings.

Security system installers arrived in four vans, then spent three days securing the facility. But if Scarman was inside, it wasn't much of a deterrent. The other frequent visitors near the end of construction were a tech company whose van logo and slogan insinuated an expertise in computer infrastructure and networking.

Scarman was either after the tech, the people behind the

tech, or was using the location as some sort of headquarters. Whatever his reasons, none of them were a welcome mat.

Damien needed to do more than walk up to the building and hope to punch Scarman in the face. He'd need backup. A lot of it.

That was Dex's job. Damien gave him a mission, and he trusted the soldier would complete it before Ted's fate was sealed.

In the meantime, Damien waited and dealt with a shirt that smelled of a thick body odor and pants like urine. These were some of Dex's "clean" clothes, which he evenly swapped for Damien's blood-splattered polo shirt, grass stained jeans, and a favor.

Damien kept his shoes. The homeless man's feet were one size smaller than his. Besides, the sneakers were the last gift Raquel had bought Damien. He was keeping them until the stitching fell apart.

Even though Dex said he hadn't seen any newcomers among his fellow street dwellers, Damien wasn't taking any chances. Scarman could have easily planted his men in the area weeks earlier as scouts, or simply paid some of them to be his eyes and ears.

He avoided as many of them as possible, following a road less traveled. He made his way inside the abandoned Hayeston Herald building, in which were moldy four-foot rolls of paper and metal typeset letters scattered across the floor. The warehouse was silent, like a morgue. The sound of a whisper would travel from one side of the structure and back with little resistance.

Instead, nothing.

In the back corner, near a bathroom stall, appeared to be where Ted had waited, hiding from roving bands of desperate people looking to take advantage of Scarman's fifty-thousand-dollar reward. The dusty floor and the lower section of an adjoining wall were clean where he leaned, no doubt suffering the pains of his broken leg.

If only Damien had arrived sooner.

His mind wanted to retrace his steps and force him to acknowledge every decision that cost Ted his freedom, but Damien refused to give in. There was still time. Scarman would not kill Ted in secret. It would be in front of a crowd, soaking in the adulation of his followers.

If Ted was still hidden, he was still alive.

Damien peered out of a cracked window, down a long alley to the front door of Digital Slate. He could see little else. From this vantage point, he could spot one guard. He looked like he had dressed down from the uniform Dex had described earlier. Now, Scarman's thug appeared more like an upscale security guard than a mercenary soldier.

The thug was big and muscular, his black t-shirt barely able to contain his vein-bulging biceps. His holstered sidearm sat on his hip, and he wore a generic black hat emblazoned with "Security" stitched in white letters.

He was formidable and, according to Dex, far from alone.

Damien considered his situation. He was unarmed, smelling like he'd bathed in raw sewage, and had to break into a heavily armed building to save his best friend from a psychopath who'd ordered his death and that of his wife.

Just like I planned it.

After wrenching a piece of metal rebar from the crumbling warehouse foundation, Damien held it like a bat. It was better than nothing.

A frontal attack alone was akin to suicide, so Damien slid out a back door of the newspaper shop and scurried down the road, parallel to Digital Slate. He hoped to flank the men guarding the building by working his way down the block, out of sight, then around them, moving in and through the warehouses lining the street to the left of the technology startup. There would be no easy way to sneak inside and find out where they held Ted, but he hoped he'd find a blind spot in the soldier's coverage to get a closer look.

Damien had been thinking about Scarman day and night since Benita's clothing store. Once he got past his anger, Damien began to study him, what he had said and done. His nemesis wanted to see the world burn. He loved chaos. He nurtured it, fed it, raised it, and willed it into existence. It was his child, trained to follow in his footsteps, but Scarman was arrogant. He thought he could contain the chaos and direct it to do what he wanted, but not all children did as they were told. Like fire could form a will of its own, the child of chaos could be equally unpredictable.

Scarman was using this offspring for revenge and as a message to the rest of the world. He was also using it to cover whatever was going on inside Digital Slate. Damien knew he had to remain patient. If things were to go as he hoped, Scarman's offspring would be coming home to roost.

Damien was counting on it.

He looked up at Digital Slate's sign hanging above the front door, searching his unreliable memories for hints as to what the business did behind closed doors. He was able to piece together some thoughts. The tech company was founded by two friends who grew up in the area. They graduated from MIT. Their names escaped him, but he could only assume one of them was scribbled on the paper Damien found in Leash's pocket.

Steven West.

Damien hadn't crossed paths with him or his family. They must have lived in the higher end of town, where only the seasoned and near-retiring cops patrolled. The drug dealers, beating husbands, and instigators were left for the young cops until they did their time and earned assignments in safer locales.

Damien remembered when West and the other man, whose name still escaped him, headed out to California.

Silicon Valley. It was big news in a small rural town. After a couple of years learning the ropes, the local boys came home, bringing their excitement and genius with them, but Damien's mental fragments didn't recall why venture capitalists invested over a million dollars on Digital Slates' version of the next big thing.

Damien could compile the who, where, and why of the small startup, but not what Scarman was after. No matter the goal, Damien didn't believe Scarman was a fan of subtraction. Everything occurring in town was connected somehow, each element adding to the other.

The bounty on Ted and his family. The riots in the streets.

They weren't just a smoke screen for what was playing out inside the tech company. He felt it was all part of a symphony Scarman was conducting for his own amusement.

Still, there were questions. The man with the odd scar was smart. A brilliant manipulator, motivator, and a zealot for a cause that earned Hayeston's destruction. Scarman came into the city like a storm, moving through with a purpose, but to what end? What was this cause he and his followers spoke of?

The day's events were going to be national news. Governmental agencies would flood the town and dissect Scarman's every move, interrogate anyone who had heard his voice or seen his face. They would retrace his steps, identify his associations, track his money, and follow his online activity. He would be one of the most investigated people on the planet.

The soon-to-be FBI's most wanted was less than one hundred yards away. Damien wanted to kill him before any agency had a chance to look the bastard in the eye.

In the distance, he began to hear voices. Grumbling. Angry. They were chanting.

Damien smiled.

It was time to bring Scarman's child home.

THE STREET in front of Digital Slate began to flood with hundreds of vigilantes holding up wanted posters and screaming for justice. Dex had done his job. He'd spread the word that their fifty-thousand-dollar prize was hiding inside Digital Slate. Their payday was only a guarded door away.

Scarman wanted bedlam, and he'd gotten it.

As the crowd approached, the guard with bulging biceps took shelter inside, locking the door behind him. Within seconds, Scarman's misguided followers surrounded the entrance, some banging on the door while others tried to break through the Plexiglass windows.

Damien slipped into the crowd, pushing his way to the front, surprised to find Dex waiting near the door.

"What are you doing here?" Damien asked.

"The mission's not over," Dex said. "I finish the way I start."

The mob was a convincing distraction, but they also wanted Ted's head. Damien had to get inside and find his friend before the crowd found him first. It wouldn't be much of a rescue if Ted was killed before Damien got there.

Damien noticed shadows moving on the roof. Scarman's

soldiers fanned out, their rifle barrels pointing down at the crowd.

"Guns," Dex yelled, pointing up.

"They're going to shoot us!" someone in the crowd yelled.

"We have to go," Dex said to Damien.

"No," Damien said. "This is what I wanted."

The chaos turned to panic. Chant's for Ted's death turned to screams. The crowd scurried in opposite directions, most of them running down the alleys and streets.

A fanatical section of the mob remained, using the threat from Scarman's guns to embolden them.

His child was having a tantrum.

Damien stoked the fire.

"Give us the cop," he yelled. "Give us the cop!"

Dex joined in.

"Give us the cop!"

Other voices soon followed until the crowd raised their fists in unison, punching the air with each word.

"Give us the cop. Give us the cop."

While the crowd screamed around him, Damien pulled a couple of the more muscular protestors toward him and motioned for them to help break down the door. They charged the entry in unison and rammed it with their shoulders, the loud *thud* covered by the howls for justice.

Damien felt the door weaken. They nodded and tried again. *Thud.* And again. *Thud.* Gaps began to form between the door and the frame.

"One more time," Damien said.

"Look out," Dex said, pinning Damien against the wall as shots rang out.

Shots whizzed by Damien's head, the buzz of each bullet followed by the sounds of ripping flesh and bones shattering.

Blood sprayed into the air. Bodies dropped.

Scarman was killing his young.

Dex kept Damien covered as the shots continued to rain

down. Most of the crowd ran for cover, their hardened hearts melted by self-preservation, but a few remained near the door, hiding under the lip of the building's edge.

"You're one crazy motherfucker," Dex said with a smile. "Feels like I'm back on the battlefield."

"Welcome home, soldier," Damien said. He leaned toward the others hiding next to them. "Don't give up. Don't let them take away your victory."

The angry remnants charged, the force of the impact ripping the door off its hinges. Like a pack of feral cats, they squeezed through the opening and raced into the building.

Damien and Dex followed the wave inside.

Mr. Bicep was waiting in the lobby, his pistol off his hip and pointing at their heads. His barrel shifted from one person to the next as if he were counting the difference between the number of people and the bullets in his clip.

"This is private property," he warned with a deep, impatient voice. "Turn around and exit the premises or there will be consequences."

The room remained silent, save for anxious panting.

The guard's mercenary friends on the roof had no qualms opening fire on them. Damien was sure the man with bulging biceps didn't either.

"We're here for the cop," Damien said, stepping forward. "Just like the sign said. Dead or alive. That's what they promised."

"We know he's in here," another yelled. "We want our reward."

"Kill the cops," another cried.

"Fuck that," still another said. "Kill everyone!"

The small mob rushed the guard, who got off two shots before being overcome. The remnants unleashed their reply with angered fists, ignoring their fellow protestors bleeding at their feet.

As the mob devoured the fallen guard, Damien and Dex slipped away, darting into the hallway.

"Keep them here," Damien said to Dex. "Give me time to find my friend."

Dex locked the door to the lobby. "I'll do my best," he said.

It wouldn't stop the mob for long, but Damien only needed a few minutes.

The hall was long and wide. As Dex had said, the front of the building had been converted into rooms, but they were inset into a massive warehouse. The eight-foot walls only traveled a third of the way to the high ceiling that hung above him. Sixteen feet of open air circulated over the constructed spaces.

Sound would travel. Moving unnoticed, nearly impossible. Especially when smelling of urine.

Damien ripped off Dex's putrid shirt and tossed it on the floor, his white undershirt retaining only a hint of the foul odor. Gripping the rebar in his hand, he moved down the hallway, pausing in front of each opened door.

The crack of gunshots continued overhead, Scarman's soldiers making easy prey of the scattered mob outside, their screams silenced by the sound of gunfire.

Damien glanced into the rooms for clues as to Digital Slate's purpose. Whiteboards were covered with handwritten schematics and acronyms he didn't recognize. Terms like *digital lake*, *data pools*, *virtual mirrors*, and *regeneration* were surrounded by shapes and connected by arrows like a hidden path through a maze of ideas.

A few of the spaces were stuffed with unopened, labelled boxes from their move out of Silicon Valley. Another office held racks of servers, blinking green and red, as if sending Morse code with Christmas lights. Drives hummed and the air conditioning whirred.

Rooms of technology, office furniture, scribbled ideas, and unpacked boxes, but no people.

No, wait. A sound. A moan. A weak voice calling from behind him.

"Ted," Damien said.

Following the sound to one of the box-filled rooms, he peered over the stacked cardboard squares. On the ground, he found a man, late twenties or early thirties, shot twice, once in the chest, once in the stomach. He laid on the ground, the beige carpet around him now a thick crimson. His eyes were open and his lips were moving, but no voice followed.

Damien jumped over the row of boxes and bent next to him, checking a security badge on the lanyard hanging around the man's neck.

Shane Masters.

The name jolted Damien's memory.

The other cofounder of Digital Slate.

Masters continued to speak in silence, and Damien lowered his ear next to his mouth.

"I don't want to die," Masters whispered. "I don't want to die."

"You're not going to die. Help is on the way," he lied. "Why did they target you? What are you working on?"

"Erasing… memory."

"Erasing memories?" Damien asked. "Our memories?"

Masters shook his head. "No," he whispered. The bullet hole puncturing his chest and the blood that was invariably surrounding his lungs made it difficult for the dying man to catch his breath.

"We were so close," Masters said. "So close. Would have made millions…"

"What were you erasing?"

"Everything," Masters said with a smile, as if what could have been was his final victory. He closed his eyes and his head slumped to the side, his last shallow breath escaping into the air.

Damien was tired of incoherent thoughts and incomplete information—from his mind, a homeless vet, and a dying CEO. He needed answers.

Damien flipped the covers off the boxes nearby, then rifled through the papers and drawings inside. He wanted to understand why Scarman was willing to kill so many for what was here, but he didn't have time to decipher the technical information in front of him. None of the documents in his hands offered quick answers to the growing number of questions, and time was running out to find Ted.

He continued his search for his best friend, while Masters' final words settled in his mind. Erasing everything? But not memories. Erasing what? A cryptic hint that opened to endless possibilities, none of which were comforting when put in Scarman's hands.

The pulse of pounding footsteps echoed from the far stairwell. The armed men on the roof were heading back down. Damien hurried in their direction. Only a few more rooms to check between him and them. He'd have to hurry. Ted had to be in one of them.

The next door, a storage closet.

Small office.

Break room.

All empty.

Behind Damien, the locked door holding the remnants at bay gave way.

"They're coming!" Dex yelled.

The frothing horde sprinted down the hall toward him. For a moment, they appeared as mindless zombies driven by impulses no living man could understand. Demented and relentless. They tried to push by each other, knocking the person next to them against the walls, yet moving forward together with a single purpose on their minds.

"Kill the cop."

Damien opened the last door. Inside was the large, open space of the warehouse, which was as of yet unfinished. It was bigger than Dex had estimated. It was fifty yards long, twenty yards wide. Above, metal beams zigzagged across the ceiling, holding up the flat warehouse roof, from which hung dim lights reflecting off the polished cement floors.

Across the indoor expanse, in the far corner, a rolling door waited to welcome items dropped off on the loading dock.

In the middle sat two men, bound to their chairs. One was wearing khaki pants, a blue polo shirt, and a black cloth bag covering his head. The other, the bright blue police uniform.

Behind the hostage stood the tall man with long hair and a scar weaving around his right arm.

Damien stepped forward as the horde arrived and poured in around him. In the shadows, Scarman's soldiers from the roof appeared and white-hot flashes exploded out of their rifles, illuminating the expansive room in a strobe-light effect. Bullets danced around Damien's head as if choreographed, flying in formation to their intended targets. A flurry of projectiles whizzing by, all within inches of Damien's face.

He dared not move, praying Dex wasn't behind him.

The flashes stopped as abruptly as they started, and the smell of gunpowder overwhelmed the stench of Damien's shirt. The bodies of the mob, the last of Scarman's children, laid at his feet, their warm corpses surrounding him. The improvised gun play was over, and only Damien remained to take a bow.

"Hello, bluebird," Scarman said to him. "What a pleasant surprise."

CHAPTER
THIRTY-FOUR

SCARMAN STEPPED over the bodies at Damien's feet and extended his hand, pulling him from the carnage.

"Admiration is not something I often feel," Scarman said. "But your persistence is impressive. Driven by revenge, no doubt. Predictable, yet ingenious in execution. Leash. He's dead, is he not?"

"Yeah," Damien said, approaching the bound men, Scarman's hidden army tracking his path from the shadows.

"He said you punched him in the face," Scarman said. "Quite the show you put on at the armory. I was afraid you'd missed the finale here. Is he the first person you've killed?"

"What?"

"Leash? I'm assuming you were the one to kill him."

"Yes," Damien said.

"And he was the first for you?"

"Yes," he said, still feeling nothing of the act.

"It gets easier," Scarman said.

"I don't want it to get easier."

"No one wants that at first. But it does. Human nature. It's comforting in its predictability. The more we do a thing, the quicker the shine wears off."

"Is that how you justify the death you've caused today?"

"We've caused." Scarman smiled with a nod. "Yes. But murder alone is a waste without a purpose behind it. We all must believe in something, isn't that right? It's what drives our decisions. Guides us when things don't go our way. Death is unavoidable. We all must die. The fact we sped up that moment for some means nothing in the grand scheme of things. Who was to say those people on the floor, or those outside on the ground, weren't supposed to die today? There is no public record of the time left on our lives. It comes as a result of decisions, not only by you, but by others. We all interact, cross paths like driftwood floating down a stream. It's coincidence. Luck."

"So, my wife and child were driftwood?" Damien asked.

"Yes," Scarman said. "Don't get me wrong. I didn't want to kill her. I wanted to kill *you*. All bluebirds should die," he said, smacking the back of Ted's hooded head. "But your wife wouldn't let you die alone, and I honored that love she had for you."

Scarman's twisted expression of compassion made Damien's blood boil. This was how a warped mind worked, justifying suffering as a form of sympathy. Damien didn't believe him for a minute. Scarman didn't honor her death; he'd encouraged it and enjoyed it. Damien saw his cold eyes as he jolted his body with fifty thousand volts. He saw the smirk on his face as Leash and the others beat them without pity.

"You could have let my wife go," Damien said.

"Yes," Scarman admitted. "Still, the way you clung to each other at the end. Quite moving."

Damien lunged at Scarman, wrapping his hands around his throat, willing and able to feel the madman's pulse weaken and stop by the grip of his fingers.

A bullet ricocheted at Damien's feet, forcing him to release his grip.

Scarman smiled as he rubbed his neck.

"I guess I deserved that," Scarman said. "Careful, though. Don't get ahead of yourself, bluebird. The only reason you're still alive is because I have not yet ordered your death. No doubt, my men over there are curious as to why I have allowed you to live this long. The truth is, I find your tenacity familiar. So few people are willing to see things through to the end, no matter the ramifications. Most have lines they will not cross, but you and I, we're not bound by such limitations. It's nice to spend time with someone like me, if only for a few minutes."

"I'm not like you," Damien said. "I'm here for my friend. That's it."

"Attachments," Scarman said with a sigh. "That's the difference between us. You still care about people. For all of your gifts, your mind is still limited. Some things are greater than just one lifetime. Some goals take generations to complete. Binding yourself to this world, at this time, with the people around you, retards your thinking. Too narrow. Too fleeting. A persistence of vision and the will to wait for the right moment to move forward is not for the impatient, but the fervent. Settlers came to this nation in the sixteen hundreds, when the average life span was thirty-five years. It took nearly five of their lifetimes for America to claim its independence. What do you believe in that requires that much diligence and effort? Anything? Nothing?"

"What do *you* believe in?" Damien asked. "What is so important that it's worth the destruction of my town?"

"A new world. Tell me, what would this planet look like if you had a hand in its creation? What would constitute holiness and sin? What aspect of human nature would change? What part of our societal structure would you improve? If you could change the world into your own likeness, what sort of world would that be?"

"What's the point?" Damien asked. "It won't change anything. People are the same as they have been since we started walking upright. Trying to figure out another way is a waste of time."

"That's where you're wrong," Scarman said. "For most of humanity's existence, we have followed certain tenants. Survival of the fittest. Thinning the herd. The strong ruled, the weak followed. Such a world was strong. It purged itself of unnecessary indulgences and honored the smartest, the strongest, and the ruthless."

"Sounds like Eden," Damien mocked.

"Thousands of years ago, dangerous influences injected themselves into the social fabric, undermining a world that had to be earned to be gained, not given without cost. Toxic ideas corroded at the foundation of our culture. The unintelligent were given a voice, the perverse given refuge, the clueless the ability to govern. False compassion masked the sickness taking over the planet, allowing the cancer to take root and grow. Humanity was not created to share, but to rule. To demand, not ask. There are those with gifts and those without, a pecking order of who is worthy of remaining and those burdening the good."

"Don't tell me," Damien said. "You're the smartest guy in the room with the power of life and death, deciding for the poor rest of us of who is worthy of your generosity."

Smiling, Scarman lowered his head. "No, no, no. I am not worthy to stand in their presence. As I have said to you before, I am but a soldier, nothing more. I follow orders. I see the tasks through to the end."

"Then what are you doing here?" Damien asked.

"What I was told."

Scarman motioned to the hidden soldiers, who, in response to his call, rushed over in formation. One yanked Ted to his feet while another pulled the second man with the covered head out of his chair.

"What are you going to do with Ted?" Damien asked.

"A trial, of course," Scarman said. "A public one, so that justice may be seen and felt by those wronged and injured."

"You're so full of shit."

"Maybe," Scarman said with a smirk. "But it will be a spectacle."

"And Steven West," Damien said. "Why is he so important?"

Upon hearing his name, the bound man tried to yell through the black cloth covering his face, but his words were stifled by what must have been tape or a gag.

"Why do you want his technology?" Damien asked. "What do you want him to erase?"

"Everything," Scarman said.

The loading dock door opened, and Ted and West were each thrown into two separate windowless vans. The soldiers split and followed them inside each vehicle, then sped away out of the alley.

"Well, my work is done," Scarman said. "I like to take a moment when I've finished a difficult task to be grateful for my part in a much bigger play."

He slid a device from his pocket. It was about two inches long with a switch, a light, and a button.

"Sadly, I can't indulge in such a simple pleasure," Scarman said. "Duty and sacrifice above all things. Right, bluebird?" He flipped the switch, and the light glowed red. His thumb hovered over the button. "I'm not a superstitious person, but I must admit, I have one fear."

The light from the opened loading dock door illuminated the once-hidden features of the warehouse. Damien could see yellow cords intertwined with the metal rafters and followed them to small packs attached along the walls, spread out ten feet apart. There were hundreds of them.

The building was rigged to blow.

Scarman held up the trigger. "I don't want to die alone."

DAMIEN STARED at the detonator in Scarman's hands. If the madman pushed the button, he and Damien would die, but that didn't bother Damien. What irked him was the scarred bastard would get away with everything. No arrest. No trial. Scott free, just like his father.

His mind leapt back to his father's grave, overwhelmed with the same disgust. He remembered looking at the new sod taking root over his dad's coffin six feet under and wanting to dig until he reached the sealed wooden box. With strength he had been hiding his entire life, he wanted to rip the lid off and wrench his corpse from the tomb.

With tight fists, he would grab his father's best suit and yank him to his feet. He would shake his father's cold body with the force of an earthquake and scream into his hollow face, staring into his empty eyes, and demand he pay for all he had done.

Scarman would call that an unnecessary attachment. Damien called it his drive for justice.

Staring at the detonator, Damien knew he may have had only seconds to live. If so, he wanted his life to end the same way Raquel loved him.

Being a cop.

"One more thing," Damien said to Scarman, whose thumb still hovered above the detonator. "I'm going to have to place you under arrest."

"What?" Scarman scoffed.

"I can't let you kill yourself. Committing suicide is against the law. I can't let that be the last crime you commit today."

"I've committed no crimes, at least none I recognize, written as unjust laws and enforced by corrupt bluebirds. Whatever consequences you think are owed by me are about to be paid with my life."

"Suicide isn't payment," Damien said. "It's cowardice. You're not facing your judgment—you're hiding from it."

"Still trying to enforce the law, bluebird?" Scarman asked. "I thought you had evolved beyond that."

"I have. I'm a murderer, just like you, because of you. I have my own crimes to pay for, but I'm not paying for them here because you pushed a button."

"You amuse me," Scarman said. "Since we first met, you've always acted as if you've had control. You were nothing more than an excuse, another symbol of all we should hate, and an example of all that is wrong with our society."

Damien sighed. "You do love to hear yourself talk."

"You live under the facade of civility and the lie of lawfulness," Scarman continued. "Illusions that only work because people have not been shown the truth of what they really are and who they can become."

"Your cause will show them this, no doubt," Damien said.

"Yes. And it will be glorious."

Scarman raised the detonator, a slow smile creeping across his lips.

"Goodbye, bluebird."

A HAND REACHED out and struck Scarman near the neck, the fingers digging deep into the nerves behind the collar bone. The instant pain forced Scarman to his knees, and the detonator fell from his hands.

A foot kicked the detonator to the side, and Scarman twisted to confront his attacker.

Dex stood over him, holding the security guard's pistol in his shaking hands.

"Special forces, asshole," Dex said. "Retired. I could have twisted your neck and dropped you like a lifeless doll, but my partner had the idea of arresting your sad ass, so I let you live."

Scarman looked Dex up and down. "I must say, the entry requirements for law enforcement have dropped considerably since my first visit. They are taking human refuse into the academy now?"

Dex struck him across the face with the butt of his pistol.

"The devil always was a smart ass," Dex said.

"Stop," Damien said. "I need him conscious."

"I can hurt him a hundred different ways without putting him under."

"Good to know."

Dex picked up the detonator and turned it off, then tapped Damien's arm with a pair of handcuffs.

"Courtesy of the bloodied security guard up front," Dex said.

Damien grinned and pulled Scarman's arms behind his back, grabbed him by the wrists, and yanked him to his feet. The cuffs made satisfying *clicks* around the scarred man's wrists.

"You have the right to remain silent, you arrogant sono-fabitch," Damien said. "Anything you say can and will be used against you in a court of law. You have the right to an attorney. If you cannot afford an attorney, one will be provided to you."

"I know my rights," Scarman said.

"You don't recognize our laws, but now you claim to understand your rights?" Damien asked. "How convenient. I'm going to make it my singular mission to make sure you make it to prison. In how many pieces is up to you."

"Your confidence amuses me. As always, you're missing the big picture. Whether you arrest me or not, I'm a dead man."

"No one is going to kill you. Not before your ass is sentenced in court. After that, you can burn in hell for all I care. But it's up to you whether you enter the prison with bruises or broken bones."

"And how's that?" Scarman asked.

"Tell me where you took Ted and we'll be on our way. Anything else and I'll let Dex revisit the old days."

"Enhanced interrogation techniques? Excellent. It's nice to see you're a police officer *and* corrupt. Exactly as I had predicted."

"I'm all cop," Damien said. "Dex, however, is a private citizen. What he does behind closed doors isn't my concern. Not unless he breaks the law."

"Torture isn't illegal in your town?" Scarman asked.

"It is. I'll arrest Dex without hesitation, if you press charges. Of course, as a material witness to such a dangerous man, we'd have to keep you in our custody until Dex's trial. For your own protection."

"I'm in police custody as either a suspect or a witness? Those are my two options?"

"Yup. You're not leaving my sight until I lock you up."

"And your families?" Scarman asked. "What of them?"

Damien gritted his teeth. "I'm trying so hard to control myself. Please don't push me with veiled threats."

"I don't threaten. I educate. Your fellow bluebird is on his way to your brother's church."

"Bullshit," Damien said.

"Father Jacob's parish is surrounded, under the watchful eye of my compatriots. After Ted is delivered there, he, along with his wife, Denise, and their children, Daniel, Ezra, and Foster, will be put on trial for the murder of Hector Martinez. The church is full of refugees, hiding under the protection of your brother, its pews filled with jurors who will decide whether Ted and his family live or die. That's their choice. Five deaths or hundreds. It will be in their hands. Justice in its purest form."

CHAPTER
THIRTY-SEVEN

IT'D BEEN A LONG DAY.

Damien had pushed his body beyond its limits. He had navigated this day relying on the damaged goods that was him.

He'd spent every waking and sleeping moment thinking about, and looking for, an excuse to kill Scarman. It didn't matter how. Bullet, knife, baseball bat, electric shock, burning, beheading, or by removing one finger, one toe, one eye, and one organ at a time.

He'd considered every option, dwelled on them, relied on them to force him out of the hospital bed and through the pains of physical therapy. His hatred and thirst for revenge drove him to visit his wife and child's grave, to try to rejoin the police force, to walk out of a burning building and into an armory teeming with Scarman's thugs. It cost Damien his brother-in-law and what little innocence he had left when he choked the life out of Leash.

His thirst for revenge was the only thing that allowed him to look in the mirror and not end his own life. Now, he stood in the warehouse rigged to explode with the focus of hate standing before him, hoping to die.

Life was funny that way, giving people what they thought they wanted just to prove how wrong they were to pursue it.

Scarman's threats to Damien's and Ted's families had the weight of experience. Their nemesis was vicious. It was his modus operandi.

Collateral damage is encouraged.

No matter what Scarman had in store for them, the only way to screw him over was to survive, with Scarman in prison facing judgement from a system he believed to be illegitimate. Perhaps Damian could gain insight into the bigger cause for which he was so willing to sacrifice Hayeston at their altar.

That would be justice.

No matter the cost, he wasn't about to let Scarman or his evil horde touch one hair on the heads of those few Damien loved.

It was time to end this.

Damien grabbed Scarman by the bicep, escorting him toward the opened loading dock doors.

"You're going to let your best friend die?" Scarman asked with a knowing smirk, one Damien wanted to punch off his face. "I can stop it. I can stop all of it."

"How?" Damien asked.

"Simple. Give me the detonator and let me die."

"No deal."

"Wait," Dex said. "This asshole is saying if we let him kill himself, your best friend and his family will live?"

"And his brother, the honorable Father Jacob," Scarman interjected.

"Mission accomplished. Let him do it."

"No," Damien said. "This guy is a puppet master. He could pull the town's strings in his sleep and we wouldn't even know it. Something else is at play here. Anything this guy wants is the wrong choice."

"Are you willing to risk their lives over it?" Dex asked.

"We could tie him to one of the poles, step outside, push the button ourselves, and watch the place come crashing down around him."

"You really think he wants to blow himself up?" Damien asked. "After all he's done, you think he's just gonna bite the bullet when there's so much glory waiting for him? This is his moment, the culmination of months of work. Look, I don't know why they rigged this place to blow, but it isn't so he could die with a flourish. Something else is going on here."

"I assure you, there isn't," Scarman said. "I've told you, my work is done. As such, my existence is a liability to the cause. I can't do anything else for them, except cause damage."

"Shut up," Damien said. "Stop trying to sound like a martyr. Your cause isn't noble, and your death isn't important."

Damien scanned the warehouse walls again, examining the wired explosives. Moving next to Dex, he whispered in his ear.

"I think he wants to wipe Digital Slate off the map," Damien said. "That's why we're surrounded by C4. I think they're just covering their tracks and destroying any way of understanding what sort of technology Steven West developed. The only thing I believe coming out of Scarman's mouth is he can cause his people damage, but not if he's dead. Or us."

Damien smacked Dex on the arm.

"We're the good guys, remember?" he said. "We've both made a lot of mistakes. This is our chance to do something right. Let's go save some people and get this asshole behind bars."

"It'd be nice to do something I'd want to remember instead of forget."

"Me too," Damien said.

Dex nodded, and they each grabbed one of Scarman's arms.

"Let's go," Damien said to him. "You're going to remember this day. Today is the day you're going to be outsmarted by a military veteran and a bluebird you couldn't kill."

"Is that a fact?"

"It is. You think you're special. You're not. You're just another sociopath."

"You get a lot of those around here, do you?" Scarman asked.

"More than you'd think. Our prison is packed with them. There, you'll realize you're no different from the petty thief, the wife beater, or the child molester."

"Of course I'm different," Scarman said. "Look at your sad little town. No one in your jail has ever done what we've accomplished today. We've brought your town to its knees."

"Playing on people's fears doesn't make you a genius."

"Of course not. Even bluebirds play on fears. What we've done is historic. Hayeston will no longer be a forgotten stop on the map. It will be remembered as the place where it all started, the Plymouth Rock of a new world, the Battle of Lexington of the next revolution."

"Our prison has a couple of people with delusions of grandeur, too," Damien said.

Smiling, Scarman shook his head.

"Enjoy this time," Scarman said. "What little of it you have left. Revel in your false victory. What you think of me or of what we've done today doesn't matter. You don't matter. You never have. Not when you were buying baby clothes and not when I ordered your death. You were, still are, and always will be, nothing."

Damien felt his hands tense, his fingers longing to wrap around Scarman's throat once again.

"You've got that backward," Damien said. "Your sacred

cause doesn't matter, and you—you'll be of interest for one news cycle, maybe two, and then no one will know you ever existed. This town is made of good people, wounded people who've been lied to and misled by you, but they will come back. We will rebuild and erase every memory of your time here. Neither Hayeston, nor the world, will ever speak of you and your cause again."

"You talk as if you have authority," Scarman said. "A little bluebird caught in a maelstrom. A rookie cop who's not even a cop playing with his homeless vet. How can you promise such things?"

"Because, unlike you, I have faith in the people here."

The warehouse suddenly echoed with a sound Damien had not heard since Scarman took control of his town.

Damien's cell phone was ringing.

DAMIEN STARED at the pocket holding his ringing phone, but he didn't move. He didn't want to answer it. Wasn't sure if he should. What if it were a hallucination—Raquel reaching out for the first time since he had told her to leave? Answering a phone no one could hear and talking to someone no one else had seen would soothe no one, especially Dex.

So Damien did nothing.

"Are you going to answer that?" Dex asked.

"You can hear my phone?" Damien asked.

"Of course I can."

"I wasn't sure it was…" Damien fumbled. "I'll get it." He pulled the phone from his pocket. "Hello?"

"Damien!" It was Jacob. "Thank God you're okay."

"How are you? I tried to call you earlier, but—"

"We've got a lot of people hiding out at my church, including Denise and the kids, but we're scared. Some parishioners have brought guns to try to keep us safe, but…"

"But what?"

"There's movement outside. People I don't recognize. A lot of them. Armed. They're surrounding us."

"Did you call 9-1-1?" Damien asked.

"Yes," Jacob said. "It was the first call I made after the lines were free, but they said their resources were stretched and couldn't guarantee anyone would show up. We're all alone up here. Please, get here as fast as you can, before it's too late."

"I'm on my way," Damien said.

Turning to Scarman, he tried to peer through his dark eyes to see if he had been telling the truth all along or if the crowd forming near the church was the result of the riots having made it that far north. Either way, it solidified one decision in Damien's mind.

He closed his fist, then punched Scarman in the face.

"What was that for?" Dex asked.

"I've thought of a thousand ways to kill you," Damien said to Scarman. "If anything happens to my brother, I will use every single one of them."

Scarman shook his head. "Punching a defenseless man?" he said. "I knew you and I were a lot alike."

"What's wrong?" Dex asked.

"We have to go."

"You won't get far," Scarman said.

Damien's phone chimed. He opened a text message to find a new wanted poster with his picture on it.

"Everyone in town got the same message. One hundred thousand dollars for the rogue cop trying to save his murderous best friend, the one whose bullet started it all."

Damien slid his phone into his pocket, continuing to pull Scarman toward the loading dock.

"Word is out that you're here, hiding. Your precious neighbors are on their way, vigilantes in search of a paycheck."

"Enough with the speeches," Damien said.

"Shh," Scarman interrupted. "Listen…"

Damien heard faint chants outside, weak, but growing stronger.

"They're back," Scarman continued. "They're building up their courage. They're scanning the dead bodies outside, wondering if they have the strength to come in, but they will. They will work themselves into a frenzy. Flow through the warehouse like a tsunami of hate, all hunting you. It is your own people who want you dead now. I won't have to kill you. They'll do it for me."

Scarman was playing the town with the predictability of Pavlov's dogs hearing a bell and expecting a treat.

The mobs were an extension of his will, like a Greek god pointing his finger down from the heavens and sending lightning bolts into the populace, forcing them in one direction, then another.

Humanity was hard-wired for survival. Scarman had figured out the triggers in the deep-seated sections of the human brains where fear activated the most primal forces within people.

As animals, humans were no different and no greater than any other species. Actually, they were worse, because their brains had more power to think of things primal brains would never dare.

Slaves had felt the whip because of this. Jews, the gas chambers. Tribes, forced starvation. Nations, ethnic cleansing.

Humanity was exceptional at making the most horrid acts justifiable victories if they could just find more pros than cons to check off their morality chart. For all of its greatness, its artwork, its operas or sculptures, its books or songs, its exploration and innovation, Scarman had mastered a shortcut around humanities' gifts and tapped directly into mankind's selfishness.

As the sounds of the approaching mob grew louder, Damien had no idea how to turn their feverish drive into a moment of sanity and calm. How could he possibly turn wrath into mercy when he was nearly as incapable of that transformation himself?

Hearing the calls for his head, Dex stared at the gun in his hand.

"I've got less than fifteen shots," he said. "And it sounds like more than that is coming."

"Partner, get behind me," Dex said, handing him the detonator.

"I'm a marksman," Damien said. "Give the pistol to me."

"Dude, I could eat your achievements for lunch. I've killed more enemy combatants than I can count. Keeps me up at night, no doubt, but when people threaten me, I have no qualms putting them down if need be. Now get behind me."

Dex pulled Scarman ahead of them, using his body as a shield.

"What do you want?" Damien yelled across the expansive space to the panting crowd, which held bats, knives, and pipes.

"You know why we're here," a voice said.

Damien tilted his head. He recognized it. The overweight and out-of-work factory worker from the auto shop.

"Charlie, is that you?" Damien asked.

"Nice to have the tables turned, isn't it?" Charlie said, holding up a gun. Damien recognized the silver badge emblazoned on the grip. Police issued. A gift from the armory. Standing next to Charlie was young Freddy, wearing the guard's hat, its white Security letters now stained with blood.

"Freddy," Damien said. "I thought we had an agreement."

"That's right," Freddy said. "You said the next time you saw me with these people you were going to kill me. I think you've overestimated your chances."

"Listen—" Damien started.

"No!" Charlie interrupted. "This time, you listen." He turned to the mob. "This guy tried to torture me today. Threatened to electrocute me if I didn't cooperate."

The mob roared in anger.

"But I didn't—" Damien said.

"But you wanted to," Charlie interrupted. "I saw it in your eyes. You're no better than us. As a matter of fact, you're worse, because you're supposed to be the someone who protects people. You're not a cop anymore. You're just a target. Now, step out and come with us so we can get our reward. No more talking. Come peacefully or we'll take him by force."

"Peacefully?" Damien asked. "Don't make me laugh. Look around you, Charlie. How many more people have to die today?"

Freddy counted Damien and Dex.

"Only two," Freddy said.

"The reward's now one-hundred K for you," Charlie said. "Two hundred K for your partner's head. We want our money. Do you know what that would do for an unemployed factory worker like me?"

"What good is it if you're dead?" Damien said. "Or in prison?"

"Nah, we got the numbers now. We're in control."

Damien sighed. "You've never been in control. None of us have all day. Please, look at the walls and the ceilings. You see those yellow wires and small gray squares?" Damien held up the detonator. "Those are explosives."

"C4," Dex said. "I've seen it work in person. This ain't no joke."

"This man we have in custody was going to blow up this building," Damien said. "He's the one behind the riots. He's responsible for all the destruction."

"Good," Charlie said. "After I collect my money, I'll buy him lunch and thank him for showing us the light."

Scarman chuckled.

"Please," Damien said. "This building is wired to explode. If you don't let us leave, it could come down on you. No reward is worth that."

"It'll come down on you, too," Charlie said.

"I don't care. I've got nothing to lose."

"Neither do I," Dex said. "Not for a long time."

"Please, just look at each other," Damien said. "Take a minute and really *see* each other. Who were you before today, before you rushed into this warehouse? Moms, dads, teachers, cooks, drivers, students? If you kill us, that life is over. You will be hunted from this day forward. You want to save your life? Then put the weapons down and leave. Or…"

Damien held up the detonator.

"One press of this button and we all die," he said. "No tomorrows. This is it, the end of your lives. Your clock runs out right here, in this building, unless you let us go."

Charlie and Freddy faced the mob behind them, each of them really studying the other, probably for the first time. They were silent. No words, just nods and shrugs.

Then, as if parts of a single body, they turned and rushed at Damien.

THE RACING HORDE of twenty appeared more like forty as it ran at them, weapons gripped in their hands so tightly their knuckles showed white, their eyes glowing a fiery red.

Damien ushered Dex ahead, then gripped Scarman's arm and pulled him toward the loading dock door, keeping him between himself and the mob.

The detonator in Damien's hand felt light and cheap. Made of plastic, it reminded him of a child's toy, like one of the fake guns he and Ted used to play with as kids.

They reached the loading dock door, the mob only seconds behind them. Even though Charlie was carrying the gun, he hadn't pulled the trigger. There was a good chance he was too afraid to try, but it didn't mean someone else wouldn't grab it from him and start firing.

Adrenaline was both an ally and an obstacle. In the heat of the moment, it could give increased strength, focus, and drive, but while coursing through the veins, it wasn't something that calmed a shaking hand or allowed a novice shooter to suddenly become a marksman.

Repetition and muscle memory enabled military and police to take moments of intense stress and perform at a high level. Hours and hours at the gun range, training in live-action drills. Damien was hoping—no, *counting*—on the fact that whoever held that gun had never shot another human before.

"What do you want to do?" Dex asked. "I don't want to fire on these people."

"Let's get outside," Damien said. "Find a vehicle and get to the church."

As they scurried to the loading dock door, Damien was surprised Scarman wasn't putting up more of a fight. If martyrdom was his last act of sacrifice, he didn't appear anxious to experience it, at least not at the hands of a weaponized mob.

It appeared Scarman's allegiance to the cause had limits.

At the entrance to the loading dock door, Damien heard a voice behind him yell, "They're getting away! Shoot them! You have a gun, use it!"

Damien glanced back as a man in his forties tried to grab the gun from Charlie. He was wearing a dirty uniform, a delivery man of some sort who had decided today was the day murder was the right choice and he was the right man to do it. That man woke up, got dressed, and was probably in the midst of his daily deliveries when Hayeston erupted. Just hours later, he was ready to kill for money.

"Permission to fire," Dex asked.

"No. We have to find a ride out of here."

"On it."

Had the delivery man always fantasized about killing or did he feel the circumstances and a hefty payday gave him permission to redefine right and wrong?

Sanity never felt so tenuous.

Damien, Dex, and Scarman stepped into the light of day.

The loading dock overlooked a docking bay where semi-trucks backed in to unload their goods. Jumping off the dock to the ground with a man in cuffs would not be easy.

Damien hit the button to lower the loading dock door as the grumble of a diesel truck approached.

Dex was behind the steering wheel of a propane delivery truck, its rusted side sporting the same logo as the one on the delivery man's uniform.

The wanna-be killer had just given them their escape.

"C'mon!" Dex yelled.

Damien gripped Scarman's arm.

"We're gonna jump down together," Damien ordered.

The wind was suddenly knocked from him, and he tumbled forward.

He and Scarman landed at the edge of the loading dock as a few men tackled them onto the hard cement.

Damien turned back to find more people trying to squeeze under the closing loading dock door.

"You're mine," one of the attackers yelled, while the other grabbed for the detonator.

Damien tried to pry the man's hand from his own. Their fingers overlapped. He could feel the attacker's hand move up the device, switching it on.

"Stop!" Damien yelled. "You're going to kill us all!"

The man didn't listen, couldn't listen. In the frenzy, he was only focused on one thing. Killing him.

Damien tried to twist from the man's grip, but his powerful hands remained wrapped around Damien's.

Below his fingers, Damien felt the detonator button depress followed by a simple, yet terrifying sound.

Click.

DAMIEN HELD HIS BREATH.

He expected to feel the vibration of each C4 pack exploding, the deafening sound of a sixty-thousand-square-foot warehouse shattering into small pieces of cement, wood, and metal.

But nothing happened.

Damien lurched his knee into the groin of his attacker, punching him in the face with his free hand. The man groaned and curled into the fetal position, releasing his grip on the detonator and grabbing his crotch.

"The button has been pushed!" Damien said. "Why hasn't it gone off?"

The other attacker froze.

Damien swiveled to watch Charlie, then Freddy, squeeze through the lowering loading dock door before it closed completely. The rest of the group banged on the metal door from inside the darkened warehouse, unsure how to open it again.

Scarman raised his wide eyes up from the ground, but his voice remained calm.

"Don't let go," he said. "It's a dead man's switch. Release the button and the building comes down."

"Another little perk you came up with?" Damien asked.

"I wanted to keep my options open."

Damien held out the detonator to Charlie and Freddy like a shield, and they stopped their approach. Reaching down, he grabbed onto Scarman and pulled him to his feet.

"Now, I'm taking this man into custody," Damien said. "You're going to let us leave. If I release this switch, we all die."

Charlie gazed toward Dex waiting in the running truck at the end of the alley. Damien could see the hand of the factory worker tighten around the pistol.

"Don't do it," Damien said.

Charlie raised the gun, but pointed it at the propane truck.

"The poster said I get the reward if you're dead or alive," Charlie barked. "That's what it said. And I could shoot the truck and blow it up. That'd end your escape and I'd get my reward."

"No," Damien said. "No, Charlie. It doesn't work that way. It won't blow up. That only happens in the movies. Those trucks are designed to survive heavy impacts, like car accidents. A bullet from your pistol won't even pierce the side."

"You're lying."

"No, I'm not, but let's say you're right. Let's say you shoot the propane truck and turn that innocent man into ash. What would that blast do to you and me? And to this?" he said, holding up the detonator. "Think, Charlie. You didn't get on that bus to die today. You just wanted the money to help your family. You're here for your family. You still have a chance to go home and be with them. If you pull that trigger, your entire life changes. The second you fire, you become a murderer. And, if I die, a cop killer. Another second after that, you become a corpse."

"But the reward," Charlie said. "My family would get it, right?"

"Charlie, look around you. The man who would pay you is in my custody. You pull that trigger, you kill your reward."

"Don't listen to him," Freddy said. "He's bluffing. Cops, always lying. That's what the man with the scar was trying to tell us all along. Cops can't be trusted. Be a man, Charlie, and shoot."

Damien could see the struggle on Charlie's face. The delusion of a payday fighting against the pressure of the mob.

"Man up," Freddy said. "He ain't holding no detonator. He's bluffing. He's a liar. Pull the trigger, man, or give it to me and let me cash in."

Damien heard the electric whir of the loading dock door opening behind them. They were about to have company.

"Charlie, just put the gun down," Damien said. "Just put it down so I can do my job and deliver this man to the authorities. You and I, we don't ever need to cross paths again. You take the next bus home and you stay in Percy. Put in that application for the job at that other factory and enjoy the rest of your life."

"What do you know about our struggles?" Freddy said. "You don't know shit. You get to go home to your nice house and a steady job. We get to go home to nothing. We need to get paid. Nothing's gonna stop us, especially you."

Freddy turned to Charlie.

"I'll show you, Charlie," he said. "I'll show you he's bluffing."

With youthful speed, Freddy charged Damien.

Scarman jumped in front of him, knocking against the lean teen, but not hard enough to stop his momentum, forcing Scarman and Freddy over the side of the loading dock. As they fell, Freddy reached out and grabbed Damien by the arm, pulling him over with them.

Damien landed on the warm asphalt with a painful *thud*, the impact shaking the detonator in his hand. He kept his grip firm and the button pushed, his fingers tightly wrapped around the plastic.

Freddy quickly hopped to his feet and gritted his teeth in anger, kicking Damien in the side.

"All. Cops. Should. Die," Freddy shouted between clenched teeth with each kick.

With his hands behind his back, Scarman couldn't stand, but was able to reach his leg forward, trying to block each of Freddy's kicks.

If things were different, Damien would have found it funny. Self-preservation. It brought the desperation out in everyone, even Scarman.

The next time Freddy's sneakers impacted Damien's side, he felt one of his fractured ribs break. Pain shot through his body with blinding intensity. He instinctively curled to protect himself, his hands grabbing onto his side.

Damien was once again overwhelmed with flashbacks. The store. The attack. He thought, for a moment, he had felt Raquel's presence near him as she was before, but was too afraid to open his eyes, fearing he would see her laying on the ground, bruised, bleeding, her hands protecting the life that once grew within her womb.

Time appeared fluid as he moved back and forth between Benita's store and the loading dock, the flurry of blows propelling him months in the past, then back to the present. A torrent of sadness and helplessness, failure and regret.

Nothing had changed.

His anger had brought him no fulfillment. His pursuit of Scarman, no closure. His attempts to save his best friend, as fruitless as saving his wife and child.

Laying on the pavement, struggling to breathe. All he had done to avenge his loss was in vain.

When Damien opened his eyes, he found Freddy standing over him, holding the detonator. Somehow, in between kicks and pain, he had pried it from Damien's hands, all the while keeping the button pushed. With immense pride, he held it over his head.

"I told you the cop was bluffing," Freddy yelled. "Now I'm gonna prove it to you."

"Stop," Charlie yelled, pointing the pistol at Freddy. "Don't do it. I'm tired. I'm so tired. I just want to go home. I want to sit in my recliner, pop open a beer, and try to forget this day ever happened."

"What's wrong with you?" Freddy asked. "You turning traitor on us?"

"No, I just… what if the cop was right, just this once?"

"But he's not. None of 'em can be trusted. That's the way it is. It's time we did something about it, stood against the machine."

Freddy spoke with the vigor of someone who had felt driven by a purpose for the first time in his life. He was part of something bigger and was never going back.

Even though he was still breathing, Freddy had become another casualty of Scarman's war.

As Charlie and Freddy debated, Damien slowly rolled onto his chest and pushed himself up, helping Scarman do the same. They moved quietly away from the building, one urgent step at time.

Behind Freddy and Charlie, Damien watched the loading door raise until the rest of the mob spilled out onto the dock in the midst of the heated debate.

"I'm not a traitor," Charlie said. "But things aren't as black and white as you think it is. Not all cops are bad. Not all are corrupt. Some are just guys like me, trying to do a job and go home. They're not all against you, Freddy."

"Listen to him," Freddy said to the mob around him. "He was never one of us. He was just playing make believe, hoping his fat ass could tag along and get an easy payday. Well, fuck you and your kind, Charlie. You're not one of us. You never have been."

He pointed the detonator at Charlie's face.

"All the cops are liars."

Damien continued to pull Scarman down the alley, quickly moving away from the building.

"I'll show you," Freddy said, sliding his thumb off the button.

The sky above Damien felt like it had shattered into a million pieces.

THE GROUND MOVED beneath their feet in waves, the asphalt undulating as each packet of C4 exploded behind them. The consecutive bursts shook the air, one after the other, like a spectacular finale during a Fourth of July celebration.

Debris began to fly past them.

Damien and Scarman's legs moved in unison, sprinting at full speed toward the end of the alley, the aches of Damien's broken rib hidden by panic that propelled him forward.

The heat from the continuous explosions grew hotter as the path of the destruction chased them down the alley, each burst faster than each step, the wave of wreckage about to overtake them.

"Hurry," Dex yelled, his voice barely audible over the shattering cement and twisting of metal.

Dex's face lit up with pulses of yellow and orange, the colors growing brighter as the explosions neared.

As they approached the truck, Damien scanned the high step and small door, fearing there wasn't enough time to maneuver Scarman into the truck cabin, then himself, and pull away before the blast caught up with them.

As shards of wood and couch-sized pieces of metal cross-beams fell around them in a dust of disintegrated cement, Damien chose a more immediate option. He pulled Scarman under the truck directly below the massive propane tank.

Above them, they heard the crashing of debris against the thick metal cylinder holding thirty-five hundred gallons of flammable gas, praying one of the sharp pieces of metal wouldn't pierce the side and expel fumes into the air, needing only a single spark to turn them into an explosive finale.

"Don't move," Damien heard Raquel yell. "Don't move an inch."

As she finished her sentence, a massive chunk of cement crashed at his feet, missing the tanker by inches.

Damien dared to peer toward the building as pellets of brick and cement rained like hail. The packets of C4 continued to blast in succession, moving from the roof line to the floor, its design meant not only to level the building, but annihilate it. Instead of falling inward, the structure was blasting outward. Computer servers blown into the air, splintered desks, reams of paper dispersed like snow, smashed doors all tossed by concurrent waves of detonations.

Nothing would be left to examine. The secrets of Digital Slate would remain solely in the mind of its kidnapped founder, spirited away in an unmarked white van by mercenaries of the cause.

Once the deafening chorus of explosions ceased, Damien grabbed Scarman by the arm. They crawled out from under the propane truck, its long metal cylinder dented and scratched, but left whole after the barrage of debris.

"Dex, you okay?" Damien asked.

"Yeah," he heard mumbled from the cabin. The windows had shattered, the glass sprayed across the seats, with several having nicked Dex's face.

"I'm fine, too," Scarman said. "In case you were wondering."

"We weren't," both Dex and Damien said in unison.

The sky clouded with cement dust began to settle, revealing the ground littered with wreckage. A bloody baseball cap floated down near Damien's feet, the black material and white Security letters singed by heat.

Freddy. Charlie. The propane delivery man. The rest of their mob, the brothers and sisters, husbands and wives, who chose to believe it was better to hunt down a cop than to defend one—they'd lost their lives chasing money they would never receive, for a cause they didn't even understand.

"This shit is getting too real," Dex said, his voice quivering. "It's like I'm back in Mosul all over again. The building looks like it got hit by a fucking missile strike."

"It fells like hell on earth," Damien mumbled.

"I like the comparison," Scarman said. "Myths can be a powerful motivator. Nearly as much as fear."

"Shut up," Damien said, punching him in the face.

Dex's eyes fixated on the remnants of Digital Slate, his head twitching with nervous tremors.

"I'll drive," Damien said.

"No," Dex said, waving him off and handing Damien the pistol. "I'm no coward. I finish the way I start."

The cabin whirred with the sound of grinding gears, shaking with the rumbling of the loud diesel engine in front of them.

"We won't make it," Scarman said. "I've told you, they won't let me survive. You should have let me die in the warehouse."

"Keep the bullshit to yourself. I'm tired. I hurt. And I just want a little peace and quiet, okay?"

"You'll see."

"That's not shutting up."

Scarman closed his eyes, leaning his head against the seat. Dex and Damien shared a look, shaking their head in disbelief.

What a day.

The rough tumble of heavy tires against pavement drowned out the rest of the world, and Damien enjoyed the respite. His ears were ringing, and his side throbbed. Will weakened, even his mind was exhausted.

He just wanted it to be over.

The short silence was interrupted by the sound of a chime on Damien's cell phone. Another text. He read aloud.

"One million dollars for the death of disgraced officer Damien Hill, as well as the prisoner currently in their custody and anyone else offering him aid. Hill is traveling from the warehouse district in a propane truck, heading toward St. Simon the Cyrene's church. No survivors are required. Collateral damage is encouraged."

Without opening his eyes, Scarman shrugged. "I told you."

DAMIEN'S first night on patrol was July seventeenth.

He was assigned to the area of town known as the Drink and Pink. It was the nickname of the location where drug dealers and prostitutes lived and worked. It wasn't a big place. Nothing in Hayeston was, but it was one of the seediest parts of town.

Patrolling that area had become an initiation of sorts for rookie cops. Hazing, law enforcement style.

That night, the thick humidity kept the heat in the air long after the sun had set. Tempers on the street were short, and the night workers had little patience for a rookie cop interfering with their prime business hours. They greeted him with middle fingers, choice words, and collective snarls.

"Let them see you and let yourself be seen," his shift commander told him. "Your job tonight is to remind them we're here. Otherwise, leave them alone. You can save the world tomorrow."

Damien had sighed in relief.

That July evening, Raquel was a mess. She called or texted Damien all night long, checking in and making sure he was okay. When she couldn't get a hold of him, she'd call Ted, who was assigned to a neighborhood nearby.

It was kind of adorable, the way she worried. Her passions were like that. She was an all-or-nothing kind of girl. When he had time to call her back, he heard the concern and pride in her voice. It reminded him why he was driving around town at an hour often void of people with good intentions.

The first half of the night was relatively quiet. A domestic violence call, a car theft, and a bar hopper who vomited in the back of his cruiser while complaining about the state of his love life. Damien felt like a janitor, cleaning up society's shit, but at least he'd come home in one piece.

With the end of his shift in sight, things got interesting. A code forty-one at the Quick Pit convenience store.

Robbery in progress.

The Quick Pit was owned by a Pakistani immigrant called Bhaskar. After calling for backup, Damien pulled into the far end of the parking lot, lights off, siren silent. Inside, he could see Eddie Orr, shirtless, sweating, and holding a bloody knife in one hand and the store's owner in the other.

Damien knew Eddie before his life went south. He peaked in high school as the team's best defensive end. When college scouts were less impressed than the girls at Hayeston High, his decisions and his life spiraled downward.

Damien had seen him around town, usually working as a bouncer at a few of the nightclubs and strip joints. His size worked to his advantage. Tall and thick.

Word was he got a taste of meth and couldn't shake it. Like a lot of people working the fast scene, he fell for its temptations. First, he lost his job. Then his girlfriend. Then everything else.

Inside the Quick Pit, harsh fluorescent lights cast a green hue on Eddie. He'd lost some weight, but was still a bull of a man. His khaki shorts were dirty and loose and appeared to be stained with drops of blood down one side. Damien wasn't sure if it was his or someone else's.

Eddie paced and screamed, growling like an animal, and accused Bhaskar of selling demons in his drinks. He'd cut open bags of chips, eating them in a frenzy. He guzzled a two-liter coke, the sticky liquid pouring down his torso as much as it did his throat.

Damien had read about this sort of behavior, from meth or, more likely, smoking or snorting bath salts. This was a new thing in Hayeston, but it was growing. More and more incidences were mentioned in the daily briefings in the Read-Off at the station.

Users overheated and tore off their clothes. They could display super strength and symptoms of paranoia. They were often disconnected from reality, hearing hallucinations and suffering from violent delusions.

Contain and secure. That was Damien's job.

Easing out of the cruiser, he removed his taser from his belt. He'd felt the jolt of one tase during his training. It only lasted a second, but had felt like an hour. Superman would drop to the floor after getting hit by one of those. Even high on drugs, Eddie was no superhero.

Ted's cruiser rolled to a stop next to him, and he exited his car.

"Is that Eddie?" Ted asked. "Seriously?"

"Yeah," Damien said. "He's high on something."

"Meth or salts?"

"Either or both."

"How do you want to handle this?" Ted asked.

Damien forced a smile. "I'm going to disarm him with my sparkling personality."

Ted groaned. "Please tell me you have a plan B."

Damien held up his taser. "I always have a plan B."

As Ted exited his cruiser, Damien's cell phone vibrated. No doubt another text from Raquel.

"If you don't text her back, she's gonna call me again," Ted said. "She's been doing that all night."

"It'll have to wait," Damien said. "I'm surprised Denise hasn't been checking up on you, too."

"Oh, she has," Ted said with a chuckle. "She promised me a fun night in the sack if I make it home in one piece. What did Raquel promise you?"

"If I don't die, she won't kill me."

"Looks like I win," Ted said.

They kept low, ducking below a thick border of beer advertisements, and neared the front glass door. Damien slowly reached for the handle, knowing an electric chime would announce their entrance once he pulled it open.

Damien jerked the door open, and he and Ted quickly rushed into the store. Damien stepped into the aisle where Eddie stood, gripping Bhaskar around his neck with one hand, his other filled with a handful of candy-coated peanuts. The knife sat on the shelf next to him, laying precariously on the edge, as if the slightest shake would knock it to the floor.

Damien gripped his taser.

"Eddie," he said.

The shirtless, sweaty man looked up and grunted. His eyes were wild, like a beast, and he threw candy at Damien to keep him away.

With Eddie distracted, Ted quietly maneuvered down the adjacent aisle, keeping his head below rows of cereal boxes and bags of potato chips.

"Eddie," Damien said. "Why don't you let Bhaskar go?"

Eddie snapped his teeth, clicking them together as he bit into the air. Ted creeped up behind him, taser drawn, ready to stun him, when, as if with a sixth sense, Eddie spun around.

With inhuman strength, he tossed Bhaskar toward Ted like a rag doll and they both fell to the floor.

Damien rushed Eddie.

There was a struggle, taser jolts, swings of a bat Bhaskar kept behind the counter, and a desperate, losing battle between three grown men and a sweaty, ex-bouncer high on salts.

Things in Damien's mind cleared up when he found himself in Eddie's grip, the knife edge against his neck, feeling the burn of the sharp edge cutting into his skin.

Ted pulled his gun, screaming for Eddie to drop the knife. Bhaskar, now bloody somehow, waved his bat wildly in the air.

Amidst the chaos, the room grew quiet and Damien thought how disappointed Raquel would be with him for having died that night, bleeding out on the dirty floor of the Quick Pit. She expected more of him than to go out in such an undignified way. Not in a hail of gunfire. Not saving the world, or a child, or anyone, for that matter, but at the hands of drug addict under the influence.

Such a rookie mistake.

The next sound Damien remembered was of Bhaskar's bat striking the back of Eddie's head. There was more fighting, fists, and tasers, a shelf of toiletries knocked over, and the smashing of a cheap bottle of whiskey against Eddie's face. The alcohol splashed across Damien's neck, and it felt as if his opened cut had been lit on fire.

When it was all said and done, pinned under Ted, Bhaskar, and a pile of merchandise worth three hundred and fifty dollars, a dazed Eddie had the fight beat out of him and Damien clicked his cuffs around the ex-lineman's thick wrists.

Paramedics arrived and had plenty to do, tending to everyone involved. Out of the four of them, Ted survived with the least damage.

The cut on Damien's neck wasn't too deep, but less than an inch from his jugular vein. A little more pressure, a smidge more to the left, and Damien's fear of an unseemly death would have been realized. A few stitches on site and a promise to visit the doctor in the morning was all he needed to end his shift early.

Before he got home, he returned to the station, cleaned up, and changed his shirt. When he walked through his apartment door, Raquel was waiting, frantic that neither he nor Ted had been answering her texts. With eagle eyes, she spotted the bandage through the dim morning light.

"What happened to you?" she asked, her eyes filled with worry, her voice teetering on tears.

For the first and only time in their marriage, Damien lied to her. He made up a story about getting nicked by a broken window while breaking up a domestic disturbance.

He could tell she wasn't ready to be married to a cop yet. Not really. Not with all the shit that came with it.

He and Ted earned a lot of respect that night from their fellow officers. The sergeant was easy on Damien for the following few days, giving him patrol duties in low-crime areas. By the time Damien's rotation placed him near the Drink and Pink again, Raquel had grown accustomed to marriage with a law enforcement officer. The crappy hours, eating dinner for breakfast, having sex during her lunch hour.

The only benefit of that first night was the passionate love-making he and Raquel shared in their bed. It was wonderfully hot, sweaty, and had lasted for hours. The benefits of a wife who loved at one hundred percent.

Ted and Denise had nothing on them.

After having talked with experienced police officers, Damien was certain that night was going to be the worst shift of his career.

And it was, until Scarman entered his life. Now Damien found himself sitting in the cabin of a propane delivery truck next to a terrorist with a million-dollar bounty on his head.

The ride from Digital Slate had been quick and uneventful so far. They'd made it to within a mile of the church with no gunshots or threats.

Damien wondered if the text was a psychological ploy to twist the knife in their exhausted psyches or for the enjoyment of their man in custody. The last gift to a dedicated and loyal soldier, watching his captors squirm at imaginary threats.

For a second, Damien had hope.

Until a bullet ricocheted off the propane tank.

THE SHOT CAME from the right, somewhere between a bank and the homes next to it.

Damien pulled his gun and leaned against the seat, trying to shield his face from the direction of the shot, hiding out of sight behind the thick metal door.

"Do you see him?" Dex asked.

"No," Damien said. "Floor it."

The heavy truck lurched and its engine growled, thick diesel smoke pouring from the exhaust like dissipating thunder clouds.

Scarman wasn't lying. His cause wanted them dead.

A million bucks for Damien? Eastern European mobs didn't invest that much money, time, and spectacle to kill an ex-cop who was nothing more than a nuisance. A quiet night, a moment alone, and a silencer would do the trick for a lot less money and publicity.

Didn't make sense. They already had Ted as their sacrificial lamb. No. Surviving Digital Slate was the problem. A reward that size could only mean one thing.

Scarman was the real target. Damien and Dex were just additional prey for the hunt.

In their new world order, those who had outlived their

usefulness, like Scarman, were to be given the honor of a public execution. Those who got in the way, like Damien and Dex, had earned their wrath.

It was the spectacle. The final act of their show. This was all part of the learning process, teaching the citizens of Hayeston, and perhaps the world, what life would be like under their merciless thumb.

Survival of the fittest.

The sound of the first shot at the propane truck sounded light. A pistol. Maybe a twenty-two caliber. Not powerful enough to pierce the double-sided metal propane tank.

The whiz of a second unseen bullet shattered a quarter-sized hole in the windshield, exploding into the seat between Damien and Scarman.

The impact was quickly followed by the loud crack.

"Holy shit!" Damien said.

Definitely large caliber. It sounded like a rifle from a distance. Maybe one of the sniper rifles stolen from the armory.

The closer they got to the church, the better the chance they were heading into a gauntlet.

Damien pulled Scarman down and laid on top of him, protecting him.

Damien looked down at his prisoner.

Scarman's eyes were closed, content, as if dying by friendly fire was as acceptable as blowing himself up.

"What do you want to do?" Dex asked.

"We're almost there," Damien said. "Just a few more blocks."

Bullets suddenly rained down on the truck. Side windows shattered. Shots ricocheted. The distinct, pungent smell of natural gas began to fill the cabin.

"The tank's been compromised!" Damien yelled over the gunfire.

Dex ducked below the steering wheel and swerved to the

side of the road, veering the truck into an empty parking lot and crashing into a closed dry-cleaning store in the middle of an aging strip mall.

Gunfire continued like a string of firecrackers, whizzing bullets impacting around them like Kamikaze hornets.

Damien grabbed Scarman, scrambling out of the cabin. From beneath the truck, he saw Dex stumble out and crawl deeper into the store.

Damien and Scarman followed behind him, charging through the debris, staying low. They crawled into a supply closet, surrounded by storage shelves stacked with rows of plastic bottles labelled perchloroethylene.

Pieces of drywall turned to dust as bullets tore through them like paper. Behind them, at the entrance of the store, the smell of escaping gas increased, and they could hear the impacts of gunshots pinging off the metal propane tank.

"One lucky shot…" Damien started, "One spark and this whole place is going up."

"It's worse than you think," Scarman said. "The chemical in these bottles is toxic. If the explosion didn't kill us, these bottles on fire would."

"You'd like that, wouldn't you?" Dex said.

"I had already picked my exit. You were the ones who changed it."

The hail of bullets continuing unabated. "We have to find a way out of here," Damien said, ignoring Scarman.

He army-crawled to the storage room door. Peering out, he spotted a glowing exit sign in the far back corner.

"Follow me," he said.

"I can't," Dex said.

"Why not?"

The homeless veteran lifted his hand from his side, his fingers and palm covered in blood.

DAMIEN TOOK the pistol from Dex's hand and slid it into his pocket. His hand was shaking. He was spent. He'd been running on adrenaline all day. Bullets were flying. Dex was stretched out on the ground, bleeding. Scarman, still cuffed behind the back, was difficult to move. The church was still a distance away.

Standing between them was a small, impatient, and well-armed army.

So far, the shots into the dry-cleaning store were quantity over quality. Random hits with little consistency. Damien would have to try to get Dex and Scarman out of the building in between rounds of fire.

It wouldn't be easy.

"Show me the cuffs," he said to Scarman.

"You're letting me go?" Scarman asked.

"Not quite," Damien said. He uncuffed one hand, but immediately clicked it around his own.

"Now, here's what's going to happen," Damien said. "We're going to lift Dex up between us and carry him out of here or I will cuff you to the front bumper of the truck and light the gas myself. You could die quick, or you could die slowly as your skin burns off your bones. Any questions?"

Scarman paused, glancing back to the leaking propane truck.

"I thought my arrest was your crowning achievement?" Scarman said. "After all this, you'd still kill me?"

"I'm done with your games," Damien said. "You either play by my rules or you die. Simple as that. Take your pick, but make it fast."

Scarman answered by offering his free hand to Dex. He and Damien lifted the ailing vet between them. Dex was heavier than Damien had anticipated. Despite his frail manner, he still had a lot of muscle hidden behind his unkempt appearance.

"Dex, we're going to have to run," Damien said. "It's gonna hurt."

Dex moaned as he lifted his arms up, clutching onto each of their shoulders. "So is dying," he said. "Let's go."

Damien led the way, peeking one more time toward the illuminated exit sign. Motioning a silent count, he started out of the storage room, hurrying down the hall, bullets grazing the floor and truck, each ping a spark waiting to ignite.

Dex grunted in pain as they shuffled toward the back exit, his feet dragging on the floor as Damien and Scarman carried his weight.

They kicked the door open. Without stopping, they rushed down the small alleyway behind the building, finding a hiding spot behind a green metal dumpster.

Dex's light skin was starting to grow white. He was losing too much blood.

Damien peered down the alley toward the church, wishing he had visited his brother more often. He had no knowledge of the neighborhood or its streets, nor the people living in the small houses surrounding them.

Did they like cops or hate them? Were they churchgoers or heathens, like Damien?

The cracks of the gunshots began to diminish, and he could hear voices approaching.

Damien cautiously glanced around the side of the dumpster through the open back door of the dry-cleaning shop, the smell of propane growing stronger.

He could hear the voices, louder every minute. A lot of them. Ten people, maybe more. In the chatter, he could also hear the clicks of clips being slapped into rifles and pistols being reloaded.

They were coming in to retrieve the corpses and secure their million-dollar reward.

Damien slid back behind the dumpster.

"I can't keep my eyes open," Dex said. "I'm not going to make it."

"Sure you are," Damien said. "The mission's not over. You start as you finish."

"Yes, sir," Dex said with a fading voice. "Ready for duty, sir."

Damien spotted a red plastic lighter tucked in Dex's pocket. A handy thing when living without electricity. Damien would buy him a zippo with the Special Forces logo for the trouble.

"I'm gonna borrow this," Damien said, taking the lighter from Dex. A few swipes later, a flame flickered out its top.

He picked a few small thin sticks off the ground and pressed them into the side of the lighter's trigger, forcing it open. When he released the trigger, the flame continued to glow.

Damien turned to Scarman, feeling an unexpected grin blossom.

"I'm beginning to like this explosion thing," he said.

Damien tossed the lighter around the dumpster into the dry cleaners back door, covered his ears, and waited.

CHAPTER
FORTY-FIVE

HEAT AND LIGHT filled the sky, the blast wave slamming against the dumpster like a tsunami of air, knocking Damien, Dex, and Scarman to the ground.

A plume of fire and smoke ascended into the air above the small strip mall as chunks of ceiling tile and pieces of drywall fell around them.

Damien rose, poking his head around the dumpster to find the propane truck flipped over, the blown-out, twisted metal of the tank resting against the crumbling outer wall, the truck cabin at a forty-five-degree angle, upside down, leaning on the storeroom, the containers of toxic dry cleaning fluid melted around it like plastic puddles beginning to form, its liquid contents sprayed and incinerated in the air.

Damien held his breath, waiting for the wind to disperse the harsh fumes. Inside the store, flames flickered around the bodies of Scarman's army. Some were whole, some in parts.

The sight was horrifying.

As the intense ringing in his ears started to subside, it was replaced by the screeching of fire alarms wailing from the strip mall.

They had to get out of there.

The sounds, smells, destruction, and confusion were the perfect distraction for them. It would take survivors, if there were any, time to sort through the charred dead before realizing their payday wasn't among them.

Unsure if the others' hearing had returned, Damien motioned in an emphatic gesture for Scarman and Dex to stand. As before, Dex propped himself between the two men. They started their laborious trek down the alley toward the church.

Scarman showed no tears for the lost warriors incinerated in front of him, nor the protestors, both local and bussed in, who had lost their lives so far that day. He was the coldest man Damien had met since his childhood friend-turned-serial-killer. Both had a confidence and arrogance.

They were narcissists. Psychopaths. Killers.

Neither felt a thing. Damien still did. Maybe, in the cloud of war, he had found a light of hope.

As they continued through the alley, Damien could sensed Dex's grip on his shoulder start to weaken, so he grabbed the vet's hand and held him up, replacing Dex's weakness with his own strength.

"It's all right," Damien said to Dex. "We're almost there."

With each step, Damien knew there was a real possibility the hero who served his country and saved Damien's life was going to die in his arms, but he refused to accept it. Not after all they had been through. Not after all they had done to try to save Ted.

The mission wasn't over, and Damien couldn't stomach losing another good soldier to the fight.

Their slow pace away from the burning building was stopped at the sight of a man and a small boy, both holding rifles, standing in the alley in front of them.

Shit, Damien thought.

They were sitting ducks.

The rifles in their foes' hands were wood grained with long barrels. Hunting rifles. Not from the police armory. Not military. Civilian guns, less sexy, but equally as powerful. The boy appeared comfortable holding a rifle nearly twice his size. He was the spitting image of the man next to him. No doubt father and son. The dad's naturally tan skin had a weathered look of someone who worked outside.

Their clothes appeared old.

Poor, if Damien had to guess, with nothing much to lose.

And their lottery ticket was standing thirty feet away from them.

The man waved, inviting them closer.

"Do you know them?" Scarman asked.

"No," Damien said.

"Then what are you going to do?"

Since Digital Slate, Damien had the sense Scarman was analyzing him, observing him like a curious scientist, assisting Damien to see how he would respond to stimuli, like a test subject in an experiment.

Damien didn't care. So far, the terrorist was helping, not hindering, and that was all that mattered.

Damien scanned the armed man and boy, unsure of their intentions, when Raquel appeared from behind them, as if she were standing just out of sight the entire time.

Damien's heart leapt.

He thought he'd never see her again, but there she was, in the flesh, smiling. She looked peaceful, as if he'd never kicked her out of his life. As if she had never died.

"We're trusting them," Damien said to Scarman.

"How can you be so sure?" Scarman asked.

"I have my reasons."

The man waved more urgently. Damien started toward them, carrying Dex and pulling Scarman with him.

As they approached, the man tilted his head.

"You're the ones everyone is after?" he asked.

"Yes," Damien said.

"You cause that?" the man asked, pointing toward the burning strip mall.

"Yup," Damien said, eyeing him and the boy more closely. The man, curious. The boy, nervous.

"Dad, we have to hurry," the boy said.

"We're on our way to the church," Damien said. "Look, my friend's been shot. Can you help us?"

"Come with me," the man said. "Quickly, before they see you."

The boy led the way, jogging to a high wooden fence before pulling open a creaky gate made of the same worn wood.

The man trailed Damien, Dex, and Scarman, periodically checking behind himself, eyeing the smoke rising above the strip mall. With his rifle butt against his shoulder, he sighted down the long barrel, his finger on the trigger, covering them, waiting for someone to follow in their footsteps.

"This way," the boy said.

In the hustle to get out of the alley, Damien lost sight of Raquel, but he could feel her presence now. She was with him, and Damien promised himself he would never push her away again. As with the first time they'd met, where ever she went, he'd follow.

She was his north star.

Damien and Scarman carried Dex into a backyard littered with old cars, some rusted, some incomplete.

"Do you live here?" Damien asked the young man.

With a nod, he began to lead them through a well-used path between the dead autos to the back porch of a small craftsman-style home. Damien guessed it was built in the early part of the twentieth century. It was old, but well maintained. It could use a new paint job and a few pieces of wood siding needed to be replaced, but overall, it was an attractive home.

The father followed them, pulled the wooden gate closed, and secured it with a small metal lock.

Confident they weren't being followed, he joined Damien on the porch and led them inside his home.

"My wife is a veterinarian," the man said. "She may be able to help your wounded friend."

"What's your name?" Damien asked.

"Eli. Xavier is my son, but we just call him X."

Inside, he placed his rifle against the wall next to the porch door and lifted Dex away from Damien and Scarman.

"Mindy," he shouted. "I need your help."

A plump brunette with naturally rosy cheeks and warm eyes rushed into the kitchen.

"Another one?" she asked.

The kitchen table had been covered with a faded pink bedsheet. A small pile of towels, stained with blood, lay in a crumpled heap on the floor.

"The world has gone crazy," she said. "Townsfolk used to care for each other, but now everyone's turning on their neighbors, like they all got a sickness."

Eli placed Dex on the kitchen table as X retrieved a pillow and placed it under his head.

It was obvious they'd done this routine before.

Mindy smiled at Dex, tenderly touching his face.

"Poor man," she said. "You rest now. Mindy will take care of you."

"They're the ones everyone is after," X said.

Eli filled two glasses from the tap, then offered them to Damien and Scarman. As he held them out, he paused when he noticed the cuffs on their hands.

"Who are you two?" Eli asked.

"I'm Officer Hill. This is my prisoner. He's the man responsible for the wanted posters, the riots, everything. Me and my partner were trying to bring him into custody when word got out."

"A million dollars," X said. "Dead or alive."

"You got the text, too?"

"We all did," Eli said.

"It's a sickness," Mindy repeated, cutting Dex's shirt away from his wound. "Whew, he's a ripe one."

"He's been living by the railroad tracks since he got back from his last tour, but he's a good man. An honorable man."

"X, go get some of Daddy's clothes. He'll wake up looking nice."

X ran out of the room as Mindy pushed Dex's scraggly hair away from his face.

"Poor, poor man," she said.

Eli escorted Damien and Scarman into an adjoining living room. Damien paused at the entrance for one more look at the weakening veteran, wondering if it would be the last time he'd see him alive.

There was nothing else he could do.

Damien pulled Scarman to a couch. As Damien eased into the soft cushions, he surveyed the room. It was nicely furnished. Nothing was new, but it was filled with well selected mid-century furniture from the nineteen fifties. Sleek and low with clean lines, the end tables, a leather chair, and a matching love seat filled the space nicely.

Eli had great taste.

Damien guzzled the cool water before holding out his glass. "Can I get another, please?" he asked Eli.

"Sure," Eli said, taking the sweating glass from his hand and reentering the kitchen.

With his free hand, Damien pulled his cell phone from his pocket and called Jacob. The church was less than two hundred yards away. It felt like a mile.

The phone rang once and was immediately answered. The

line was open, but no one spoke. Damien could hear murmuring and muffled conversation, but no Jacob.

"Hello?" Damien asked.

"Mr. Hill," an unfamiliar voice said. It was raspy and deep. "You and your prisoner have ten minutes to get to the church or everyone here dies."

CHAPTER
FORTY-SIX

THE MAN on the other end of the call hung up. Damien gazed forward, motionless, his tired mind and sore body trying to muster up the strength to move.

He was weary of playing their game, sick of running and hiding, of being their victim and pawn.

He wanted to sink into Eli's comfortable love seat, enjoy another cool glass of water, and soak in a few more seconds of normal.

But rest would not come today.

When Damien stood, Scarman silently followed him to his feet, like an obedient dog.

Damien met Eli at the entrance to the kitchen.

"Something wrong?" Eli said, reading Damien's eyes.

"What isn't?" Damien said.

He took the glass of water, enjoying each cool gulp as it cascaded down his dry throat, making sure not to waste a drop. With a deep exhale, he handed the glass back to Eli.

"Thank you," Damien asked. "How is my friend?"

Mindy answered, the front of her blouse smeared with traces of Dex's blood. "He needs a hospital, but I think I've stopped the bleeding. I don't think the bullet hit any major organs. Just through the side near the edge, in and out. Of course, I don't know for sure. It could have done all sorts of damage in there, but we wouldn't know without opening him up."

"Can you take care of him while we're gone?" Damien asked.

Eli and Mindy stared at Damien, but didn't say anything. The silence, Damien's eyes, the rhetorical nature of the question—it told them all they needed to know. The odds of a friendly reunion were slim.

"Yes," Mindy said. "Of course. You do what you have to do. We'll take care of your friend."

Damien's lips curved into a sad smile. "You're very generous," he said. "I wish there were more of you in the world."

"Most people are good," Mindy said. "We just don't boast about it."

Damien nodded. "My brother would agree with you," he said.

"I believe Father Hill would," she said, surprising Damien. "You look like him, except…"

"Except what?"

"Your eyes. They're harder."

He turned to Eli. "You're a lucky man. You have something special here. Don't ever take them for granted."

"I don't," Eli said. "Listen, there's a few of us in the neighborhood who stayed behind to help get people to the church. We can get you there quickly and out of sight."

"That would be much appreciated."

Damien took a few steps toward Dex, then grabbed his warm, limp hand. "Your mission is complete, my friend," Damien said. "You finished as strong as you started."

He motioned to Eli, tugging on Scarman as they followed him through the kitchen to the back porch.

They stepped into the crowded backyard and walked behind a detached garage, weaving through overgrown grass, stepping over car axles and around stacked tires buzzing with mosquitos.

Behind the garage, they ducked under split slats of fence and approached the house next door.

It was similar in design, but the owner had different, eclectic tastes. The backyard was cleanly trimmed and maintained. From a single large oak tree, a number of hummingbird feeders hung like Christmas ornaments. A gaggle of wrought-iron pink flamingos posed on either side of the stairs. Above the porch railing hung seven wind chimes, playing different notes. Yet, together, they sounded like a single song.

Eli hurried up the porch steps, then rapped on the door with a series of timed knocks. An older woman with gray hair and wrinkled skin, which looked as if it could be stretched to encompass someone twice her size, opened the door.

"Eli, you have more visitors?" she said.

"Good evening, Mrs. Lawson," Eli said. "This is a police officer and his prisoner. They need to get to the church in a hurry."

"Of course." She glanced from side to side, distracted by the tune orchestrated through the wind chimes. "I miss when people weren't in such a rush. You could sit on the back porch, have a drink, and talk about our days. Now, everyone is too busy running around, but never seeming to get anywhere."

"Please, Mrs. Lawson. They must hurry."

"Yes, yes," she said. "Please, come in."

Mrs. Lawson led them into her house, the air filled with stuffy odors of old clothes and mothballs. Her feet shuffled across the floor like sandpaper lightly grazing the hard wood below them.

"I sure wish you boys could stay and talk," she said. "So many people coming through today, but none had time for a conversation. Shame. I love company. I got a coffee cake in the refrigerator in case anyone drops by. Have to throw it out occasionally and get a new one, but that's okay. My father told me to always be prepared. And my mother said that being polite took as much effort as being mean, so I should invest my energies wisely. So I do. I have coffee cake and a witty joke ready in case anyone drops in to surprise me."

She led them through the kitchen to a closet near the front entrance. Inside was a panel that, when pushed, opened, revealing a thin staircase. She pulled on a string, turning on an exposed light bulb. Grasping a railing made of one-by-twos nailed to the wall, she steadied herself and started down.

"Do you want to hear my joke?" she asked. "It's funny."

"Not now," Eli said, following behind Damien and Scarman.

"You're always so serious, Eli. I'm going to tell it anyway. I think the police officer would find it funny."

She winked at Damien before continuing down the stairs.

"Two cannibals were eating a clown. After a few bites, one of them turned to the other and asked, 'Does this taste funny?'"

She slapped the fragile handrail and cackled, laughing so hard it inspired a coughing fit. Her small body shook with each hack and she leaned forward, trying to catch her breath. Damien reached out and grabbed her arm, keeping her from falling forward.

"Are you okay?" Damien asked.

"You're not laughing," she said in between coughs. "That was funny stuff. My husband, Larry, would have split a gut over that one."

"It was funny," he said. "I'm sorry."

"My Larry, he loved to laugh. You could hear it no matter where you were in the house. A bellow more than a laugh. I miss it. He brightened up every room he entered. All his joy left this house when he passed."

"Not all of it," Damien said. "You're still here."

"Yeah, but you didn't laugh, son. Looks like I got to practice my timing."

Damien admired her spirit. Amidst all the chaos, of using her home to move people from danger to safety, she still found reasons to laugh. She kept her pleasures simple. A joke, a short talk, or sharing a piece of coffee cake. She didn't ask a lot of life, and it didn't demand much in return.

They continued into a small room. It was cool and dark, the walls made of cement and covered with empty wooden cubby holes the size of a wine bottle.

"Larry had an idea to make this a wine cellar," Mrs. Lawson said. "It isn't pretty, but it kept the vino nice and chilled."

She pulled on one of the sections, opening a hidden door that led to a small passage under her property.

"Rumor has it this was built to move slaves through the Underground Railroad," Mrs. Lawson said. "Shame almost a hundred and fifty years later, we're doing nearly the same thing. You follow this to the end and go up the stairs. It will take you to the garden shed behind the rectory of the church. Mr. Tomey will be waiting. That is unless he went to take a leak. Prostate problems. Poor fellow has a prostate the size of a watermelon. His bladder had to make room for the expansion."

She stepped into an indentation in the wall to let Damien, Scarman, and Eli pass.

"Thank you," Damien said.

"You'll come back, won't you?" she asked. "I'll have coffee cake and a good joke ready when you do."

"I'll be back," he said. "And I'll bring you some wine for your wine cellar."

"Larry would've liked that."

Damien stepped deeper into the thin hall lit by a string of miniature white lights hung down its length. They headed into the tunnel single file, with Scarman behind Damien, and Eli covering the rear. The dirt above and to the side of the tunnel was held in place by old timbers attached one against the other, keeping the weight of the earth from falling in on them. It was hard to date the construction of the tunnel. It may have been built to free slaves or, some years later, to move moonshine during Prohibition.

It was sturdy and cool, though the air rarely moved. When the entry to Mrs. Lawson's house disappeared behind them, the passage began to feel smaller. Compressed. Stifling. Damien had never felt so closed in before. He grew impatient for the opening at the other end to appear. Certain the oxygen in the hall could no longer support them, he began to panic.

Three grown men were too big for this space, taking in too much precious air in a place where new air rarely entered. Damien started to pant, growing lightheaded. He had to hurry.

He glanced behind him. Scarman and Eli seemed unaffected by the space, their breathing, normal. No panting or sweating, no fear in their eyes.

Damien clenched his teeth. He'd never been in a space this small for this long. It was a terrible time to find out he was claustrophobic.

He had no time for weakness. Lives were depending on him. He quickened his pace and slowed his breathing. There was still work to do and no one else to do it.

A few moments later, an old wooden ladder appeared against a far timbered wall. Built from two-by-fours, it looked worn, but sturdy.

Damien grabbed on with his free hand and started up the ladder, forced to bend awkwardly to allow Scarman to climb below him. At the top of the ladder was a closed hatch, which Damien was able to push open with his head until he could see inside the garden shed. It appeared empty. He grasped the hatch frame and climbed out. Scarman and Eli followed.

The shed was small. Ten feet by six feet. Rakes and shovels leaned against bags of fertilizer and an old mower sat in the corner, a red plastic gas canister by its side.

"Where's Mr. Tomey?" Eli asked. "He should've been waiting for us."

Damien noticed dirt on the stack of fertilizer had been wiped off. An indentation dipped in the middle. That must have been where Mr. Tomey sat while he waited.

"Maybe he stepped outside," Damien said.

He walked to the shed door and slid it open, peering out. They were about twenty yards behind the church. Between them was a small prayer garden with a statue of the Virgin Mary in the middle, holding the baby Jesus in her arms.

Damien couldn't see any other people, either residents or Scarman's army.

He pushed the door open further and led them outside.

To his right, Damien caught sight of a pair of tennis shoes, laying toes down, sticking out from the side of the shed.

He cautiously peeked around the corner to find an older man dead, his body twisted on the ground, the top of his pants unzipped and a bullet in the back of his head.

Mr. Tomey was dead. Killed while taking a leak. It would have been funny if it were a joke, but his death wasn't a punchline.

Murder had reached the church grounds.

DAMIEN STARED at Mr. Tomey's dead body. Another casualty. Another coffin. Another gravestone.

He turned back toward the shed.

"Eli, go home. Lock your doors and don't come out until the National Guard takes control of this town."

"But I can help," Eli said.

"No, you've done more than enough. You go home and love your wife. Raise your son. That's all that matters."

Eli accepted Damien's request and started back into the tunnel.

"We will take care of your friend," Eli said.

"Thank you."

When Eli disappeared into the tunnel, Damien closed the wooden hatch behind him.

"Why did you lie to him?" Scarman asked. "You know once you go into that church, you're going to die."

"You think they want me dead? Tell them to get in line. A lot of people have tried to kill me, including you. You've all failed."

"So, you think you're invincible?"

"No," Damien said. "But when I die, it'll be on my terms. No one else's."

Scarman chuckled.

"You confuse luck with providence," he said.

"There's one way to find out."

He held the pistol and headed out of the garden shed, pulling Scarman with him. Scanning the grounds as they approached the church, he felt as if the statue of the Virgin Mary was staring at them as they passed.

In the evening sun, the stained-glass windows running the length of the building looked dead from the outside, their dim figures sleeping until light from within gave them life. What was going on inside the church, on the other side of the glass, was something only the saints portrayed in the windows could see.

The size of Scarman's army had fluctuated all day. Along with the core members of the cause he brought with him, Damien had no idea how many converts were left. Ten, a hundred, or a thousand.

He felt as vulnerable as he did during his first night on duty. Overwhelmed. Overmatched. Those old fears crept in with a newfound intensity. Anxiety threatened to paralyze him.

Damien tried to shake it off, but he had no ability to contain it. Like rage, hate, and love, he had no control over what emotions rushed through him. For most of the day, he was driven by revenge and concern for Ted.

Now, Damien was inundated with an onslaught of conflicting emotions. He paused next to the church, unsure of what to do, his torrent of feelings both driving him and hindering him at the same time.

If police psychologist Doctor Jones were here, staring at him through her oversized glasses, she'd have a new word to describe him.

Unstable.

Physical exhaustion. Mental fatigue. Erratic emotions. He

was losing control, heading into the most important moment of his life on the brink of psychological collapse.

Just a few more minutes, he thought. *Keep it together for just a few more minutes.*

Damien opened the handcuff from his wrist, then put both on Scarman, securing his arms behind his back. Where they were headed, Damien needed both hands free.

His prisoner didn't protest.

Through the prayer garden, they followed a path of stepping stones to the side of the church, stopping at an arched trellis that led toward the grand front stairs and wooden doors carved with the image of a man assisting Christ as he carried his cross.

He took a few steps up the stairs, waited and listened. The church was quiet. For a building that was supposed to be packed with people seeking refuge, it was as silent as a cemetery.

Scarman was also quiet. He spoke no words about his revolution or his inevitable death. He followed Damien like a shadow, mute and ever present.

Damien continued up the steps. They were free of blood or bullet casings. There was no sign of struggle or gunplay, of anyone or anything.

He eyed the brass handles on each wooden door. The one on the left was dark and tarnished. The one on the right, bright and worn from thousands of hands pulling it open.

It reminded him of Scarman's boasts. Human nature. So predictable.

The worn brass handle was cooler than the evening air. Damien yanked it toward him, the heavy, thick door gliding outward, its hinges resisting with a soft creak.

Damien leaned his back against the open door and made sure his fingers gripped the pistol firmly, his index finger poised on the trigger.

Directly inside the church was a small ornate room, like a lobby. Damien tried to remember its correct name. *Narthex*. Jacob had mentioned the narthex to him before. It was exceptionally small in comparison to the rest of the building, and it appeared to be a buffer between the outside world and the church inside.

The last time Damien had stepped into one of these was at his father's funeral. He remembered how uncomfortable he'd felt seeing the casket in front of the altar. His dad never went to church. Never cared about God. It didn't feel honest to put him there at the end.

No matter how much Damien tried to bury the thoughts of his father, he saw too many of his traits in his own actions to forget him. Like his dad, it seemed odd to be back at the church as a stranger, not seeking some divine wisdom or guidance, but to try to stop the execution of his best friend.

Between the narthex and the church were more stained-glass windows depicting images of St. Cyrene's walk, his face happily carrying the burden of a criminal's cross on the way to his execution.

Damien gripped another worn brass handle, then opened the door leading into the church.

The pews were full, like on Easter or Christmas. Everyone was silent, facing the altar, their heads down, as if in prayer. Some tilted and peeked at Damien and Scarman, but didn't dare look up.

Ted sat in the chair normally used by the priest during mass, if memory served. The chair had been moved center stage, in front of the altar. Adjacent to Ted, who appeared worn and beaten, stood a tall man with a gun. Down the steps of the altar stood Jacob, accompanied by four armed men, one of whom held a gun against Damien's brother's ribs.

The tall man behind Ted was lean and tone. His face had hawk-like features with a sharp nose and flaring nostrils. His chin was pointed, extended with a patch of hair just long enough to braid. His hair was short on the sides and spiked on top.

He could have passed as a fresh-faced programmer at Digital Slate, save for the pistol poised at Ted's head.

His smug arrogance reminded Damien of a younger Scarman, standing on the steps above Jacob, lording over the church full of frightened people.

A wellspring of hate boiled within Damien. He tapped the barrel of his pistol against his hip, wondering how many more inches away from Ted the gunman needed to be before he'd feel comfortable putting a bullet between the thug's eyes.

Kneeling at the base of the altar at the communion rail were four people, a woman and three children, next to each other in order of size. Their backs were to Damien, but he knew who they were.

Ted's wife and children.

Damien started up the center aisle, scanning the church as he moved toward the altar. No one looked up from the packed pews, all kneeling in deference to the man threatening Ted. Over their bowed heads, Damien could see the expanse of the interior of the church, from the side doors to the narthex to the altar. No other armed men in sight.

If it were Damien, he'd have some hidden amongst the people in the pews, keeping their full numbers hidden from view. If these were Scarman's thugs, he'd expect no less. If they were vigilantes looking for a paycheck, they probably wouldn't have thought that far ahead, not when they had the leverage to cash in.

Something about the thugs standing on the altar bothered Damien. This church was Jacob's world, and they were showing it disrespect. Damien could never grasp Jacob's hopeful outlook, but he envied it.

In Jacob, Damien saw a better escape from their childhood. His little brother who would add to the world, not take from it.

Their mere presence of those men on the altar felt blasphemous to a God Damien wasn't sure was real and an offense to the brother he knew he couldn't lose.

Scarman followed behind Damien, cuffed and silent. He didn't lead Damien toward his compatriots on the altar, nor walk beside him as an equal. He remained a step behind, hiding from the thugs' direct line of sight.

Damien glared into the gunman's eyes, pinpointing his rage at his best friend's captor.

"What's your name?" Damien asked.

"I'm the executioner," the tall man said.

ONE OF THE armed thugs approached Damien, jabbing a pistol into his broken ribs. Damien twisted away from the pressure, reluctantly relinquishing his Glock.

The thug pushed Damien and Scarman over to the communion rail, then forced them to kneel. Damien plopped next to a gagged Denise to his right. Beside her, Ted's children were also gagged.

Scarman knelt to Damien's left.

Behind them loomed the thug with Damien's pistol. Four armed men stood between Damien and Jacob.

The self-proclaimed executioner slammed the butt of his pistol against the altar three times, each clack echoing in the quiet church. Damien spotted the police shield on the grip. The executioner had Ted's gun.

"The court will now come to order," the executioner said. "The trial of Officer Ted Sherman against society. The charge? Murder. This carries with it the penalty of death. How do you plead?"

Ted raised his head, his left eye swollen, but not shut. His mouth was bloodied. His bright blue uniform stained with his own saliva and blood.

"How do you plead?"

"Fuck off," he said, then grimaced apologetically at Jacob. "Sorry, Father."

Jacob nodded, forgiving his choice of words.

The executioner swung the pistol, striking Ted in the back of the head. Ted groaned, but did not cry out.

"So noted," the man said. "Officer Sherman is accused of the cold-blooded murder of Hector Martinez, a small business owner who was on his way to work. Driven by racial profiling and a duty to protect their own, Officer Sherman shot Mr. Martinez in the chest. He was dead before he hit the ground."

A woman began to sob behind Damien. Suffering cries, unable to muffle her pain.

"The prosecution will present its first witness. The mother of Hector Martinez."

The sobbing woman was escorted to the podium where Jacob read from the Bible during Mass, her arm held almost gently by one of the thugs.

"Mrs. Martinez," the executioner said. "Please tell us about your son."

"Hector was a good boy," she said into the microphone, her voice quivering. "He was my youngest. A good boy. He helped me around the house. He was thinking of going back to school."

"He was a drug dealer," Ted said. "He was wanted for selling crack to teens, one of which, Tammy Allen, overdosed during a party in the groves."

The executioner struck Ted again.

"Out of order," the executioner said.

"I don't know about those things," Mrs. Martinez said. "He didn't tell me what he did when he left the house. But he was always home by dinner. He mowed the yard. Fixed things. He was a good boy. He was my youngest." She began to weep again. "He was my son."

Damien watched Mrs. Martinez give her testimony.

Despite her ignorance of Hector's life, either willful or truthful, Damien recognized the pain in her eyes. He had seen it every time he looked in the mirror.

As the executioner paraded Hector's family and friends to the witness stand, and those who had been mistreated by the police in years past, Damien refused to gaze upon the spectacle in front of him. He had learned from Scarman that the shiny object was rarely the object of desire.

The show was for others. Those in the pews hoping to survive the day. And those on the altar holding a mock trial in a false court.

Damien had watched the master at work. He'd seen Scarman lead his men, order them to do heinous things, and never blinked at the carnage that was to follow.

The executioner was no Scarman. This show was as much for him as it was for the others, to garner enough courage to do what was required to earn the million-dollar reward. He was capable of pulling the trigger that would end Ted's life or else he wouldn't have gotten this far. He'd cobbled together his own small force, then led them to this pinnacle moment.

Yet, there was something in the executioner's eyes. Something Scarman seemed to be born without. Something Damien lost the moment he choked the life out of Leash.

Remorse.

Still, a man in power with no judgement but his own was dangerous.

Damien examined the thugs on the altar near Jacob. They stood in uniformed positions, their heads scanning the crowd, their hands crossed in front of them at the waist. For the uninformed, they seemed intimidating, but their hands were away from their guns. They weren't on guard or afraid. They believed they were in complete control.

Anyone with any real training knew there was no such thing. There were only variables which people tried to control, but no one could plan for everything.

Especially a sociopathic cop.

"Does anyone wish to offer a defense for Officer Sherman?" the executioner asked.

Denise and his kids squirmed at the communion rail, trying to talk through their gags.

"I'm sorry, I can't make out what you're saying."

"They're saying I don't need a defense," Ted said. "The people of Hayeston know me. They know the truth. And they know you're a joke. Just get this shit over with before you bore me to death."

"You're bored?"

"Of course I am," he said with a chuckle. "I've known people like you my entire life. Bullies. You think you have power that lets you do whatever you want. Real power comes from having it and not using it. And real men know the difference. You're not a leader; you're a showpiece. A wannabe. A bully with a pistol. Well, do your duty and get it over with. I'm tired of hearing you talk."

Damien smirked. He couldn't have said it better himself. That was the man he'd known since they were kids, the boy with passion and an immovable sense of right and wrong who dreamt of being a police officer.

"So be it," the executioner said. "I hereby find you guilty, Officer Ted Sherman, of murder in the first degree. Your punishment, death by the same gun you used to kill Hector Martinez. Any last words?"

Ted remained silent.

Denise and his kids cried.

"I have some," Damien said.

The thug with Damien's Glock approached from behind.

"Motion denied," the executioner said.

Damien kicked the thug in the shin, spun to his feet, took his Glock from the thug's hand, then shot him in the head. Screams filled the church as the body landed with a *thud*.

The executioner froze. No one from the pews rushed up to

assist. No hidden army. The men on the altar were the only ones left.

Damien hopped over the communion rail, shooting the thugs standing between him and Jacob in quick succession. Hayeston's best marksman had earned his title.

As the executioner lifted Ted's gun to fire, Damien charged toward him, tackling him into the altar, and then struck him across the face. He swept the gunman's feet out from under him, then slammed him into the marble stairs.

Damien stomped on his wrist. The crack of the man's breaking bones was followed by the wail of his screams.

Ted's gun fell from his hand. Damien snatched it up, put it in his pocket, and then yanked the executioner to his feet.

Jacob rushed over to help Ted from the chair, escorting him to his family and free them from their binds. Ted and Denise greeted each other with a desperate and loving hug.

Damien returned his attention back to the executioner.

"I've seen killers up close," Damien said, holding his gun against the man's head. "I've seen vengeance in the eyes of a teen boy named Freddy and the look of a coward in a factory worker named Charlie. I've seen malevolence in the eyes of my prisoner, and I've even seen murder in my own eyes in the mirror. Yours tell me you're not a killer. You're greedy. You're a conman or a thief. You don't take lives, you take things."

He examined the man up close, scrutinized the sweat beading above his lip, his eyelids twitching in fear.

"I don't recognize you," Damien said. "Where did you come from?"

"I-I-I came here on a bus, from Traverson."

"That's four hours away from here. Who do you work for?"

"I don't work for anyone. I'm an electrician. I'm a freelancer—"

"Shut up," Damien said. "This isn't a job interview. Tell me about the cause. How did you become a part of it?"

"The cause? I don't know anything about a cause."

"I am tired of *lies*," Damien screamed. "I'm tired of the stench of your kind, and I will excise all of you from this town one way or the other."

Damien pushed the gun harder against the man's head, forcing him to his knees.

"Damien, stop," Jacob said.

"This isn't a time for saints, Jacob."

"Damien—"

Damien motioned to Scarman, who rose and joined him next to the altar.

"These men are the cause of our pain," Damien said. "Not Ted. Not even Hector. These men and those outside are the ones who have taken our town away from us. It's time we take it back."

Damien placed the gun to the back of the executioner's head.

NEXT TO HIM, Damien heard laughing. Small, quiet chuckles that grew louder and more boisterous. It was a sound he had heard before, in his memories and nightmares. It echoed in his mind from the first moment he heard it.

Damien turned to find Scarman smiling and clapping, his hands uncuffed.

"Wonderful," Scarman said. "What a wonderful creation I have made."

Damien spotted the opened cuffs lying on the marble floor, realizing his nemesis could have escaped at any time.

"Just a few months ago, you were a naive rookie police officer," Scarman continued. "Now, before me, stands a cold-blooded murderer guilty of…" He paused to calculate. "Four, plus the one from before, equals five. Five murders. And if I had waited a few seconds more, you would have executed number six without a second thought. That doesn't even count the ones you blew up at the dry-cleaning store, but for those, I'll give you a pass. We'll call that self-defense. But the five people you killed in cold blood…. you, bluebird, are my greatest experiment yet."

Damien lifted the gun. Pointed it at Scarman.

"I'm nobody's experiment," Damien said.

"Oh, but you are. Your survival has been a windfall of good fortune. To see you evolve from one of them," he said, pointing to the pews, "to one of us is a watershed moment. You have given the cause a blueprint on how to make more die-hard soldiers for their mission."

"I'm not one of you," Damien said.

"True. Ideologically. You're too independent. More concerned about justice than revenge. Otherwise, you would have killed me by now."

"There's still time."

"You've had all day. Yet, here I am. You see, psychologically, you are a perfect example of how it can be done. How we can grow more people just like you. Next time, we'll be more selective. With you, I picked from the wrong tree, but the fruit of my labor will be repeated with more appropriate crops of fragile men and women."

Damien circled Scarman, who stood proudly, his chest high and his arms crossed. Smug and smiling, resembling a leaner version of Mussolini.

Hatred seeped from every pore in Damien's body. This was still a game to Scarman, and Damien had become his most valuable chess piece.

"You want to kill me," Scarman said.

"It would just be body number six," Damien said.

"Would you really execute me, an unarmed man, in front of witnesses?"

"I was about to kill him," Damien said, pointing to the executioner. "Why not you? Besides, you escaped." Damien pointed to the cuffs on the floor. "You tried to attack me."

"Is that what you'd tell the authorities? Are you absolutely certain that everyone in this building would corroborate your story after they've watched you kill four men? Unlike you and me, murder is new to them. What you have done will be etched in their minds for the rest of their lives. They won't forget anything. They can't. Every second will be memorized, and they will have to tell someone. Trauma requires a release, and they will tell the story about how you executed an unarmed man in their presence at the foot of the altar."

"I'll take my chances."

"Damien, don't," Jacob said.

Damien ignored his brother's voice. He'd been the angel on his shoulder his entire life. Today, Damien was only taking suggestions from the devil.

"But why risk it?" Scarman asked. "You still have the chance to be the hero." Scarman held out his hands. "Take me into custody. Turn me in."

"You'd just escape again."

"No," he said, crossing his heart with his finger. "I promise. I'll go quietly as I have all day. There are witnesses of how docile I've been since you arrested me."

Damien felt the tug of Scarman's strings, directing him like a puppet, urging him to pull the trigger. The scarred man wanted to die a martyr. Now he had another chance to do it in front of a church full of Hayeston's innocents. One last chance at corrupting them. One more dagger into the heart of the town.

Knowing this didn't diminish the drive to put a bullet through his brain. Damien had long lost the ability to force right over wrong, and all of his twisted impulses were directed at his finger on the trigger.

"On your knees," Damien said.

Scarman raised his hands, got on his knees, and lowered his head.

"Do it," Scarman said. "For your wife. For your child. Do it. Don't be a coward, not when the sweet taste of vengeance is within reach."

Damien closed his eyes, listening. He heard nothing over the beating of his racing heart. He waited for a whisper. A plea.

He hoped Raquel would stop him, to tell him to put the gun down and forgive.

But she was silent, mute. Certainly if she were truly dead in a place where God existed, she would try to convince him to stop.

Yet, nothing pierced his ears or moved his heart.

If Raquel were an aberration, a hallucination, a corpse with no soul, no life after this one, then Damien's actions had no consequence beyond this world.

Existing without her for eternity was a life he was willing to forfeit.

Jacob's God had become little more than statues and colored glass, for only a cruel God would leave Damien alone when the fate of his soul hung in the balance. In this place of worship, God should have sent a messenger to prove he wasn't insane.

Still, Raquel remained silent.

As Damien opened his eyes, he felt a pull on his pant leg. Startled, he glanced down to find Billy at his feet. The four-year-old stared up at him with the same inquisitive eyes as he'd had in Benita's store.

"Go away," Damien said.

"But you're one of the good guys," Billy said. "You protect us. Like you did before. You saved us from those bad men with guns. That's what you do. Remember? But you don't kill unarmed bad guys. That's not what cops do."

Damien glimpsed Benita standing next to the front pew, holding her hand out to her son.

"Come here, baby," she said, sounding panicked.

"Go to your mother," Damien said. "And don't look back."

"If you come with me," Billy said.

"This isn't a negotiation."

Huffing, Billy crossed his arms. "Then I'm not going anywhere. And you can't make me."

Damien clenched his teeth. "Billy, go back to your—"

Damien motioned to Benita, but stopped, frozen.

Raquel stood behind her, wearing her wedding dress. A long white veil covering her hair, a bouquet of yellow and white flowers grasped in her hand.

She was radiant, almost glowing.

"What are you…" Damien started. "Why are you wearing that?"

Benita's brow furrowed as she gestured at her sweatpants and t-shirt. "This? It was the only thing clean. It's laundry day."

"No, not you," he said.

Benita turned to see who was behind her, as did the eyes of the entire church.

"Then who are you talking to?" she asked once she'd faced forward.

"My wife. Raquel. Why are you dressed like that?"

"To remind you," Raquel said. "Remember the man who first saw me in this dress. Remember the man I fell in love with. Remember who you really are."

"I'm not that man anymore."

"You keep saying that, but I know better."

She walked down the aisle toward the back of the church. Damien followed, as if in a trance, moving past a confused Benita.

"Where you going, honey?" Benita asked.

Damien remained silent, following the angelic form of his dead wife until she stopped midway down the aisle and placed her hand on the end of the pew. Sitting there was a Hispanic family, who watched Damien as he approached.

"See them and you see me," Raquel said.

Damien squinted at his wife, confused.

She placed her bouquet in the lap of a woman at the end of the pew. Hector's mother.

Hector's death had triggered everything.

He had a long rap sheet and a penchant for hitting women, but his mother's pain extended beyond her son's misdeeds.

She and Damien were connected through violent deaths at the hands of others. They weren't enemies, but wounded souls sharing the worst parts of the human experience.

Emotions welled up in Damien. Rage and anger were washed away by grief and lamentation.

Falling to his knees, he reached out and grabbed onto the woman's hand. The feelings once muted at his wife's grave rose like a geyser. Tears flowed freely down his cheeks as he heaved cries of anguish, his wails echoing against the stained-glass windows and holy statues.

The death of his wife and son were fully realized in him, the emptiness he'd been filling with vengeance again barren. His soul felt hollow, his world surrounded by infinite loneliness. His grief flowed like a broken dam and his tears dripped next to his knees, pooling on the red carpet like drops of blood.

As his body trembled with waves of sorrow, he felt a gentle hand on his shoulder. It was warm and comforting. He reached for it. Felt soft skin and long fingers, one wrapped in a diamond ring he recognized. It was small and round. The only one he could afford on a cadet's salary.

Raquel.

His grip on her hand tightened as he wept.

"I love you," she whispered in his ear.

"I love you, too," he said.

The deluge of sadness began to subside, and Damien's eyes started to dry.

Raquel's hand slipped from his, and he opened his eyes to find Hector's mother wiping her own tears from her cheeks.

"I'm sorry for your loss," he said to her. "I'm so sorry for everything."

"As are we," she said.

"He was lucky to have had a mother who loved him as much as you did."

Damien gave Hector's mother's hand a squeeze before rising to his feet. Turning back to the altar, he saw the tall man being held by Ted. Scarman still knelt, his head down, waiting for his execution.

Jacob moved from the altar, but kept his distance, no doubt wondering about his brother's sanity. Damien couldn't blame him.

With renewed energy, Damien placed both cuffs on Scarman's hands and pulled him to his feet, escorting him toward the rear of the church.

"You're under arrest," Damien said. "Again."

"I could spend years studying you," Scarman said. "But there won't be enough time for that."

"I'll visit you in prison. You can study me all you want."

"You and I know I won't live long enough."

"You won't die at my hands," Damien said.

"I know. Such a waste."

"I'm happy to disappoint you."

Damien escorted Scarman through the narthex. When he opened the church doors, he found a number of gun barrels leveled at their heads.

"ON YOUR KNEES," a voice yelled. "On your knees now!"

Damien and Scarman were surrounded by men in camouflage uniforms, aiming military-grade weapons. The National Guard had finally arrived.

Damien lifted his free hand, aiming his gun in the air. "Don't shoot. I'm a police officer with the Hayeston police department. This is my prisoner. I'm taking him into custody."

"On your knees," the voice yelled again.

"This man is very dangerous," Damien said. "I cannot let him out of my sight. I'm a cop, for God's sake!"

"Show us your badge!"

Damien grimaced at the memory of handing it over to Dr. Jones. It was probably in a desk drawer under a building worth of rubble.

"I don't have it with me," Damien said. "It was lost at the police station when it was bombed *by my prisoner*."

"Sir, either drop your gun and get on your knees or you will be shot," the soldier said.

"Fine! Fine," Damien said.

He tossed his gun to the side, lowering himself to his

knees. Scarman laughed as he settled next to him.

"Put your hands in the air," the soldier commanded.

Damien's fingers tightened around the cuffs behind Scarman's back.

"Put your hands where I can see them, or I will fire."

"You don't understand—" Damien started.

"You have one second, sir," the soldier said.

Damien released the cuffs, then raised his other hand above his head.

Boots clunked on the ground as the soldiers swarmed and tackled them. With their faces pressed against the sidewalk, Damien met Scarman's gaze. His nemesis winked, reveling in Damien's failure.

"You did your best," Scarman said. "It just wasn't good enough."

"We'll see," Damien said.

They were jerked to their feet as one of the soldiers clicked cuffs around Damien's wrists.

"There are people hiding in the church," Damien said. "Officer Sherman and Father Jacob will be able to help you."

Some of the soldiers peeled into the narthex as others escorted Damien and Scarman toward the parking lot where a Humvee waited for them.

"I'm Officer Damien Hill, badge number one-nine-zero-nine," he said to the tall, bulky soldier leading them. "Look it up."

"There'll be plenty of time to sort things out after we secure the town," the soldier said.

"Look, this man is extremely dangerous," Damien said.

"So you've said."

"He cannot be left alone. He has valuable information that must be extracted or else what happened here will occur elsewhere."

"Sir, this isn't our first rodeo."

"Keep him under watch in isolation. He's a valuable asset, and the people he works for want him dead."

"We'll take every precaution."

"If I may say something," Scarman said.

The soldier stopped and turned to him.

"What?" he asked with a sigh.

A blood-red dot appeared on Scarman's forehead.

Damien wrenched away from the soldier and dove in front of Scarman as a bullet tore through his body. Both men landed on the ground as a rifle shot cracked through the air.

THAT SMELL. It was back.

Bleach. Feces. Plastic. Soap. Damien was in the hospital. Again.

He bolted up in the bed, a pain shot through his chest and back and he struggled to catch his breath.

"Easy," Raquel said. "You're not invincible."

"Is he alive?" he asked.

The room was different then he expected. It was small with gray cement walls. And there was a tell tale sign that his bullet wound was the least of his problems.

Damien's hand was cuffed to the bed.

"Where am I?"

"County jail," she said. "Infirmary. They patched you up at the hospital. Once you were stable they shipped you over here."

"What about Scarman? Did he survive? Is he here?"

Raquel sat on the end of the bed, motioning to the cuffs.

"You sure that's what you want to talk about?"

"Is he here?"

"That's not for me to say. Now, take it easy. The bullet went through your back and left lung. You don't want to start bleeding, internal or otherwise."

"Did Scarman survive?"

"That's not for me to say."

"You can be so frustrating some times."

"I don't make the rules," she said.

Damien winced as the pain from his injury overtook him.

"The bullet did more damage leaving your body that it did going in," she said. "The surgeon did a fine job of patching you up. Said it was a miracle you survived."

"Don't tell Jacob that. I'll never hear the end of it."

He closed his eyes and pressed his head into the pillow. "Did they get the shooter?"

"Who are you talking to?" a familiar voice said.

Ted stood at the door, crutch under one arm and a fresh cast wrapping his leg. The swelling on his face was down, but the discoloration from the bruises still tinted his skin.

Damien must have been out a couple of days. "It hasn't been four months. What's the rush stopping by?"

"Because I don't feel guilty about *you* being here," Ted said with a wink.

Damien rattled the cuffs against the gurney.

"Can you get me out of these things?"

"You were lucky you were unconscious." Ted held up a small key and uncuffed him. "It took this long to prove you were who you said you were. At least, to the federal government's satisfaction." Ted slipped the cuff key into his pocket. "Was that Raquel you were talking to?"

Damien glanced at Raquel sitting at the foot of the bed.

"No," Damien lied.

"How about in the church? How about then?"

"How about you answer my question? Did they get the guy who shot me?"

"No."

"Did the scarred bastard survive?"

"Yes. And he's waiting for you."

TED HELD a Hayeston police officer shirt up as Damien eased his arms through the sleeves. He hadn't been reinstated. He wasn't a cop. He'd never be one again.

This wasn't for himself. Or Raquel.

This charade was for Scarman.

Damien panted with shallow breaths as his fingers struggled to slip the shirt buttons through the holes.

Ted brushed his hands aside and finished for him.

"You sure this is necessary?" Ted asked.

"The man is arrogant. Believes he's always twelve steps ahead of us."

"So far, he's been right."

"If he were right, he'd be dead, not in custody. No, I have to show him all his work has been for nothing. I'm going in there as a decorated hero while he sits opposite me in an orange jumpsuit. I want him to know we've won. While we honor the dead, he'll be a forgotten number in the penal system."

"Don't gloat in there too long. The feds weren't happy about this. They're looking for a reason to pull the plug on your interview, so keep it short."

"I just need to look in his eyes and show him, prove to him, he's lost everything."

"What about wanting to watch them put a needle in his arm?"

"There are far worse things than dying," Damien said.

"Like what?"

"Living as a failure with no chance at redemption."

————

Damien stood at the door to the interrogation room. His legs shook beneath his pressed pants. He could barely stand.

"Do you have a handkerchief?" he asked Ted, who offered him one.

Damien wiped the sweat from his face, then slapped his pale skin to give it some color.

"How do I look?" he asked.

Ted eyed him with a sad smile.

"Like you've earned that uniform."

Damien thought of Leash's last, gurgling gasps and knew better.

He stood straight, the soreness in his chest emanating down his body. He hid the grimace from his face and opened the door.

Inside, Scarman sat at a table bolted to the floor, feet cuffed, hands as well, attached to a hook and chain in front of him. He fidgeted like a caged animal, the knowing smirk replaced by a hardened scowl. In many ways, he looked more dangerous than ever.

Damien stepped with confident strides and sat across from him, plopping into the chair as the vibration nearly took his breath.

"Orange is not your color," Damien said. "Clashes with your olive complexion."

"So, now you're a beauty consultant?"

"They say it's in the eye of the beholder and, I gotta tell you, seeing you chained like a dog is a beautiful fucking sight."

Scarman leaned his head to the side and scanned Damien's uniform.

"I see you're a Sergeant now."

"Bringing you to justice has its rewards."

"They promote killers in this town?"

"Why, you looking for a job?"

Scarman sneered. "So, what, you're here to brag?"

"I thought you might have something to say to me."

"You think this is a victory? That you've beaten me? Beaten us? You have no idea who you're facing. I singlehandedly brought this town to its knees and I am nothing, a foot soldier in a cause that lives and breathes in every community, city and institution in the world. You've thrown a pebble at a tsunami. You've stopped nothing. The wave is gathering speed and it will crest, descending upon the world, cleansing it of people like you."

"I thought you were going to say, 'Thank you for saving my life.' But, a long-winded threat is more your style."

"I'll offer thanks the day I get to watch you die at my hands. Until then, I owe you nothing."

"Well, you're welcome."

Scarman lurched and grabbed Damien's arm, pulling him forward. Damien slammed into the table and a short whimper escaped his lips.

"I knew it," Scarman said. "This is nothing but a show and you, a hollow shell. Just like the first time we met. An empty uniform, an echo of a man."

Sweat started to bead on Damien's brow. "And you're nothing but a number now. You wanted to die? You'll get your wish. You'll never see the light of day a free man again. You'll spend the rest of your life behind bars of a justice system you despise, knowing that this hollow shell, this empty uniform, put you there."

"Yes. How unfortunate for me, surrounded by broken men, angry and anti-social with a complete disregard for this life you cherish so greatly. Inside your prison I'll recruit to my cause the most dangerous, the most lethal of them. I may never see the light of day, but I will make sure those that will, do so at my behest. And they will come for you."

"Do it, and I'll take them down as I did you. One at a time."

Scarman leaned forward.

"You'll need an army."

Damien matched his glare.

"I look forward to it."

The door behind Damien opened and two men in suits tapped him on the shoulder.

"Time's up," one of them said, guiding Damien from his seat.

"I'll be waiting," Damien said as he was led out of the room.

He turned and stared into the scarred man's eyes one last time as the door behind him closed.

DAMIEN SAT ALONE in a FEMA trailer in a hard plastic chair next to a card table with a desk phone, an empty pad of paper, and an expensive black leather chair. Though, technically still under arrest, he was free of cuffs and chains, waiting for a federal psychologist to arrive.

The evaluation was inevitable. Talking to his dead wife in a church full of people after killing a group of armed thugs hadn't given the authorities much choice.

It'd been weeks since the National Guard took over the town and Scarman had been whisked away to an unnamed holding facility.

His scarred nemesis had remained a mystery. Before his departure in a windowless van in the dead of night, the authorities hadn't yet uncovered Scarman's true identity. His prints or DNA weren't in the system and he had zero digital footprint. With no work history, birth certificate, financial transactions, social security card, or property, he was a ghost, manufactured by the cause. In today's world, that was virtually impossible, unless powerful forces were at work, forces that made Hayeston their first battlefield.

Watching through the county cell window, Scarman's exit

was satisfactorily unimpressive. The mouthpiece of the cause was silent and no one knew he'd gone.

He'd left Hayeston as quietly as he'd arrived. Invisible.

Damien thought seeing him spirited away, under the full weight of America's justice system, would have given him greater satisfaction, but the darkness within him longed for vengeance.

It was an appetite Damien would have to starve if he had any chance of becoming the man he'd once been.

He was relieved to find that Dex was alive and recovering in the hospital. Mindy had saved him after all. Her stitch work on the kitchen table stopped the bleeding long enough for help to arrive.

Jacob visited twice since his arrest, but hadn't mentioned what happened in the church. Not yet. Damien could see he had things he wanted to say, but couldn't muster the courage to spit it out.

In between the awkward silences, he did relay the news of a miracle. Raquel's brother, Robert, had survived the shootout at the police armory. He fought them off and killed them all, or those who hadn't accidentally shot each other in the panic following the release of the tear gas. It was hard to tell. Too many bullets. Too many guns. As the lone survivor, he was stuck in the armory for two days, surrounded by their corpses.

The National Guard freed him, arrested him, interrogated him, and released him. Jacob said the event changed Robert. His machismo had been replaced by a quiet humility.

The consequence of taking lives.

Tired and impatient, Damien stood and stretched his legs, the bandage under his shirt beginning to itch. A good sign. The wound was healing.

Staring at the blank notepad, he wondered if they'd find Dr. Jones' psychological evaluation of him. She wrote on a similar yellow pad and slipped her notes into his official employee file, but he was curious if she had entered her findings into the police system.

Was there enough time between him leaving her office and Scarman's bomb exploding?

Probably not. Which was likely why the feds had set up this follow-up evaluation.

Damien wasn't going to lie this time. No point faking it and trying to say what they wanted to hear. It didn't matter. He was going to prison, probably for life. The haze of war didn't apply in the streets during a riot. The rule of law didn't bend due to circumstance. It was what he loved about it.

The door behind Damien opened, more warm sunlight flooding the room. A man in an off-the-rack dark blue business suit entered wearing sunglasses. He was sweating profusely, wiping his face with his white pocket square.

"You people actually live down here?" he said. "On purpose? It's like hell with a view."

Damien watched with amusement as the man slammed the door behind him and fanned himself with his handkerchief.

"Oh, thank God," the suited man said. "Air conditioning has to be one of the best inventions in the history of mankind."

"I think math, science, and indoor plumbing may beat that," Damien said.

The man plopped into the leather chair and leaned back.

"Just give me a second," he said, panting. "Another second or two. I just need to control my metabolism."

The man closed his eyes and took deep breaths, in and out. His behavior surprised Damien. He was in a room with a sociopathic killer… and the first thing he did was put himself in a vulnerable position and close his eyes? Damien could kill him before his next exhale.

Who the hell is this guy?

The plastic chair squeaked as Damien sat across from him.

"So, where do you want to start?" Damien asked. "My childhood? Because you'll need more than one pad of paper for that."

"What?" The man opened his eyes, leaning forward and flopping against the table. "I don't need to interview you. I know everything I need to know."

"Aren't you a psychologist?"

"Oh, God no. My mother was a psychologist. She was not a pleasant person. Funny, but not fun, if that makes any sense."

"Not really," Damien said.

"Thirty minutes with her and you'd know exactly what I mean."

"Who the hell are you?" Damien asked.

"I'm Harold Winniver."

"Have you come to interrogate me? Kill me? Lock me up?"

"No, no, no, nothing like that. I'm from a certain agency that would like to remain nameless at this point. Your work with the scarred man—it was impressive. You've come closer to the cause than anyone alive, for the simple fact they usually kill witnesses of your caliber. Then again, the Hayeston incident was, by far, their largest effort yet. No doubt their rules of engagement have changed. Perhaps because they don't fear the repercussions."

"If you're not going to toss me behind bars, then what are you doing here?"

"Sorry, Mr. Hill, I thought I made that clear."

"Well, you didn't."

"I'm here to recruit you."

DAMIEN STOOD, gazing out over the scenic overview above the Braden River where Leash's car had been driven over the edge. It was gone, along with all evidence of his death. There was no longer a crime scene to investigate, either here or in the tall grass where Damien had choked him to death. Like sins after a good confession, his crimes were erased. Jacob would have admired their thoroughness. They cleaned the slate nearly as well as God.

"Do you trust them?" Raquel asked, suddenly standing next to him. She wore sneakers, sweatpants, and a tight t-shirt with the Hayeston High School logo on it. Her hair was lifted into a sloppy bun, and her face had no traces of makeup. Just the way he liked her. Naturally beautiful.

"I don't know," Damien said.

"They have a lot of pull. I mean, look at what they've done for you already."

"I know."

"Just because they've hidden your crimes doesn't mean they've forgotten them. If they cleaned up after you, they could keep that evidence to hold against you whenever they want."

"I know."

"Is that all you're going to say?" she said. "I know?"

"What do you want me to say?" he asked. "They're another puppet master pulling my strings. I would cut them if I could. But there's nothing left for me here, and they're giving me a way out."

"You have your brother here. Your mother. And Ted."

"Which is why I need to get as far away as possible. You heard Scarman."

"Do you believe him?"

"Can I take that chance? Jacob, Ted and my mom, they're all I have left."

"Have you talked to your mother lately?" she asked.

"I tried calling her when I got out of prison. The nurse put the phone next to her ear, but I only heard breathing. I don't know if she remembers me anymore, which, in her case, would probably be a good thing."

"Don't say that," Raquel said. "Your mother loves you."

He sighed in resignation. "And where has that gotten anyone?"

He looked out at the thin, steady stream of water flowing toward the bay, felt the warm, dry air caressing his face. Damien closed his eyes and smiled, enjoying the quiet.

He'd miss Hayeston. It held his greatest dreams and greatest sorrows. A small blip on the map, but the center of his entire world, and home to the first battle against the cause. He may never come back to this town, but it would never leave him.

"So where to now?" she asked.

"I have a couple more places to visit before I go. Are you coming?"

"Where else would I be?"

———

Damien met Dex in a waiting area at the end of Dex's floor. Still wired with fluids and monitors, he shuffled across the white tile in yellow cloth booties, wearing a white and blue hospital gown.

He'd shaved his beard and washed his hair. He looked ten years younger.

Damien helped him into the stiff chair, then sat in an identical one next to him.

"You look good," Damien said.

"Well, I'm breathing," Dex said. "That's a start. I've been trying to get released for a week, but it turned out the bullet nicked my bowel, released toxins into my system. They opened me up, flushed me out, and pumped me full of antibiotics. Fever's gone. They think they got it all before it started attacking my other organs."

"Better late than never, I guess."

"Yeah," Dex said. "I've been living on the fringes between life and death for a while now. I guess a few more weeks won't hurt."

"You're stronger than you think," Damien said.

"I am now. And I have you to thank for it."

"For throwing you into a firefight? Nearly getting you killed?"

"For giving me another chance to wrestle the devil on the battlefield. This time, I won."

"You saved my life out there," Damien said.

"And you saved mine. We're even, in my book."

Damien held out a brand-new Zippo with the Special Forces logo. "I owe you a lighter," he said.

Dex took it and flipped it open, smelling the lighter fluid on the cloth wick. He flicked his hand, and the metal lighter clicked closed.

"I think I'm giving up smoking," Dex said. "After all this, if I get healthy again, no point in trying to slowly kill myself."

"Keep it. It has other uses. I didn't exactly use your old one to light a cigarette."

Dex nodded, wrapping his fingers around the gift.

"Thanks," he said.

Damien smiled. "What's next for you?"

"After I get out of here, I'm going to Tampa. A buddy of mine got me an entry-level job at the VA. Could be something."

"One step at a time. I hear that's a thing."

"Better than living in a box."

"No doubt."

"What about you?" Dex asked.

"I'm heading out of town, too. We'll see what happens."

"Something good?"

"It's something," Damien said. "It may not be good, but it's good enough."

Nodding, Dex extended his hand. "To good enough."

They shook.

"To good enough."

———

The padded kneeler creaked as Damien knelt in the small, dark room. On the other side of the screen was the silhouette of his brother.

"Forgive me, Father, for I have sinned," Damien said. "It has been… shit, like my entire life since my last confession."

"Damien?" Jacob asked.

"I shouldn't have said shit. Sorry."

He could see Jacob's smile through the screen.

"I'm just glad you're here."

"So…" Damien started. "How does this thing work?"

"You tell me your sins, I offer you absolution, assuming you are sincerely sorry for offending God."

"Come on, Jacob, I'm not even sure God is real."

"Then you're not asking the right questions."

"What does that mean?" Damien asked.

"That's a conversation for another time. What would you like to confess?"

"I'm leaving town…"

Damien waited for a response, but Jacob remained silent.

"I'm a sociopath, clinically speaking. I killed five people on purpose. Four in this church and one by choking him to death because he was going to kill me. I know in my head that killing people is wrong. I was a cop, after all. But I feel no remorse. I don't know if that's due to my beat-up brain or because I really don't give a sh—I mean crap. I don't know much of anything anymore."

Damien paused. Still silence.

"I see my dead wife often. She tries to help me. She sees me the way I was, before I changed. I think she's trying to save me somehow. I don't know from what. Maybe myself. It's hard to tell. She doesn't know why she's allowed to stick around either. If God is really there, he's keeping his reasons close to the chest. I smell her perfume. I've felt her touch. I sense her love for me. I believe she's real. I doubt anyone else would agree with me, even you."

"Go on," Jacob said without judgement.

"Raquel and I had sex before we got married. I stole money from Mom's purse once to help pay a debt Ted's sister owed a dealer. In high school, I told Polly Atkins you were gay because I wanted to go out with her. Didn't work. I've looked at porn. I haven't gone to church since Dad's funeral. I'm not great at forgiving people. I think you're insane for being a priest, but just as proud of you for doing it. And… I think I helped Dad bury a dead body when I was a kid."

Damien could hear Jacob sigh, not out of boredom or frustration, but discomfort.

"Is that all of your sins?" Jacob asked.

"All that I can remember."

"And you are truly sorry for these transgressions?"

"Yeah," Damien said with more sincerity than he expected. "Yeah, I am."

"God, the Father of mercies, through the death and resurrection of his Son, has reconciled the world to himself and sent the Holy Spirit among us for the forgiveness of sins; through the ministry of the Church, may God give you pardon and peace, and I absolve you from your sins in the name of the Father, and of the Son, and of the Holy Spirit."

Damien sloppily made the sign of the cross. "Is that it?" he asked.

"The weight of your sin is heavy, so your penance will not be easy."

"That's fine. I'm game. Give me your best shot"

"Go to church on Sundays," Jacob said.

"I can probably do that."

"And forgive Scarman."

'What?" Damien asked.

"Forgive your enemy."

"What the hell is wrong with you?" Damien nearly shouted. "You want me to forgive the man responsible for killing my wife and son, destroying this town, and nearly killing you and Ted?"

"Yes," Jacob said calmly.

"You're out of your mind. Your collar has cut off oxygen to your brain."

"You have a decision to make, Damien. Either you are like your enemy or you're not. They show no mercy. They don't value life. And they don't forgive. I'm not saying you have to forgive Scarman right this second. I'm saying you must be open to it. Otherwise, you are no better than he is."

"Then maybe I'm not," Damien said.

"Of course you are. You're here, aren't you?"

"You and your stupid religion," Damien muttered.

"*Our* stupid religion," Jacob said.

"Whatever. Look, I'm not promising anything. But…" He swallowed his anger and took a deep breath, forcing the next few words out of his mouth. "I'll try. Okay? Is that good enough?"

"Yes, for now."

"For now," Damien grumbled. "It's never enough for you, is it?"

"You'll thank me one day," Jacob said.

"Maybe. But not today."

"Oh, and one more thing," Jacob said.

"Great," Damien said. "I can't wait."

"Find out if Dad really did kill someone."

CHAPTER
FIFTY-FIVE

PACKING up the apartment was hard. Putting away clothes that smelled like Raquel and toys meant for Nicholas was like burying them one more time. However, there was a finality to it this time. Damien was moving on, away from his hometown, his family and friends, and his wife and son's grave.

He had a sense he would never come back. Whatever his new employer was to require of him would probably take him far away from here and into circumstances more dangerous.

In many ways, he was their perfect asset. A sociopath bent on justice.

Damien stored the boxes in Ted's garage, bought the motorcycle he'd borrowed from the police auto shop from a mechanic named Toby, and made one last stop on his way out of town.

As promised, Mrs. Lawson's coffee cake was fresh, her coffee warm, and her jokes funny. The one about the pool boy, the psychic, and the terrorist on a desert island was, by far, the funniest of the bunch. They were joined by Eli and Mindy and their boy Xavier. Before the afternoon ended, Damien thanked each one for all they had done. They weren't the only unsung heroes to rise to the challenge, but they were responsible for the few fleeting moments from that day Damien didn't want to forget.

Damien kicked the motorcycle to a purr, waving as he sped away from Mrs. Lawson's house. As he headed toward the setting sun, he wondered what the cause had in store for Digital Slate founder Steven West.

What was West working on? And what would the cause do with his technology? There were still so many questions. So many things to do. Hayeston was the initial salvo of an impending borderless war, and Damien was about to lead the charge against its faceless leaders.

He'd rather be buying a bunch of baby clothes with his wife, looking forward to the birth of their child, and preparing for one more boring shift on the job.

That was another life. Long gone.

As Damien leaned into the wind, he felt Raquel's hands wrap around his waist. He could feel her weight shift forward. Heard her soft voice whisper in his ear.

"I love you," she said.

Damien smiled. Maybe this new life wouldn't be so bad after all.

His cellphone rang.

He answered.

Through the buffeting wind, the conversation with Winniver was barely coherent, but he could make out one thing.

Damien had his first assignment.

SHARE YOUR EXPERIENCE

Book reviews are incredibly valuable to independent authors by helping thriller fans discover the book. Please take a moment to leave a quick review. Stars and a few words is all that's necessary.

Leave a review for TRIGGER here.

RECOIL
CHAPTER ONE

Damien sat in a dimly lit room gripping his Beretta, waiting patiently in the stranger's home, like death about to cast its shadow over another soul.

He fidgeted with the pistol in his hand. He missed his police-issued Glock. It had felt more natural, like an extension of his arm, it's grip contoured to his palm. The Beretta felt clunky, like an awkward first date, but the Agency didn't provide Damien any alternatives. They weren't the most obliging type.

The Agency, capital A, was his new employer. Their size, unknown. Their influence, also a mystery, but from its extensive access to real-time information, seemingly deep pockets, and its near-imperceptible nature, Damien sensed the company was powerful.

He'd met his handler, Harold Winniver, and no one else. Damien had been through training alone. Empty gun range. Empty weight room. Empty obstacle course. Hand-to-hand combat was instructed by a man who neither spoke nor revealed his face. Instead, he wore a cloth mask during each of their sessions, teaching through example and expectation.

It was unclear who was paying Damien's bills. Whether

the Agency was government or a private contractor, Damien had their full attention, or maybe they had his. The Agency was either an army of one or an invisible force of thousands.

The isolation was to hide their numbers, Winniver explained, and to keep one asset from affecting another. Each member of the Agency was its own individual ripple, which, collectively, guided global forces in directions the Agency felt was in the best interest of the United States.

That was the spiel, and it flowed from Winniver's mouth with near-perfect authenticity.

Damien was new to this autonomous, anonymous life. He felt odd, still pulled between the man he once was and the man he was hired to be. Yet, obscurity suited him. It kept those in his former life from getting hurt, either by him or others.

No good would come from Damien's newfound moral ambiguity.

The Agency hadn't asked a lot of him yet, but he felt it was only a matter of time before they did. They wouldn't have recruited him—wouldn't have hid his past sins— without demanding repayment through obedience.

He leaned back into an oversized leather chair, staring out at the spacious penthouse apartment. The brown, or maybe black, high-backed armchair was comfortable. He couldn't tell its color. Not in this light. The leather was worn and soft. The padding, plush yet firm.

He could sit there all night, if necessary. Tonight, his job was to wait. He wasn't there on Agency business. That bell hadn't rung yet.

His handler didn't know about his investigation into a case Damien would never let grow cold. If he was aware, Winniver was quiet about it. Probably because he knew they couldn't stop Damien, not without killing him.

Damien scanned the room, admiring the open concept and

the resident's design style. Classy, yet functional. Simple. Clean lines. Nothing ostentatious belying the wealth necessary to exist on the highest floor in one of the tallest buildings in the city.

The penthouse was owned by a ghost. A figment. A shadow. The floor itself didn't exist. Not in the building plans. Not in the main elevators. It was tucked away, invisible, in plain sight of everyone who looked up. It was the perfect place to disappear.

Damien might need to do that one day. In his new line of work, getting out was more important than getting in. People like him, people like he had become, didn't fit in the world others moved through in the daytime. They existed at night in strange rooms, in the dark, waiting.

He still had dreams about his life before this one. Once pleasant, they had devolved into nightmares of unachievable happiness. He'd learned the hard way that the world didn't offer second chances. It pushed forward with or without him, giving him opportunities to reinvent himself, but never the ability to forget his prior failings.

The past was stone, the future like air. He could only wade through the present with the hope to redeem himself through the blood of others.

Beeps of alarm codes traveled across the room.

This was it. Showtime.

He sat up, straightening his tailored vest over his silk shirt, then nudged his tie under his chin. In his opinion, he felt the professional look worked best. It was more intimidating. Indicated he was there on business. He wasn't there for shock and awe. That was for people less skilled at nuance. He was a closer. The final bell in a fifteen-round bout.

He'd decided to leave his suit coat in the car. It just got in the way. Small pockets didn't offer any practical use. Not in moments like this, not in the event things went sideways.

Besides, he didn't want to explain any drops of blood to his dry cleaner.

The approaching footsteps were steady, unconcerned. Two sets. One heavy, one light. No hesitation. No cautious, measured pace. Just a relaxed stride. Coming home after a long day. Tired. Hungry. No worries.

Lights brightened, and it took a moment for Damien's eyes to adjust. He quickly checked the room and smiled, satisfied the decor looked as good in the light as he'd imagined in the dark.

The footsteps weaved through the kitchen, framed with floor-to-ceiling windows that showcased the impressive skyline, before strolling effortlessly into the living room.

"Do you know how much money I can get for a cadaver?" Damien asked.

The woman jolted, instinctively pulling her three-year-old daughter toward her, her keys falling and clanging at her feet. She stepped backward, still clutching her child, and nearly stumbled with her to the floor, eyes wide with terror.

It was the appropriate response.

———

Read the second thriller in the Damien Hill origin trilogy. Get RECOIL today.

**Want to know about Damien's
first investigation before TRIGGER?**

Read the crime that changed Damien's life.

CHAMBER takes place months before the Hayeston riots. Damien is in the middle of his cadet training when a local murder turns out to be more than anyone expected. Damien's called to join forces with the department's seasoned detectives to stop a copycat serial killer targeting young women in his small town.

(You may have to turn the page to see the cover)

You can get this page-turning ebook for free at petebauer books.com/damienfan.

AFTERWORD

For me, writing is all about fear. I write what scares the crap out of me.

I see this crazy world we live in and wonder what would be the worst day of my life, then amplify it by infinity, then put it to paper.

My heroes allow me to make sense of the senseless. They are stronger than me, more focused, more dedicated, relentless and, most of all, fearless. I wish I were them, or parts of them, when facing life's uncomfortable realities.

Damien's primary challenge is the one I fight the most - whether to be selfish or selfless. Do I sacrifice or indulge? Do the ends justify the means or does what we do and how we do it matter more? How do we overcome our own bad wiring? How do we fight life when it forces us down paths we never wanted to travel?

Sometimes the world craps on us and our job is to make fertilizer out of that steaming pile of dung.

It's not easy. Escape is more preferable to confrontation. Floating downstream is always easier than fighting the currents.

Yet, our greatest successes are often tied to our greatest

challenges. What is hardest makes us stronger. What is most difficult makes us better.

Failure makes us successful.

Damien's victories are powerful because of their near impossibility and, once through them, he becomes a better man.

He tries to remain one and, for the reasons mentioned above, he'll often fail.

Yet, Damien is tenacious.

He never gives up.

That gives me hope.

Heroes like him, flaws and all, help allay my fears for having faced them through the eyes of a broken man like Damien Hill.

ACKNOWLEDGMENTS

Writing is a solitary endeavor, but publishing is a group effort. I'd like to thank my family, Dea, DC and Gabe, for their continued support and assistance.

For Cynthia Shepp for her ninja editing skills and Jun Ares for his powerful book cover designs.

For my fellow authors who have been so generous with their examples and guidance.

And, as someone of faith, I must also thank the Author of all things for allowing me to dip my toe into the pool of creation.

I would never presume to equate myself to the Almighty, but creating worlds, people and relationships... I get the attraction.

ABOUT THE AUTHOR

Pete Bauer is an award-winning writer whose love of Hitchcock, Koontz, Meltzer and Patterson inspires him to create page-turning suspense thrillers.

He's been writing since he was nine years old and, having grown up in Florida, has seen the crazy and the amazing, both of which he tries to sprinkle into his books.

When he's not finding ways to put his heroes through hell, he enjoys the 3 Fs - family, faith and football.

Connect with Pete

petebauerbooks.com
damienhill@petebauerbooks.com

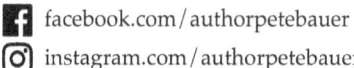

facebook.com / authorpetebauer
instagram.com / authorpetebauer

ALSO BY PETE BAUER

ACTION THRILLERS

Damien Hill

Chamber

Trigger

Recoil

Blowback

STAND ALONE THRILLERS

Cold Storage

YOUNG ADULT THRILLERS

Gabby Wells

Kneel & Prey

Lost & Found

Sins & Suicide

Gods & Martyrs

AMDG